CORRUPT FIRE

ANGEL FIRE, BOOK 5

MARIE JOHNSTON

LE PUBLISHING

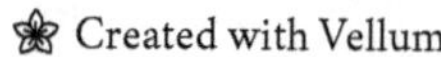 Created with Vellum

One minute the angel Tosca is a respected enforcer having a drink with someone she considers an ally. The next minute she wakes up beside a dead body, red-handed and blackballed.

Now enforcers she used to call friends are calling her a murderer. When they dredge up the past she's so carefully buried, she'll only look guiltier. Her only hope for clearing her name is escaping to Earth—and seeking refuge in the one place she vowed never to set foot in again.

One minute the angel Bronx is a frustrated warrior railing at the corruption that keeps him from doing his job. The next minute he's got free rein to hunt the bane of his existence.

The cute but infuriating enforcer has been questioning his every move and tattling to her crooked senator friends. But now that Tosca is on the run, there's nowhere on Earth he won't follow—even if it takes him smack into a nest of forgotten angels and unchecked demons who will do anything to stay that way.

Except once he finds Tosca, he doesn't know what to do with her. His gut tells him she's innocent, but he'll have to gain her trust to learn who framed her and why. Yet Tosca has no intention of letting any male dictate her fate again, even one who stars nightly in her dreams. Together they could root out the corruption bedeviling their realm—but divided they will fall prey to a determined enemy adept at killing enforcers and warriors alike.

CHAPTER 1

*P*ounding resounded through the house.

Tosca groaned but didn't open her eyes. Just a few more minutes. She didn't have to be at work yet.

It stopped and the consciousness she was avoiding faded away.

More muffled pounding. "Enforcers. Open up."

Enforcers? *She* was an enforcer. She tried to open her eyes but they were so heavy.

The distant sound of cracking wood wrenched through the day. She tried to open her eyes again. *Open, dang it.* Were sandbags attached to her eyelids?

A sliver of light peeked through. Her gritty gaze landed on an ornate dresser with a gilded mirror. A silk robe hung off the side.

I don't wear silk. Not anymore.

Neither did she have an ostentatious dresser or a fancy mirror.

With a gasp, she sat up. The effort needed nearly made her collapse backward. *What the hell is wrong with me?*

Something was off. A lot of things were off.

She glanced down. Where her clothing should be was bare skin. When had she undressed?

She couldn't remember.

A metallic tang assaulted her nose as her gaze landed on smears and splotches of red. Her fuzzy brain struggled to understand.

Was she hurt?

Her body was in a different dimension but it wasn't in pain. She was sluggish. She was tired. So dang tired.

Footsteps pounded through the house.

Frowning, she looked at the dresser. The door. Whose house was this?

Alarm broke through her foggy thoughts.

Something was wrong. So very wrong.

She twisted to swing her legs off the bed, but they were caught in the sheets. She couldn't move them. Her wings hung off her back like each feather was lined with lead. She tried tugging one wing loose but the feeling was wrong. There was a weight on her wings, holding it down.

Nothing made sense.

She turned her head and froze.

A bloody, lifeless male stared at her. His wide, glassy eyes were empty of all life. She'd seen enough dead people to know without a doubt there was no longer a soul in his body.

Her sluggish mind whirled. She had to . . . She had to . . .

What should she do?

Voices drifted closer.

Enforcers. Right. She was an enforcer.

She pried her wing from under the body and swung her legs over the bed. She stood to race for the door, to call for help—

Her legs collapsed under her. She hit the floor with an

oomph, a startled cry leaving her, and a male shouted from outside the room. They'd heard her. Footsteps approached.

She army crawled to the dresser, every move requiring more effort than it should've, and tugged the silk robe down. She covered herself just as a male in black tactical pants and a long-sleeved shirt burst in.

She should be wearing those clothes. She should be wearing those heavy boots. She should be in uniform, breaking into this house to find out what was wrong.

Where were her clothes?

"We've got a body!" the male shouted. She couldn't summon his name. Why wasn't her brain working? "It's Jean Luc."

Senator Colbert's mate. That male was Jean Luc? Tosca hadn't had many dealings with him. Why had she been naked and next to him in bed? And why was he dead at the same time?

Foggy memories surfaced. Tosca had visited Juliette. She'd wanted to check on her after Jean Luc's incarceration for trafficking angels. He'd confessed, said it was him and not his son who was guilty, the son who'd been killed by the demons Jean Luc had dealt with. But then there'd been stirrings that Jean Luc was getting out. She'd checked on the senator, then . . .

What?

She couldn't remember.

A second male spotted her. "Tosca?"

"Mmbleph." Her mouth refused to work. The male's name was Hessler. Jorge Hessler.

The first male—Clive. Clive Kont, not so affectionally called The Cunt behind his back. He'd earned the nickname.

Her synapses started firing but Clive spoke first. "Detain her. She killed the senator's husband."

Jorge didn't move from the doorway. "Clive—"

"Detain her, dammit."

Jorge approached her, his expression regretful, but confused. A tiny bit grateful this situation didn't make sense to others, she didn't like the way he was advancing on her, like she was a crook. She shook her head and scooted backward across the floor.

"I'm really sorry, Tosca."

She didn't trust herself to speak. Jorge held out a hand. It was the apology that got to her. She was sorry too, and she had no idea why. Not knowing if she could stand on her own, she reached for it.

Blood stained her skin. Her fingers were covered from the tips to her wrists. It looked like she'd splashed around in a sink full of blood.

Jorge blanched and drew back. She dropped her hand and tried pushing off the floor.

More cylinders were firing in her brain. Jean Luc was dead, and she was covered in blood in his bedroom with his body. Nothing looked like an accident. She hadn't done this. Whatever had happened, she hadn't done it.

Jorge scooted to her side and helped her straighten the silk robe. She hated the feeling of it against her skin. It reminded her of another time, when she'd been another person. A fake. *That* person would look guilty. But that was decades ago. She hadn't lived like that in a long time.

Jorge grasped her around the shoulders and helped her stand. She scanned the room. This had to be Juliette and Jean Luc's bedroom.

Her stomach twisted and bile crept up her throat when she saw the mess on the bed. She'd lain in that.

A body was crumpled on the side of the bed she hadn't lain on. The way the blood pooled under Jean Luc's body made her think his throat had been slit. And her hands were covered, like she'd been the one holding the knife.

Except she hadn't done this.

The Cunt picked up a six-inch knife from the covers. "We found the murder weapon." His grim gaze met Jorge's, then landed on her. The spark of glee in his eyes fueled a cascade of adrenaline through her veins, clearing the cobwebs from her brain. "Take her downstairs. We'll take her in and question her."

Question her. What they couldn't do was a full forensics investigation. This was Numen. The realm of angels. There was no jury. Just the senate the dead male's mate served in.

As she stumbled down the hallway, her wings dragging on the floor behind her, Jorge half holding her up, her legs strengthened with each step and her brain cleared.

Was that knife actually the murder weapon? Did the blood on her hands and on the bed match the victim's? Could they test her system for drugs? What about his?

She had to figure out what had happened to her, and to Jean Luc. It was Tosca's job.

Where was Juliette?

Many of Numen's residents thought enforcers like her weren't necessary. Why would a realm of angels need any sort of law enforcement? Tosca had grown up knowing they were as capable of crime as humans. Her job was to remind them they weren't divine. Some of them still beat the shit out of their mates. Some stole property or, worse, the weapons their kind used against demons. Some worked with humans or demons to infiltrate the realm.

Some had killed a senator's husband.

And set her up to take the fall for it.

BRONX SCANNED the Numen market as a slight breeze ruffled the dark feathers of his wings. White-robed angels roamed the stands, selecting perfectly ripened produce and cuts of meat other angels had couriered over from Earth. Still more angels ordered already prepared food at other stands.

He could've eaten at home, but his parents doted on him, almost too much. He was pushing fifty, young for his kind, but he'd been a warrior for decades. Like his father and mother had once been.

Maybe they should get back into it again.

But both his mother and father had left the warrior world behind when they'd mated and had him. He was their world, and it was stifling.

Breakfasts at the market with one of his teammates, Urban, was a good way to get out from under their smothering and do some work.

He usually tried to steer clear of this place. He preferred the human world, but after the shit that had gone down with Harlowe and Sandeen, Director Vale had asked him and Urban to spend a little more time at home. Keep an eye on things.

Ever cynical, Director Vale thought there was trouble brewing, and after Sandeen's "Hello, I'm half demon and my other half is angel and if you tell anyone, you can kiss the Daemon steel trade goodbye" announcement, the director expected more treachery. More duplicity.

Numen was a realm with secrets. Bronx understood that more than ever.

Two enforcers roamed the market, wearing the same black pants and long-sleeved shirts that Bronx and Urban wore. Bronx dismissed them. They weren't *that* enforcer. The short one with hips that flared like the ends of her short hair. The one who looked like she could be an Olympic gymnast. Just how flexible was she?

Damn, but Tosca got under his skin.

It didn't help that she didn't trust him.

He was trustworthy, dammit. And he didn't trust her.

"Why are you glaring at the enforcers?" Urban asked. "You're going to get them riled up and we don't need them crawling up our asses again."

But Bronx wanted at least one of them to crawl all over his body. He ground his teeth together. When had Tosca become synonymous with sex? Maybe since his work had interfered with his personal life until he didn't *have* a personal life, other than wandering around the market trying to catch bits of gossip.

"I want to go back to my apartment in Vegas." And actually stay in it. As a warrior, he was accustomed to a life of roaming all over the world, but ever since they'd uncovered a scheme within Numen to aid demons in breaching its borders, he'd been working nonstop. He couldn't even combine work and play anymore. Too many Numen plotting with fucking demons.

Urban veered toward a fresh fruit stand. "I have to admit, it's been kind of nice to let my wings hang out."

Yeah, Bronx would grudgingly admit that. His wings were steel gray, and a stark contrast with his pitch-black hair. His feathers had a glossy shine that drew in the females. They practically wanted to pet him, and usually he was more than up for it. But something was bothering him today. The space between his shoulder blades was tight and it had nothing to do with the weight of his wings. His stomach was knotted and he was pissy.

Maybe he'd have this kind of day until they flushed out all the traitors within the realm. He'd be terminally cranky until he had the freedom to roam Earth in his off-hours again.

He loved his parents, but damn. His mother had hand-stitched a robe for him. Between training and working and transcending to Earth, when the hell would he wear a robe?

But he loved his parents. Deeply. And there was shady shit going on in the realm, putting every angel in Numen at risk. So he'd stick around and wander the market until he was pointed in the direction of trouble.

Ordinarily, that'd be a job for the enforcers. But they'd been sheltering some of the worst traitors. Thus the reason Director Vale had asked Bronx, Urban, and their other teammate Ransom to spend more time in the realm.

Warriors worked in teams of seven on Earth. They hunted for demons and kept humans safe and protected from the secrets of Numen and Daemon.

But his team was hardly a team anymore. Bryant Vale had once been their leader, but he'd taken the position of director after the previous one had gotten injured. Dionna should be in charge, but she was still tied up with personal issues in the human realm. Jagger had gotten mated to Felicia, the sister of Director Vale's mate. Felicia was a senator, and Jagger hung around her to suss out any information that came her way. Sierra had lost her wings and mated with a human. They were secretly raising their baby in the middle of nowhere, but she still helped out with tech stuff. Her father, Ransom, had sort of replaced her, but Bronx doubted the guy knew how to open a flip phone, much less run sophisticated, realm-spanning tech and surveillance. And after Harlowe had mated a half demon, it wasn't like she and her mate could make their happy home in Numen anymore.

His team had changed, its members scattered across

two realms. The warrior dream he'd been living had shifted. What next? Find a mate and get pressured to quit and raise a family?

He suppressed a shudder and glowered at a stand of oranges. Round, juicy oranges, almost as lush as the ass he'd love to sink his teeth into—

A female enforcer rushed to the two roaming the market. They huddled together while she talked, her voice low and her hands flying.

Bronx picked up an orange and smelled it. Urban had noticed what was going on and was doing the same with the bananas next to him.

Bronx rolled his eyes toward Urban as if to say, *You can't smell a banana, dumbass*, but Urban gave him the flat stare that said he was going to do it anyway and *By the way, how's the orange sniffing going?*

Setting his orange down, he wandered to the plums that were two stands closer to the target. The enforcers were talking too low for him to catch anything, but his intuition burned like a freshly lit torch.

Persephone Nassim spotted them and sauntered their way, her gaze glued to Urban. "What are you two doing here?"

Bronx didn't know if she stuck her chest out on purpose, or if she was so used to curving her back that she'd fused her vertebrae. She sidled close to Urban, who froze with a bunch of bananas in his hand.

"Shopping," Urban answered.

Bronx strained to catch what the enforcers were saying. He recognized them. The taller man often worked with Tosca, but she'd taken to working alone a lot recently. A giant red flag. Add in how close she'd become to Senator Colbert, and it was suspicious. Tosca Smith might be cute in the sexiest damn way, but that didn't mean he wouldn't take her down if she plotted against the realm.

Bronx ignored Urban and Persephone and leaned closer to the plums, only his gaze was on the enforcers. He couldn't read lips very well, but he caught Tosca's name on the new arrival's lips, and the other two gasped.

What was going on?

Behind him, Persephone kicked a hip out. Her pewter wings were arched high. Between those wings and the way she was pushing her breasts out, she was going to lift off any moment. "You're never here shopping."

Bronx let Urban field her questions and swiveled back to the enforcers. Their voices had dropped frustratingly lower, and they leaned into each other, making it hard to see their mouths.

"Warriors get days off too," said Urban. He could just as well be talking to a wall instead of one of the most gorgeous angels in Numen. Persephone had long, jet-black hair. Her brown skin glowed almost as much as the deep brown of her eyes. Beautiful, but toxic. Both parents were respected senators, and Persephone was the stereotypical spoiled rich kid. She was aimless and liked to use her time to poke into people's lives and spread chaos. Be it gossip, flirtation, or wealth, she used what was in her tool belt to get whatever she wanted, and that didn't include anything useful. Persephone was destruction. And if she was talking to them, she was up to something.

"What do warriors do with their days off?" she purred.

The enforcers rushed away as a group. Bronx put down the plums that had somehow ended up in his grip. Shit. He'd have to take them. He'd half crushed the fruit.

He'd keep the enforcers in the corner of his eye, give them a few minutes before following them. Enough time to see if Urban fell for the dangerous beauty's game, whatever it was.

"Eat fruit," was Urban's answer.

Bronx choked back a snort. Persephone ignored him, giving him her back and a face full of downy feathers.

She picked up a banana and stroked it. If the pull to go after the enforcers wasn't so strong, Bronx would hang back and watch the show. Urban wasn't usually dense around women on Earth, but Persephone either short-circuited his brain or the male didn't want to get lured into her selfish games.

Bronx didn't have time for her. The enforcers were getting farther away. Something was wrong and it had to do with Tosca.

"Hey, uh, Urban," he said. "I want to redecorate my office before the end of the day. We should get going."

Persephone whipped around, her wing nearly smacking him across the face. "How are you redoing it? I could help."

Urban smirked behind her back. It was all Bronx could do not to glare at him. He didn't have an office. And if he did, why the hell would Persephone be interested in it?

"It's a guy bonding thing. Urban and I don't get down days too often."

She pouted, a practiced move that he couldn't believe anyone fell for. But they did. Persephone was hot. She got what she wanted.

"See you later," Urban said as he walked away. Bronx was right with him.

Bronx waited several steps before he peeked behind a wing to make sure she wasn't following them. She was frowning at the stacks of bananas. A tendril of empathy curled through him, but he didn't have time for that either. She looked lost and lonely. He'd never have attributed those feelings to someone like her.

"What are we doing?" Urban asked as they wove through the angels doing their morning shopping. Some gave them cursory looks, but he and Urban had been through here enough that most recognized them. Which made Persephone happening upon them less of a coincidence. Was it all tied together?

Was she at the market getting dirt for her own juicy fun, or for someone else?

He'd worry about it later, after he figured out what Tosca was up to.

Urban was casting glances in his direction. Right. Bronx hadn't answered him. "The enforcers mentioned something about Tosca and rushed off."

"Is she okay?"

"I don't know." But he was driven to find out.

She had to be okay. She was the biggest pain in his ass, but she couldn't just *not* be. It wasn't right. They had a warped game of cat and mouse. She was an enforcer undaunted by his warrior attitude. He was a warrior who liked to piss her off. She suspected he had a ton of secrets the senators should know. He *absolutely* had a ton of secrets that she couldn't know. Neither was sure where the other's loyalties lay.

He didn't know what he'd do if she was hurt or in trouble, but it was time to find out.

CHAPTER 2

Tosca huddled on the couch of the main room of the house. Fragments of memory returned. She'd come here to visit Juliette. They'd sat in this room and talked. Tosca eyed the wineglass on the table. There were two of them. One was the glass she'd drunk from.

She'd been drugged. It made sense. She hadn't been sleeping, she'd been unconscious. From the sluggish uploading of her thoughts and memories to the leaden weight of her body—she'd been intentionally drugged.

She'd done it enough to others to know when it'd been done to her. And there was no way to prove it. Juliette had to be behind it.

Unless the drugs had been meant for the senator?

No. Tosca recalled the brightness of the senator's eyes as she served the wine. The way she'd gushed about friendship and complimented Tosca. How the senator had focused on her, making it seem like they had a special bond. They'd all been tactics Tosca should've recognized.

"I was set up, Jorge."

He gave her a sympathetic grimace. "I'm sorry, Tosca."

He sounded sorry, but there was something in his tone. He didn't believe her. It was like he was sorry that she'd taken a tragic turn from dedicated enforcer to scorned lover. Because that was what it looked like.

Why would Juliette want to kill her mate and frame Tosca?

It'd be a handy way to distance herself from Jean Luc and his confession of trafficking females to Daemon. She'd turn suspicion into sympathy. She'd become the victim.

Tosca had been found naked in a dead man's bed. Like his death throes had knocked her out after she'd slit his throat.

The only person Tosca had been around was Juliette. Tosca had trusted her. She'd trusted the female with her career, which was everything. Everything.

It was her way to redeem herself, to prove that she was as Numen as everyone else in the realm, despite how she'd grown up.

She swallowed the burn of betrayal. Senator Colbert had been like a mentor. Tosca had admired her. Juliette had had everything Tosca wanted. She'd been respected, she'd occupied the highest position in the realm, and she'd had a mate and a son.

A son who'd been killed by demons and a mate who'd likely trafficked Numen females to those demons. And since Juliette had latched on to Tosca as her eyes and ears in the realm, Juliette was probably behind it too. She'd wanted to use Tosca to make sure no one was closing in on their family secrets. And Tosca had been too ready to do Juliette's bidding.

Tosca had been suspicious of the warriors. Specifically, Director Vale's former team. But her world had been upended and that might mean Director Vale's team were the good guys, and Juliette and anyone she was working with were the bad guys.

Except Tosca. Only how could she prove that?

Who else was working with Juliette? Who could Tosca trust?

Jorge paced the living room while Clive finished in the bedroom. He spoke into his phone. Enforcers had quickly adopted the human technology. The devices were easy to power with their natural energy, allowing angels to communicate quickly and privately, like they were doing about her now.

"Yeah, that should be enough," Jorge said. He half turned, keeping his eyes on her. As if she would attack him in nothing but a silk robe.

She wanted to wash off, but he hadn't let her do anything. She'd barely been able to get down the stairs to the living room, but she could've summoned enough energy to wash her damn hands.

"We can't let her—right. Right. Okay. You called . . . you know?"

He clearly didn't want her to hear what he was saying. As if she didn't know procedure. Clive had called more enforcers to haul her to jail. They would bring warded bands to bind her wrists and keep her from transcending as soon as she got outside. Then they would toss her in a cell.

From there, she would most likely be found guilty of killing Jean Luc. And they would take her wings. They would make her into a fallen and she would be cast out. She'd be dumped with nothing but a carved-out back in a part of Earth where she'd never been. And she'd have to start over.

She'd lose everything she'd worked for, the most

important of which was respect. The respect of her people, and her self-respect. She'd worked so damn hard.

No one knew it, but the irony was, she'd thrive no matter where they dropped her. She had skills few other Numen had, and she'd be fine. Except for the bitterness and resentment that'd eat her alive.

No one was dictating her life. She had refused to let it happen before, and she wasn't going to give up now.

She'd have to run. To where?

There was only one place she could go. She'd made Numen her sole focus for over twenty years. Was her old home even still there?

No. She wasn't going back to that place.

But she had nowhere else to go, and that place was . . . home.

That place was somewhere she could hide. It was full of people who had taught her how to lie and lie well. Habits she'd hoped to leave behind, but needed desperately right now. An area that no one in Numen knew she'd come from. After her birth was logged, there was no record of Tosca Smith until twenty-four years ago, when she'd applied to be an enforcer.

She'd never wanted to go back to her old life, and that was exactly what she needed to do now. She had no one and nothing else.

Staying hunched over, she scoped the room. A large set of picture windows loomed behind the seating area. Jorge was dutifully staying between her and the front door. She racked her brain to remember the layout of the house. The seating area. The kitchen was down a hallway, on the other side of the house with its own exit. Too far, and there wasn't a valid excuse for her to go to the kitchen. The bedrooms were upstairs, but she had to stay away from the second level and Clive. Jorge by himself was her best bet.

There was what Juliette had referred to as a powder room. It was a bathroom, but Tosca had been charmed at Juliette's term. The senator had been the worldly one, a diamond in a titanium setting, while Tosca had been fool's gold.

Tosca might still be just a fancy-looking rock, but Juliette was nothing but cubic zirconia. Crafty, but a knockoff nonetheless.

Had Jean Luc been dead before she arrived? And as soon as she'd passed out, someone, hell, maybe even Clive, had helped the senator get her to the bedroom and undressed. Then they'd ditched the place and reported a crime.

There was a knock on the door. Jorge glanced at her, his expression full of regret. But he was like her. He was a rule follower. He'd do his job even if he hated it. Because justice needed to be served.

But unlike her, he hadn't been raised to lie and steal. What had once been a detriment was now her advantage. He was expecting compliance.

She waited until his back was turned and his hand was on the doorknob before she jumped to her feet and sprinted to the hallway.

Her bare feet slipped on the marble floor, but she caught the corner of the wall with her hands and swung around.

"What the—"

Jorge's words faded as she darted down the hall to the bathroom. She slammed and locked the door behind her.

The window was decorative only. Shit!

She dug through a vanity drawer. People were yelling from the other side of the door. The good news was they were all inside.

There, a brush. She grabbed it, held it like the knife she

had *not* used to slit Jean Luc's throat and slammed it into the window. It took a few hits while the enforcers pounded on the door. It rattled on its hinges. They'd break it down soon. She had to get out.

The glass fractured and she continued to punch the handle of the brush into the window. Glass shattered. The wood from the door splintered.

She ignored the cut of the glass as she pushed the pane out and lifted herself through the opening, tucking her wings close to her body. Glass dug into her flesh and pain flared in her hands. Her blood mingled with the stains already on her skin, but she didn't care. She just had to get away from the house.

There was no time to spread her wings to slow her fall. She tumbled to the ground just as the door was breached. Behind her, Jorge was halfway through the window.

Tosca closed her eyes, morphed her blood-crusted wings for the first time in decades, and imagined the last place on Earth she thought she'd ever go again.

A BLOODIED TOSCA rolled out the window and was gone.

"What the fuck?" Urban said under his breath.

All Bronx could do was shake his head. What the hell?

They were hiding in the bushes of Senator Colbert's house like stalkers. The enforcers from the market had taken flight, and it had been hard as hell to track angels in the middle of the big open sky without being conspicuous. But they had done it—just in time to see something was seriously wrong with Tosca.

"Was she wearing a robe?" Bronx had glimpsed too much and not enough of her creamy flesh. Her wings had flared back to aid her fall and then she'd morphed them in a blink and transcended.

A dark-haired enforcer craned his head out the window, shouting back into the house.

"She wasn't wearing her uniform," Urban replied. "If I didn't know better, I'd say she was running from them. I know she's tight with the senator but why would she be in the female's house with nothing but a robe on? Do you think she's having an affair with Jean Luc Colbert?"

His hands curled into fists. That slimy male had no business touching Tosca, but an affair didn't make sense. "She's too much of a do-gooder for that. She worships the senator and that doesn't explain why it looked like she was covered in blood."

"Yeah, that one wing of hers was nearly brown."

The enforcer peering out the window disappeared into the house. More than curiosity propelled Bronx backward out of the bushes. Urban followed.

"I need more information." Bronx glanced at the property. Senators' houses were never small and this place was no exception. It was surrounded by acres of perfectly manicured lawn and trees—evergreens and weeping willows. Large trees that added more privacy. This mansion was one of the outermost of the realm and occupied a large chunk of Numen realty.

"How?" Urban asked.

Good question. How could they find out what was going on without anyone knowing they were looking? At first glance, this wasn't warrior business. Enforcers were the police force of the realm. Warriors hunted demons on Earth. Their work shouldn't mingle.

He and Urban skimmed around the bushes. Urban spotted the enforcer female who had approached the other two in the market. "That's Malin. Maybe I could find a way to talk to her."

"Did you two used to date?"

"We fucked when I was in warrior training. If she wasn't orgasming, she was talking. Maybe she's still like that."

Urban was the strong, silent type. Females loved it and tended to spill their secrets around him. Still, he couldn't ask Urban to use her, but maybe the female would still prattle on around her old fuck buddy.

Malin launched into the air, her dusky-gray wings spread for flight.

"I've got an idea." He beckoned Urban to follow him as they ran in the opposite direction. Before they trespassed on another senator's property, Bronx spread his wings and took to the sky. Urban did the same.

After making a wide arc, Bronx made sure to cross paths with Malin.

Urban must've figured out his plan. "Hey, Malin," he called. "What's up?"

She started and dipped in the air, but recovered and turned her wide gaze to them. "Oh, Urban. Hey, Bronx."

"You okay?" Urban asked as if it was a surprise something might be wrong.

She licked her lips and looked around. "I guess everyone's going to find out soon enough. Senator Colbert's mate has been killed."

Bronx nearly tumbled from the sky. Tosca was running from a dead man's house. "Just now?"

"I don't know. We only just found him." She veered toward enforcer headquarters. They didn't have much time. Malin might be a talker, but she'd be reminded to keep her mouth shut when she spotted other enforcers.

"Who did it?" he asked.

She glanced at them, then behind her. Her auburn hair fluttered in the wind. "We have a suspect, but you know how it is."

No fucking way. Their suspect was Tosca?

No way.

Tosca was too by the book. If she killed a male, he deserved it.

If she killed a male who deserved it, would she jump out a window in a robe or would she stand her ground and give a detailed report about what had happened?

Something else was going on.

Malin began her descent. "Nice to run into you guys, but I gotta get to work."

Bronx fell back, but Urban followed the enforcer. "Want to go out sometime?"

Bronx didn't hear her answer but he caught her smile. When Urban circled back to him, he asked, "Did you ask her out just to get information?"

Urban answered with a smirk.

"I owe you."

"Nah. It's not a hardship, trust me. But she'll tell me everything before we hit the sheets."

They flew a few more minutes. Bronx's mind ruminated on the information. What was going on?

"We should inform Director Vale," Urban said.

They should, but the urgency flowing through his veins wasn't because he needed to tell his boss. "We need to find Tosca."

"Where would she go? I didn't think she went to Earth that much, or ever."

Neither did Bronx. Where would a workaholic female like Tosca go to unwind? Or had she done service work for the humans? Not all angels got access to Earth, but enforcers were trusted with the security of the realm. They often got rewarded with the right to spend time in the earthly realm. Or if an angel's duties involved humans, they could get access via service work. Whether they actually did that work was another story. Angels weren't policed outside of Numen. As long as they didn't break Numen's laws, what they did on Earth wasn't an issue.

"Let's talk to Director Vale. Maybe Odessa can help us out in the archives."

DIONNA BIT into her lip before she cried out, her orgasm cascading over her, wave after empty wave. As fast as it hit, her orgasm was done. She climbed off her mate and stretched out next to him, but Charles rolled to his side and sat up with his legs hanging over the bed.

He had finished, but it'd been years since they'd cuddled afterward. There was no glow, just a dim echo of the bond they'd once had.

"I have to get to work," he muttered as he rose. His broad back flexed as he shrugged into his shirt, and his firm ass tensed when he stepped into his shorts.

The male was in even better shape than when he'd lived in their quaint little home in Numen. He hadn't crossed their threshold in so long. She quashed the melancholy thought. His work on Earth was admirable and demanding. Years of backbreaking work building irrigation systems in some of the most inaccessible places around the world had honed his frame.

Years of avoiding her and their failing sync bond.

The flat he shared with their two daughters was smaller than their place in Numen, but this space had the hominess their home now lacked. Charles preferred to rent furnished apartments. Less to deal with when moving from place to place. But several of the paintings on the wall revealed her daughters' touch. Vibrant reds and oranges overlaid the faint outline of an angel playing a harp. Exactly the type of artwork rebellious Courtney would admire—and that Charles would indulge his daughters with. A way to let them flex their wings in Accra without revealing actual wings in the bustling capital city of Ghana.

When Charles had left Numen, the girls had gone with him. Both adults, they were still young for angels. Courtney was almost thirty and Stella was twenty-two. Accra was a complete contrast to Numen. Voices filled with emotions carried on the breeze. In Numen, sound and emotion were stifled. Even the skies were quiet. The market a few blocks from the apartment was a cacophony of commerce. The market in Numen was for commerce too, but also for show—watch me select the best of the best produce, talk to the most important angels, and ignore those beneath me.

Was the market one of the reasons her family had stayed? The humanitarian work they did was supposed to have lasted a couple of years at the most.

You're never home. What difference does it make where we live?

It made a world of difference when there was no easy way for Dionna to transcend undetected into a large human city. Even harder when Charles moved around with the girls. All in the name of his work.

The last few years, it had felt like he was purposely avoiding her. As if he couldn't resist her, blamed her for their bond, and packed his bags the moment she left for another mission.

So this time, she hadn't left. She'd taken a sabbatical from her work as a warrior. But in the months since she'd been with her family, the distance between them had only grown.

"Father?" Stella called, the front door slamming.

Her mate let out a disgruntled huff and hurried through dressing. He ran a hand over short hair that was an inch longer than hers.

"Father?" Their oldest daughter, Courtney, sounded more indignant. "We were supposed to meet Daniel twenty minutes ago."

Her daughters had been out . . . doing whatever adult human women did in the big city all day. Shopping? Had they gotten a job? Dionna wouldn't know. They didn't talk to her. Too many nights away for work instead of home telling bedtime stories had made them strangers. They worked with Charles, but he wasn't in the middle of an irrigation project at the moment. She stayed in the dark while they stayed away from the flat all day.

There was a knock on the bedroom door a moment before Courtney opened it. Dionna yanked a sheet over herself. Courtney's gaze landed on her and irritation flashed in her brown eyes. "Father, we're late and how are we supposed to explain it? 'Sorry, my mother finally deigned to come home and we had to accommodate her'?"

"Courtney," Dionna chided.

Courtney just rolled her eyes. "Daniel is relying on this internship while you're wasting his time. That's not helping humanity." She spun and stomped away. Her energy and attitude were befitting a warrior, but Dionna would never mention it. A sure way to ensure Courtney shunned the profession for eternity.

Stella stayed out of view and out of arguments, like always. Dionna had grown slightly closer to her youngest since she'd been in Ghana, but the girl held herself back, as if she feared the wrath of Courtney.

"I'll be right out." Charles closed the bedroom door on their daughters and hung his head.

"Charles—"

"I can't keep doing this." His quiet tone was regretful but resolved. He turned, his hand waving at the bed with her in it. "You're a distraction. You're here and I can't think clearly. When you go, I can sort my feelings. It's always so clear."

"I'm not going anywhere. You and the girls are important to me."

"I never doubted that, Dionna. The whole realm is important to you. We're important to you. But we're no more special than anyone else."

"My job—"

"Is where you've gone to hide from us. I know you think your time here with us will repair what's wrong, but it's only revealing how deep in the foundation the cracks go."

Mating was for life. It was for eternity. What was he saying? "What if the foundation is solid, but the house built over it needs work?"

"We were the carpenters, my dear." His tone was resigned, but she refused to give up. It wasn't in her as a warrior, and it wasn't in her as a mate. "Maybe we didn't do enough quality work in the beginning."

Enough with the construction metaphors. "I left my team to work on us. Harlowe almost got killed while I was chasing you and the girls across the globe."

His measured expression didn't change. "And because you did that once, we're good?"

"It shows that I put you—us—the girls—above my team. I'm not sure what else you want me to do. Quit? Lives were on the line—immortal lives. Yet I was here."

"And so are they. What do you know, Di. They can survive without you. And so can we."

She reared back. "You want me to leave? We still have our bond. We still have chemistry." Empty sex, but only because they no longer trusted each other with their vulnerability. "We can rebuild what we have."

"What if we rebuild and you still don't choose us?"

That was his argument each time. He always laid the responsibility at her feet. "What if we rebuild and you still choose not to try?"

His inhale was sharp. "Then we are at an impasse."

"I'm not letting you run from me." There had to be some way to chisel through his stubborn pride. Some way to highlight the reality of what these continual arguments could lead to. "What if one day you turn around and I'm not there?"

Sadness leached into his gaze. "I've had several of those days, Dionna. I know exactly what it's like."

And he was gone.

CHAPTER 3

*T*osca cowered in the trees, peering through the branches at the group of people around the campfire.

She'd descended three miles away, adjusting for any expansion in the last couple of decades. The trees around the commune stretched for miles. Tampa, and its many suburbs, was the closest city. Hot, humid air clung to her, and her skin already itched from the bugs she couldn't see.

Home.

Peacequarters didn't look the same. An outsider might ask how the main building in a commune—or "mind and body holistic community"—could be so ornate, so luxurious, and so large when everyone here supposedly worked and lived off the land.

Tosca knew. She'd contributed to that wealth. Apparently, business was still good.

Once a simple building, Peacequarters was now a sprawling facility with several open-air rooms. A couple of bedrooms were for new arrivals: disillusioned angels who'd given up on the decency of Numen and didn't care to contribute to humanity's welfare. So they came to Forgotten Peace. Peace for the angels who sought refuge here, and Forgotten because their existence wasn't missed by those in Numen.

If any humans came sniffing around for their own holistic well-being, they were politely convinced this place wasn't for them.

After she'd gathered her bearings and hiked in her bare feet to the commune, she'd circled around to the side where her old cabin sat. The cabins surrounding Peacequarters were individual homes given to those who contributed to—stole for—the commune.

A group of four surrounded a campfire—two females and two males. The smoke worked its way through the trees and around her, layering a sense of nostalgia over the flight for her life.

A male rose in the group. His blond hair was braided and hung below his shoulders. He was wearing a loose white linen shirt and baggy gray linen pants. He turned to where she was hiding. "You might as well come out. I sense you lurking."

The laughter around the fire ceased. Her stomach dropped, then clenched. She couldn't hide. She had come here because she had nowhere else to go. She didn't know who else she could trust.

The only thing she could trust was that this group of Numen distrusted their own kind so much they had cut all ties to the realm. And she didn't recognize the other three with the male.

Only one male would've made her run the other direction and risk her luck in Tampa.

She edged out, wincing as scattered branches poked into her bare feet. As she picked her way out of the trees and strode toward the campfire, her back straight, she took as good of a look at her surroundings as she could in the darkness. "Hi, Papa."

Concern pinched the corners of his eyes as he took in her ragged appearance. She hadn't found a water source to wash off all the blood. It was dark out, but no doubt it was obvious she was caked in something, and the robe was barely holding up after repeated altercations with branches. An ache had settled in from holding her wings in a morph for hours. She hadn't done so for over two decades.

"Tosca?"

She didn't blame him for not recognizing her. She nodded.

"My child, what happened?" He closed the distance between them, his arms out.

When he got closer, the metallic stench covering her must've hit his nose, registering that it wasn't mud on her skin.

"I'm in trouble." Her voice was puny and she should be ashamed, but it was all she could do not to collapse into his hold and dissolve into sobs. "I had nowhere else to go. I've been framed for murder. They'll take my wings and I'm innocent."

Hostile energy poured off the other three, answering a few of her questions. People here still knew who she was. The daughter who'd abandoned them all, including her papa, without explanation.

A dark-haired female peered at her as if the blood covering Tosca glowed. Her gaze darted to Papa and he gave her a kind smile. "It's my daughter."

The others continued to regard her as a threat to the commune. Perhaps she was, but she needed to catch her breath. She needed a safe place to think. Forgotten Peace had to be safe enough for a day or two.

Papa wrapped an arm around her shoulders, heedless of getting himself dirty. "Come, come. We'll take care of you. You can tell me everything after we get you cleaned up. Megan," he called to the female he'd exchanged looks with, "you're close to my daughter's size. Can she borrow some clothing?"

Megan eyed her warily, but nodded, the long dark braid over one shoulder dipping with the motion. Tosca tipped her head in thanks but had to watch her footing.

"Stephen," the other male said, his tone grave. "We must report her arrival to Peacequarters."

Papa's grip tightened on her. "Do as you must, but realize she's been gone for over twenty years and no one has come looking for us in that time. She might've left, but she's one of us."

Anxiety churned her gut. She didn't want anyone else to know she was here, but they certainly wouldn't tell Numen. They might want her gone, but maybe not until she had a change of clothes and a shower.

Papa rushed them away from the others, toward the little two-bedroom cabin she'd never thought she'd see again, much less stay in again.

The angels who resided here felt that Numen had become a spectacle. Marble mansions, pristine yards, nothing but the best produce and supplies shuttled to the realm. Hard to see in the dark, but the light pollution from the ostentatious Peacequarters suggested they weren't above the realm they had left.

Which she'd realized right before she'd left. Everything this place claimed to stand for was a lie.

As a kid, she had been indoctrinated. Until she'd noticed that their Robin Hood mentality wasn't the humanitarian service they deemed it to be.

Papa steered her around the cabin to a wash rack in the

back. He gave her shoulder a squeeze. "I set up a solar shower for when I'm done working in the gardens. Out here you won't have to worry about getting the inside dirty. Megan's going to have words with me as it is."

"That's fine. I just want to wash this off."

"Is any of that blood yours, Tosca? Are you hurt?"

Yes, she was injured, but nothing compared to Jean Luc and his slit throat. There was no coming back from that much blood loss. His mate could've saved him. Would anyone ask where Juliette had been when Jean Luc was bleeding out? "I'll heal quickly enough from my wounds."

"You can tell me the rest after you get clean. I installed sun bladders." He gave her a proud smile. "The water warms all day. That means hot showers at night. Living as one with the land."

Except he'd purchased those sun bladders and paid for the water with money stolen from humans.

That wasn't her problem right now.

She looked forward to scrubbing herself clean. She'd burn the blood off with angel fire if it wouldn't eat her skin and destroy her in the process. "I'll try to be quick so I don't waste your supply."

"And I'll find some food for you." He faced her, putting his hands on her shoulders again. "My daughter has returned. I never thought I'd see the day."

All she could manage was a shaky smile. Papa was probably giddy that she had been driven from Numen, proving that they lived in the middle of nowhere for a good damn reason.

What Papa didn't realize was that the only thing her time in Numen had done was prove the need for people like her. People who wanted to do what was right *for the people*. People who looked for the truth. And once Tosca cleaned her wounds and recuperated, she was going to find a way to clear her name.

BRONX FACED a giant stack of scrolls. He stood in front of a massive, ten-foot wooden table. To his right was a pile of already-read scrolls. To the left was an even bigger stack he and Urban had yet to go through.

Urban pushed a hand through his dark hair and propped the other on his hip. "Do you think we're going to find anything? Or am I going to lose my sanity going through all these boring announcements?"

Director Vale's mate, Odessa, was an analyst. Numen had adopted several technological advances over the years and had converted many of these scrolls to electronic formats, but she'd already searched the database. The only odd thing she'd found was that there was very little on Tosca. A birth record, news about her mother's death in the line of duty as an enforcer, but no other information beyond that.

Tosca's father was a Xavier Smith, and he had no other information in his record other than his own birth three hundred years ago, his sync bond announcement, and Tosca's record of birth.

It was like he'd vanished with her after his mate had died. Then one day several years later, Tosca had appeared in Numen and gotten hired as an enforcer.

When technology had failed, Bronx and Urban had gone old school. Odessa couldn't be the one rooting through the archives. She had her own job, and the senate might be looking more closely at what she was doing. Director Vale knew more than they wanted him to, and Odessa was a huge factor in that.

So Bronx and Urban found themselves in a temporary window of not-quite anonymity with freedom to do as they pleased without anyone in their business. Tosca had fled the realm. The enforcers were scrambling to find her and piece together what had happened in Senator Colbert's mansion. The senate was still riled from Sandeen's blackmail.

Bronx and Urban had been at their search for hours already. They had combed through old documents that hadn't yet been included in the electronic databases. It was tedious work. While their people's natural energy ran technology, he had to carefully open each aged scroll, hold back a cough from all the dust released when unraveled, and then scan old calligraphic handwriting, only to learn not one damn useful thing.

To answer Urban's question, he said, "We're going to go insane, combing through all these documents."

Urban sucked in a breath as if fortifying himself. Just as they each reached for a new scroll, the floor-to-ceiling doors of the archives room pushed open.

Odessa swept through, her gray wings off the floor and flared behind her. The top of her robe swished around her sandals, and her brilliant teal eyes sparkled as she took in their dusty clothing and their losing battle with research.

Her knowing grin was kind but teasing. "This sight brings me back to the early days of my training. Any luck?"

"We've scoured more records, but haven't found anything other than her birth announcement." Bronx didn't know when to call off that part of the hunt. There should have been more about Tosca in Odessa's databases.

She was close to his age, yet his parents had added a shit ton on him over his lifetime. His birth. When he'd been accepted into warrior training, when he'd finished it, where he'd lived, what his favorite food was, and when he returned to the realm after long missions.

If Numen had had *My Kid is on the Honor Roll* stickers, his parents would've shingled the roof with them for all the angels in Numen's skies to see.

Odessa frowned and lifted one of the scrolls they had already checked. She nodded as if she hadn't expected to find anything new. "I agree. And the birth announcement wasn't submitted by her parents. It was from an observant neighbor."

Urban braced his fingertips on top of the table. "Why would that happen?"

Her brow furrowed as she considered the stacks of scrolls. "It's rare, but in cases where parents are quiet about their lives, someone usually informs an archivist about the news."

"We barely have the names of the parents," Bronx pointed out. "It's like they were living off the grid."

"I thought the same." Odessa absentmindedly resealed scrolls as she spoke. "That leads me to think that her father abandoned the realm with her after her mother died."

"Where would they go?" Urban looked as bewildered as Bronx felt. Was there something about Tosca's past that had put her in the senator's mansion with a dead body? He believed in coincidences, but he'd also worked around angels, demons, and humans enough to know that each kind capitalized on information for their own benefit. "We would know about them, wouldn't we? Between watchers and warriors, we would know who they are and where they are."

"There should be some record of them," Bronx agreed.

Odessa lifted a shoulder. "If they were once watchers or warriors, they'd know how to hide themselves. There've been rumors for years of angels that have never been heard from again, but we have no evidence of death. No witnesses, nothing. They weren't reported as missing, they were just . . . forgotten."

Bronx scratched the back of his neck. "You think they could have families and we'd never know?"

"The world is a big place. Cal started compiling a list before he was killed. I can find it and pass it along."

"I'd appreciate it."

She nodded and folded her arms. "I'll give the information to Bryant so people don't see us together too much. I had to come to the archives anyway today, so it's like I happened upon you."

"Thanks, Odessa."

When she left, he met Urban's gaze. "It's looking like Tosca has a secret past."

"The enforcers wouldn't have hired her if they'd known."

He cocked a brow. "Or they did *because* they knew."

A sneer curled Urban's lips. "Corrupt fuckers."

"Several of them, it seems. The big question is whether Tosca is one of them." He shook his head.

Awareness prickled the back of his neck. Nothing was wrong, but more time had passed than he'd realized. He was supposed to meet his parents for dinner and they worried if he was late.

"I've gotta go."

"Tell your parents hi for me."

"You can come over." His parents loved when he brought his teammates over. If he were less secure, it'd be embarrassing, but there were worse things than having parents who loved him.

"I've got a date with Malin."

"Getting some info?"

His friend flashed a grin. "She said to just go to her place and walk in. We might not be talking for a while."

Bronx laughed as they walked out of the archives. He launched into the air in the opposite direction of his buddy, flying past the center of the realm. His place was close to the barracks, but his parents lived in Numen's equivalent of a nice middle-class suburb.

He landed at a small wood house that wouldn't be out of place in any generic neighborhood in North America.

His mother opened the door, her brown eyes warm and her arms wide. "Bronx, I've been looking forward to your visit."

He'd been here a week ago, but each time he stopped by, they acted like it'd been years. "Hello, Mother. Sorry I'm late. I got wrapped up in work."

Concern added a century to her youthful face. She feathered a hand over the loose ponytail she'd pulled her black hair into. "We heard about Senator Colbert's mate. But you wouldn't have anything to do with that, would you?"

He shook his head, biting his tongue to keep from lying to her. Technically, no. But he was all over it. "The enforcers have their hands full."

"Especially with one of their own as the perpetrator." She pulled him into the house. Savory smells surrounded him. He had no clue what he'd be eating, but whatever his parents had made would be delicious.

They cooked together, cleaned together, went for late-night flights together. His parents were attached at the hip. Hard to believe the petite female in front of him had once been a ferocious warrior. And while his father was almost as tall as Bronx, he was lankier. *Lean, but vicious*, Director Vale had once said of his father.

His parents hadn't hunted demons on the same team.

They had met when his father had been grievously injured. The sync brand had appeared on Mother and she'd found him and healed him. Then they'd walked away from warrior life together. Half a century ago, Bronx had joined them.

"Bronx." His father's warm voice carried from the kitchen. "Come on in."

Bronx followed his mom into the tidy little kitchen. Father was at the stove, tending a pot of something tasty.

"How's work?"

He gave the same answer he always did since things had changed with his team. "Slow right now."

His father's mischievous eyes crinkled at the corners, and Bronx knew what was coming. "Even in slow times, you can find a mate."

Mother sidled next to Father and slipped her arms around his waist. Without missing a beat, Father lifted a red-sauce-covered spoon for Mother to taste. They were sweet as fuck, and they wanted that for Bronx, but he wasn't willing to trade everything for it.

When humans asked Bronx where he was from, he stuck with a large city like Vegas. If they pressed because he looked Asian, he said his family was from Hong Kong, another large city to lose details in. But he resembled his father more, making it hard not to picture himself in bonded bliss, his arms wrapped around a shorter angel with a frayed blond bob and storm-gray wings.

He blinked away the image. "It'll happen when it happens," he said. Hopefully, that was a few centuries away.

He settled into the typical routine with his parents. He told them stories—older ones now that he couldn't share what he was truly doing—and they regaled him with tales of their centuries of warrior experience.

It wasn't hard to believe these two had loved their

work. He often found his parents sparring in the small, square backyard. Yet when he'd ask them why they didn't work anymore, they'd say they'd promised the other they wouldn't.

Whatever. Bronx was almost scared to get injured in the line of work and find himself saddled with a sync mate. He didn't want to leave his job because his mate didn't want him to work anymore.

Dinner was almost ready—a stew of some sort—when his phone buzzed. "Excuse me."

He ducked into the living room. His parents respected his privacy. Director Vale's name flashed on the screen. "Yeah, boss."

"You ever been in or around Tampa, Florida?"

CHAPTER 4

Things didn't seem as bleak in the light of day. Tosca woke up in the same room she'd fled all those years ago. Her back ached and her shoulders cramped from morphing her wings so long, but she'd have to get used to it. She'd *lived* with her wings morphed before. This time frame was nothing.

The loose T-shirt she wore from Megan was from Aviator Nation—and likely stolen. No five-dollar Hanes shirt for her. The trendy, loose, navy-blue sweats were the same brand and had to be rolled up at the bottom thanks to her height, but she was covered and blood-free. Her wounds from jumping through the window had healed, but hunger twisted her stomach.

She stood from the padded pallet on the floor, and her bones protested the hard night's sleep. That was life in the commune. Whatever they could steal was quality. Whatever they had to buy was crap.

Tilting her head from side to side, she cracked her neck and went into the main room. Megan was at the table. Her hair was still in a braid, but she wore a purple summer dress with yellow flowers today.

"Evening, Tosca."

"Evening?"

Megan paged through a book that was probably as stolen as all the clothing. Her voice was soft, almost subservient, but her expression was lofty. "You slept all through the day, but granted, it took you quite a while to scrub yourself clean last night."

"Right." Tosca peeked at her hands. No blood. Good. Had she finished sleeping off the drugs and the stress?

"Your father is outside getting our supper."

"I'll go see if he needs help." Tosca hugged her arms around herself as she stepped into the fading sun. Megan seemed nice, but other than her name and her taste in stolen clothes, Tosca didn't know a thing about her. The vibe wasn't overly friendly. Given how business was done at Forgotten Peace, Tosca wasn't surprised. At best, she would be considered a newcomer, and they'd always been regarded with wariness until they proved themselves.

The only thing Tosca needed to prove was that she wasn't a murderer.

She stepped off the pebbled path onto the grass. Papa would be on the other side of the cabin, digging in the gardens.

Supplies cost money, and growing enough to sell on top of what they needed for themselves required too many rules and policies. The commune wouldn't exist if that was how they'd wanted to live. But food was a regular need, and riskier to consistently steal. So the people who lived in Forgotten Peace were expected to garden, tend to the chickens, or contribute to the food supply in some other way.

Didn't mean the neighboring farmers and ranchers

didn't occasionally find a cow missing or produce trees pilfered.

She found Papa stooped over a large square plot tilled between two of the cabins. Grateful that there were few people about, she wandered toward him. Awareness prickled over her shoulders.

She probably had eyes on her. Word would've spread that she had returned. She didn't want to think about what that meant. Who she'd have to answer to.

Who she'd have to see again.

She shivered, the possibility of confronting the reason she'd left propelling her backward in time to the scorned and humiliated female she'd been all those years ago. It would be one thing to face Carlos Montoya with a steady career and the respect of their kind under her tactical belt. But she'd be facing him with even less than when he'd painted her a fool.

A shovel was sticking out from the dirt in the corner of the plot with a pile of red potatoes on the grass next to it.

Her stomach clenched and rumbled. For all his faults, Papa made excellent potatoes. "Are you going to make fried potatoes?"

He straightened with a grin and shielded his eyes from the sun. It had sunk low, barely brushing over the tops of the trees. "They're your favorite."

They were, and he'd remembered. She had a decision to make. Did she pretend like nothing had happened to keep her away for twenty-four years, or did she rip off the bandage and bring it up? "Does everyone know?"

Papa brushed his hands off on his cargo pants. They were frayed along the seams and there was a hole by one of the pockets. At one time, they'd probably been two-hundred-dollar pants. "That you're here? Yes, by now word has spread."

She hugged her arms tighter around herself, unable to warm up despite the Florida sun. "What did you tell them when I left?"

She'd fled a ritzy hotel in Tampa only to tell Papa goodbye. At the time, only two people had known the reason she'd abandoned Forgotten Peace, and she'd tried not to think of what Carlos might've said. He wouldn't have had to lie to make it look like she'd overreacted and overcorrected, blaming him.

That'd be pretty accurate.

But before she'd left, she'd told Papa that she was sick of the lying and thieving. That it shamed her, that their lifestyle made her sick.

"Ah." He propped his hands on his hips and stared at the green carrot tops in front of his shoes. "I told them that you wanted to find out who you were, and that you couldn't do that without living in Numen for a while."

That had become true once she was in Numen, a realm she'd been taken away from before she'd been old enough to form memories. Being born on Earth was like being a dual citizen. She enjoyed the privileges of both realms and could travel freely back and forth. But yesterday she'd experienced the drawback of not having been exposed to the politics of Numen, of not having been raised in that environment. "Is he around?"

Papa didn't meet her gaze. "He's around."

Her heart twisted. A boy she'd grown up with and trusted with every feather of her wings had only seen her as a tool. Carlos had been devastatingly handsome, and she'd been too naive to consider that what he used as a weapon on others could also be turned on her. "You think there will be problems with my presence?"

"You're one of us." His determined tone didn't match the uncertainty in his eyes.

"I'm an enforcer." Might as well get that out of the way. No one here was supposed to have anything to do with Numen. They shouldn't know about her, but she wanted to be transparent.

Papa's lips thinned. A few shades of color leached from his face. "You were always so preoccupied with rules. You wanted to create more when we're all together because we shunned them. And after what happened with Carlos . . . I can see you being an enforcer. Just like your mother."

Longing dug into her chest and burrowed in. She hadn't known her mother, who'd been killed in an angel fire incident right after she was born. A domestic dispute between two warrior mates, and Mother had taken the final abuse. "I don't know if I can go back. I don't know who I can trust."

The fatherly kindness she had missed over the years infused his expression. "But you aren't exactly the type to tolerate the unfairness of it."

"I want to find who killed him, not just to clear my name, but because something else is going on up there. Something big."

He shook his head, sadness entering his eyes. "There's always something big going on there, Tosca. That was what I was afraid you wouldn't understand. You can comb over a beach and clean up all the trash, but when you come back a week later, there'll be garbage all over again."

A couple of years ago, heck, a couple of days ago, she would've argued with him. Since she had started with the enforcers, she'd thought she could make a difference. She'd thought she could make the realm a place that wouldn't drive people like Papa away.

But ever since she had been assigned protection detail for Odessa Vale, before she'd become Director Vale's mate, it had been like trying to put out a fire that would never burn itself out. The fuel was plentiful and invisible, and the source was unknown.

"I want to clear my name. After that, I don't know."

"I understand." He gave her a small smile, but glanced around as if expecting to see the leaders of the commune marching to his door. Would they? Or were they discussing how best to utilize her presence for their own gain? Carlos's mother, Cordelia, was one of those leaders. She hadn't slept on a pallet then and Tosca doubted her living arrangements had gotten less luxurious over the years.

But she could make Papa's life easier, if only for a few moments.

"I still remember your trick for digging up carrots. Need help?"

She busied herself in the garden, enjoying a familiar task that she hadn't done in a couple of decades. She hadn't needed to garden unless she'd wanted to, and she hadn't wanted to. It would've made her reflect on home too much. It was hard enough to forget all the reasons why she had left this tidy little commune. The memories didn't help the paranoia that she would be found out, that her fellow enforcers would learn she was nothing but a common criminal on Earth.

"So who's Megan?" she asked, more to distract herself than out of curiosity. Papa had messed around with females here and there when Tosca was growing up, but they'd never moved in.

"She's sometimes more than a friend." The same answer she'd gotten when she'd asked about the others.

Was every male in the commune unwilling to commit? Perhaps it was Megan, perhaps it was the environment itself. A lack of meaningful connection. Using others for gain. Those were the unspoken foundations of Forgotten Peace.

Papa cleaned the potatoes and then went inside so he and Megan could peel them for frying. Tosca stayed outside to clean the rest of the produce. That part hadn't changed.

After several minutes, she smelled meat cooking.

"Still cattle rustling, I guess," she muttered under her breath.

A shadow fell over her. She looked up, intending to ask Papa if he needed some of these vegetables for the meal, when her gaze collided with a familiar deep-brown one that had visited her dreams too many times over the last several months.

Bronx towered over her. "Of all the things I thought you guilty of, stealing cows wasn't one of them."

THE STARTLED ANGEL popped to her feet, her eyes wide and her fists up. "I didn't do it."

"I wouldn't be here if I thought you had." That was an honest answer. Bronx had no business with Tosca. He should be grateful she'd been driven from the realm. She wouldn't be a thorn in his side anymore. She wouldn't be shadowing him, trying to determine what his team was up to and tattling to the senate.

But he couldn't leave it alone, and since the reason she'd been framed seemed tied to what his team had been working on for the last couple of years, he couldn't escape a sense of responsibility. His team had missed something, and it could cost Tosca her wings.

She lowered her hands, but confusion crossed her face. He'd never seen her like this. Instead of her sturdy black enforcer outfit, she was in a loose T-shirt and sweats. This was the first time he'd seen her with her stormy-gray wings morphed. Her short hair was mussed, and she looked like she had just walked off of a college campus.

"Did you find who killed him?" There was a hopeful note to her voice.

He could see why she asked. Why else would he be here? Unfortunately, he didn't have an answer she'd want to hear. "They aren't going to look beyond you."

Her shoulders slumped and her gaze darted around. They were concealed between two cabins. No one had seen him, he'd made sure of it. Urban hadn't followed him this far. According to Director Vale, this group would be less hostile if only one of them was caught within the confines of the cabins.

Bronx and Urban had gotten a crash course in the limited information the analysts had on Forgotten Peace. This little commune wasn't as forgotten as its residents hoped. Though the missing angels had been erased more thoroughly than this place had. But that was a concern for another day.

Tosca's wings, possibly her life, were in danger.

She pushed her hair off her face. A gentle breeze blew the dark-blond locks back into her eyes. She shoved them behind her ear with a dirty finger. This was a Tosca he'd never seen before.

"How did you find me?" she asked. Her hard, no-nonsense tone was still the same.

He leaned against the cabin wall. He was still in his standard warrior gear, dressed much like she usually was. Given the others roaming through this odd—town, camp, whatever they called it, he would stand out. But for now his dark attire helped him blend into the shadows. "It wasn't easy. Urban and I scoured the archives for hours, but when it became apparent we wouldn't find much information on you or your family, our contact figured it out. These people's secrets aren't as buried as they want them to be."

"They don't want their secrets buried. They just don't want anything to do with Numen," she said defensively.

He held his hands up, palms out. "You asked, I answered."

She rolled her eyes. "Contact? Really? You mean Odessa figured it out."

He chuckled because he couldn't help himself. This female had been framed for murder and risked losing everything that resembled her life. Yet she was still throwing around attitude. "She's damn good at her job. Now, want to tell me what happened?"

Soft footsteps rustled the grass behind him. He spun, crouching like Tosca had, ready for a fight. An older male with long hair the same color as Tosca's studied him. He wasn't as tall as Bronx, but with a compact body and wisdom in his pale-blue eyes, the relation was undeniable. This must be Tosca's father.

"She might as well tell both of us. I haven't heard it yet either." The male looked from Tosca to Bronx. "We aren't going to have a problem, are we?"

"No," he answered. "I have no issues with the people here."

"We may have resentments about our former home and some of the people in it, but all we want is a peaceful life."

There was something in Tosca's expression Bronx couldn't identify. Almost like she didn't quite agree with what her father had said. But again, Bronx wasn't here for them. And she probably wouldn't like what he had to say next. "I actually want to make a deal."

Tosca's gaze grew guarded. "I've had enough with deals, thanks."

"Senator Colbert didn't make a deal with you. She conned you. She used her station to gain your trust, and then she abused it. I'm going to be very open about what I want."

Her expression didn't soften, and she didn't look like she believed him. "Go on. We'll at least hear what you have to say."

We. Her and her father. Were they a team, or was she saying it out of respect, to keep the other male from getting worked up about his presence? If the latter was the case, she was shrewder than he gave her credit for. How had the senator gotten to her?

In the end, she was the one on the run for murder. Bronx had the upper hand, but it'd get him nowhere if he didn't work with her. She clearly had a history on Earth he knew nothing about, and if she wanted to run again, he might not be able to find her. "I help you figure out who murdered Jean Luc, and if you get your position back with the enforcers, you leave me and the rest of my team alone."

Her father made a disgusted noise. "Corruption everywhere."

If his wings had been out, they would've twitched at her father's insinuation. "Call who you want corrupt, but I will stand by every member of my team. We've been the only thing between innocent angels and violent demons too many times for me to tolerate that accusation."

His outburst made Tosca soften. "I want to know what's going on—on both ends. I want to clear my name, but not at the cost of ignorance about what you and your team are hiding."

Her adamant tone resonated. She was clueless about what had been done to her and why. She was afraid of it happening again. "I can't make that call. But I can talk to Director Vale."

She exchanged a look with her father. "How many people know where I am?"

He shrugged unapologetically. "The only people I trust in this world are my team."

She narrowed her eyes. "What about their mates?"

"Same." His loyalty was unwavering. Tosca had reason to be wary, but she had to rely on someone or she wouldn't get out of her situation. "My teammates' mates are like an extension of the team. I trust them to make good decisions with my life and theirs. And their mates have helped save all our lives at different points."

"I don't really have any bargaining power."

"I don't need to bargain, I just need you to tell me what your working relationship with Senator Colbert was like and the events that led up to Jean Luc's murder. Anything you can tell me about her or anyone else in the senate you've interacted with might lead in the right direction."

She exchanged another look with her father. Disapproval radiated from him, but he was in a similar situation. It was either play ball or Bronx could inform the realm about this place. Not all the residents in this realm were innocent victims of Numen circumstance. Tosca was on the run. Others might be in hiding because they *weren't* the victims.

"Fine," she relented. "But you're helping me clean these vegetables."

DIONNA CRANED her neck from side to side. Her back ached. She spent a lot of time in the human realm, but never in this long of an unbroken stretch. Her wings had been morphed for weeks, and it grated on her.

So did not doing her job.

Her mate hadn't let his wings down for years. He'd endured the discomfort to maintain distance between them.

The sun beat down on her. The market was loud, hot, and busy. Women walked by with large baskets or circular trays full of items on their heads. Men and women peddled their goods on each side of the street—clothing, art, jewelry. Dionna wished all she had to do was make a few purchases and go about her day.

She recognized the seller who'd spoken to her mate last week about an old buddy who needed an irrigation system on his oil palm farm.

"Hello, Dionna," he greeted. "Did I change your mind about a new dress?"

She eyed the bright-yellow-and-orange wrap dress with peacock-blue accents, complete with large pockets. Each one was sewn by either his wife or his daughters. They were exquisite, and nothing like Dionna usually wore.

She was a warrior. Her uniform was black pants and black shirts, a color that hid blood better. If she was hunting a demon among humans, then she wore what the locals wore, true. But even so, her wardrobe was necessity based, and there was no need for material that looked like heaven to wear.

She wore a dress now. Nothing as festive as the yellow-and-orange wrap dress. Hers was brown, like her sandals. Cheap attire she'd procured for what was supposed to have been a short stay.

As much as she admired his wares, she wasn't here to shop. "No, thank you. Have you seen Charles?"

It wasn't unusual to wake up in bed without her mate. Since she'd come to Ghana, Charles hadn't exactly been welcoming, but he'd been there more days than not, and the quick couplings in the dark before reality wedged between both of them had kept her hopes up.

There was a time he would have lit up like a candle when she walked into a room. But as time had marched on and she'd continued her work as a warrior, he'd grown more distant. As if it was a slight that she spent time saving the souls of humans instead of hanging out with him in the clouds.

He might've left Numen, but he hadn't left Accra while she'd been here. Now, he'd been gone since yesterday morning. Since their argument. Either he was in danger, or he had left her again.

She'd overheard him discussing a possible new irrigation project with their daughters, so she knew which scenario was more likely—and more convenient for him. She tired of being hurt by someone who should be her biggest supporter.

The man screwed his face up. "He's at my friend Afi's farm. That project will take days, maybe even weeks."

She had familiarized herself with the geography around Accra. The village was an hour outside city limits, even without factoring in zones of heavy traffic. Given the commute, he must've left knowing that he'd be staying on the farm for the duration of the project. Hurt and irritation mixed inside of her.

She could hear him sneering, *How is it any different than the missions you go on? A month on Earth? Two months? You leave and you don't know where you are going or how long you'll be gone.*

The man snapped his fingers. "My son, he drives a cab. He'll take you."

She held back a sigh. She could afford the round trip, but she hated to take someone away from their job just because her mate had ditched her. "Thank you for the offer, but no. I don't want to take him away from work that long. He won't return until late."

"It's okay. He likes the long fares. He's trying to build a photography portfolio, and small trips give him new scenery. You'd be doing him a favor."

Well, when he put it that way. She hated to chase after Charles, but she needed to make sure he was okay.

One of them had to care.

How many nights in the last several years had she returned to their empty home in Numen, bruised and beaten from a demon fight? Mates could aid with healing. Mates could be emotional support through the ugliest parts of a warrior's job. But not long after their youngest was born, Charles had started with the comments. Why did she have to be gone all the time? Why was she constantly putting herself in danger when they had a small family? Did she love her work more than them?

The questions had infiltrated their daughters' thoughts, and it wasn't long before they had started asking the same questions. When they'd been old enough to learn to hold their wings in a long-term morph, Charles had moved them to the human realm for humanitarian work.

If you're not going to be home, why should we?

"Where can I meet your son?" The market didn't allow vehicle traffic.

Charles's friend pointed to the end of the booths, where the pathway opened to a sidewalk that bordered a city road. "I'll call him and see when he can be here."

"All I need is time to grab a few things."

Her gaze caught on the dress he'd tried to sell her. She was a tall female, but the garment would sweep the top of her ankles, as if the dressmaker had known she preferred more coverage over less. The peacock blue against her dark-brown skin would be a stunning combination, and the pops of yellow in the pattern were like jewelry. Perfect for someone like her who didn't wear accessories—unless she counted her weapons. The only adornments Dionna wore were her dagger holsters and the chain she kept her vial of angel fire secured with.

No. This wasn't her world. She worked here, she didn't live here. She'd waited for Charles to talk to her. For a way to meet in the middle. But in the end, she'd been the one to bend.

She hadn't broken. She could bend further, and she needed an advantage. "Actually, I'd like to buy the dress before I go."

Would a pretty garment help catch Charles's eye? Who knew? She wouldn't question it, otherwise she'd ask herself a question she'd been avoiding for the last couple of days.

If her mate would rather avoid her than work on their relationship, why should she stay?

CHAPTER 5

*H*ow had he found her so fast? Even with Odessa's help, it had barely been a day since she'd fled. But Bronx had found her exact location.

As a warrior, he had an advantage. She hadn't traveled far from Forgotten Peace and Tampa during her time on Earth. Bronx would've been all over for his job. He would've been able to transcend close to the commune and drive the rest of the way. The trees would've concealed him while he'd searched for her, and she hadn't been out in the open, but Papa's cabin was on the edge. She'd unknowingly made it easy for Bronx to spot her.

Papa had set a plate for Bronx. While they ate, Megan watched Bronx like he was a cobra ready to strike.

Papa wasn't as intimidated. "Who were you born to?" He might be nosy, but she detected nostalgia in his question too.

Bronx finished chewing his potatoes. Surprisingly, the male had manners. They'd had an adversarial relationship for so long she hadn't thought of him as anything other than oppositional. But he hadn't made a comment about the crystal goblets they drank water from, or the gold-rimmed plates, or the real silverware. She'd grown up with these table settings, often forgetting Papa had scored them off a rich, dying widow's estate. But even if Bronx didn't know his C. Parlon from his Corelle, the difference between the dinnerware and the surroundings had to be obvious.

His love for his parents was clear when he answered. "My parents are Robert—Bobby—and Roxanna Lee."

Megan's head tilted like she didn't recognize them. Papa thought for a moment. "Both warriors?"

Bronx nodded. "I come from a long line of warriors, but my parents both retired when they bonded."

"And your name? A combination of theirs?"

Surprise flitted across his face. "Yes. Not many put that together."

"Many in that realm have lost their capacity to care beyond themselves."

Bronx's smile was pleasant but tight. "Many haven't."

"Yet you're in my home, taking advantage of my hospitality, helping my daughter for your own benefit."

"The answers behind what happened to her could save more innocent angels. Angels who dedicate their lives to helping humans." Bronx's point wasn't subtle. He knew the people living at Forgotten Peace didn't aid humanity in a darn thing. What he'd noticed within hours had taken her years.

Megan abruptly stood and jerked her plate off the table. She hadn't talked much to Tosca last night, and today was no exception. Bronx's presence had only added to the tension.

When Megan stormed out the front door, Papa said, "Please excuse her. I won't discuss her background, only that the presence of a warrior is deeply upsetting to her."

Bronx's forehead creased as he processed the information. She expected more obstinance, a blanket defense of his fellow warriors, but he surprised her again. "I understand."

Papa rose, eating the last of his food as he did. He took his plate to the sink and carefully set it next to Megan's. "I'll let you have some privacy to talk. But I can't offer you a place to stay tonight."

"Understood."

Tosca took another bite. She'd been little more than a spectator for most of the meal. The flavor of the buttery potatoes dusted with chives fell flat on her tongue. Tonight could've gone worse, but it could be going better.

Bronx pushed his empty plate away and reclined in the chair. "Start at the beginning."

She speared a carrot. The urge to clean her plate was stronger than ever. When the commune had to either grow their own food or steal it, waste was not appreciated. "Juliette invited me over—"

"No. The very beginning."

She couldn't keep annoyance off her face. "There was a sperm cell that was faster than all the others—"

"Tosca, this isn't funny."

She dropped her fork on her plate. The clatter rang between them. "Don't you think I know that? I was drugged by someone I trusted and thought was a friend. Then I woke up next to her husband, covered in his blood. My coworkers, people I should be able to trust with my life, tried to arrest me. They all thought I was guilty." She poked her chest. "Me! I've never woken up in any bed that wasn't my own." She picked her fork up and stuffed the carrot in her mouth before she could say more.

Bronx was quiet for several moments. A relief, since he usually enjoyed pestering her.

Finally he spoke. "I don't know what could be important. Maybe start a little later than the moment when the sperm met the egg, but gloss over the early years."

His gentle, professional tone slowed her racing heart. Usually, it was easy to dislike him. Tonight was different. *He* was different. And after yesterday, she was different.

"This place shuns Numen rules and restrictions. Mostly that means they don't like the senate, or they don't want to do any of the jobs available to them, but they think they are better than helping humans all day."

"I knew people like that. I always wondered what happened to them when they dropped out of warrior training camp."

"Walk around the camp and you'll probably see a few familiar faces." She scooted her chair farther away from the table and leaned against the wall, kicking her legs out to cross her feet at the ankles. His gaze dropped to her ankles. Dirt was smudged on her skin underneath the straps of her Birkenstocks. "My mother was an enforcer and she died on a call when I was a baby. Papa couldn't stand living in a realm where her killers weren't punished. An *accident*, they called it."

"The records said she was responding to a domestic dispute."

"Between two warriors," she said flatly. "Two warriors who were threatening each other with their angel fire, and then it got dumped on Mother. All the senate said was, 'Oops.' For Papa, it was either murder them or move here."

His brows dropped down. He crossed his arms over his chest, and she forced her gaze to stay on his face. He had a nice body. Lean and strong. And he knew it. Tosca detested arrogant males who were far too aware of how good they looked and the effect they had on females.

But he wasn't using his charm on her, and that was the biggest reason she'd decided to work with him.

That, and she had nowhere else to go.

"How did you come to live in Numen if that was where your mother died?"

"I was an angel in a human world. My wings hadn't seen the sun." She would leave it at that. Just like she would gloss over the next stretch of her life. "When I was an adult, I wanted to know where I came from. I wanted to know that side of me."

"And since they knew your mother, they probably didn't check on you, or ask where you'd been."

She snorted. "I doubt they even knew Papa was gone. He was a supplier, bringing goods from Earth to Numen. He didn't show for work one day and someone took his place. I don't think anyone thought to look for him."

He considered her information, or lack of. "When you became an enforcer, what was it like?"

Lonely. "I did my job. It was cliquish, which makes sense now. I wanted to enforce the rules, and others wanted to enforce the personal agendas of senators. But I was left to do my job."

"Which involved?"

Bronx's clinical demeanor helped her answer. He wasn't questioning her character, or trying to prove that she was lying. He was the closest thing to an ally she had.

"I investigated vandalism and theft. Petty stuff, mostly minor squabbles between angels, and the typical poor decisions young angels make. Being put on Odessa's guard detail was a big step up for me." And she'd been thrilled. Finally, she could provide a service that protected her people instead of their produce and lawn ornaments.

"After Stede was gone, then what?"

"I was made supervisor. I reported to the senators, and

Senator Colbert took me under her wing. It seemed like a natural progression."

"What did you think when Jean Luc got out of jail?"

She'd trampled her suspicions and paid for it. "I planned to follow up on it. He said he'd lured those angels to the human realm and sold them to demons. Then he said he'd only confessed to save his son's good name. But his son was already dead. That was a convenient retraction, and I thought I should look into it."

"Did Senator Colbert know you were going to investigate her mate?"

She shook her head. "He had just gotten out of jail. I barely had the thought before I was passing out."

Bronx reclined in his chair and worried his chin between his thumb and forefinger. It was such a mature move for a guy who looked like he was still in his twenties. He had long, elegant fingers. The angles of his face were harsh in some places, soft in others. A square jaw with a sharp chin. He was a hard male not to take notice of, and many females loved to do more than notice. Tosca didn't love it, but she couldn't help it. "Do you think she poisoned you and killed her mate?"

"Yes."

His brows shot up as if he'd expected her to defend the senator. Her only redeeming quality was that she didn't get fooled by the same person twice.

"She might not have wielded the knife herself, but she had help and I was convenient. Juliette probably wanted to distance herself from her mate to retain power in the senate."

Bronx leveled his stare on her. "Juliette, eh?"

She gave him a falsely sweet smile. "She said I could call her that, right before she served me drugged wine and framed me for the murder of her mate. She's no senator in my book."

"Then there are more people involved than we thought. We need to know who they are and what they're planning."

A commotion sounded outside the door. Raised voices. Papa was telling someone to stop and wait.

Megan slammed the door open. Carlos was behind her.

Of all the ways to add salt to her wounds, it would be for Carlos to see her like this. Disgraced and slinking back to the commune after she'd gone off on him in a righteous rage. Not only that, she was in borrowed clothing and getting interrogated by a warrior. And she still had dirt on her feet.

While he'd been naked the last time she'd seen him, he was now dressed in ash-gray slacks and a white button-up shirt, as if he'd been dragged out of a board meeting. His hair was dark as Bronx's but with a slight curl over his brow. His gaze was more intense, more worldly, and the power that emanated from him said that more than his mother was now in charge of the commune.

Megan jabbed her finger in the air toward Bronx. "He has to go."

Papa edged past her into the house as if he was afraid he'd have to jump between Megan and her target. "He is my guest."

"It's either him or me under this roof." Megan's voice shook. Tosca didn't know what had happened to her, but Bronx's presence was deeply upsetting.

Carlos's amber gaze swept down Tosca's body, leaving an oily feeling on her skin wherever it touched. Safe to say, she was over him. Had been as soon as she'd walked in on him and some flighty heiress he'd been scamming.

"Leave it to you to bring one of them here," Carlos sneered in that cultured tone he'd worked to develop when they were younger. Young and cocky and despising the rigidity of Numen.

"I brought myself here." Bronx rose and stood next to her, facing off with Carlos. Tension radiated from Bronx, but outwardly, he oozed calm. She could barely see Carlos around the warrior. Bronx wasn't as muscular as Carlos. "But hey, I wondered what you wanted to do after your training didn't work out."

Carlos's face flushed red. "I don't remember you."

"It's not usually the winners you remember."

Megan was shaking her head like she was trying to dislodge a squirrel from her hair. "I won't stay here. This is supposed to be a safe place. It's supposed to be safe. Carlos, you promised no warriors here."

Carlos twitched like he wanted to fight Bronx but knew better. He'd lose. Megan was nearing hysteria and Papa was rubbing her shoulders, trying to keep her anchored to the present. Tosca summoned all of her training, trying to figure out a way to defuse the situation.

Bronx spoke first. "May I have two minutes to talk to Tosca before I leave?"

It was like cool air flooded into the cabin and swept out the hostility. Megan sagged against Papa and hid her face in his shirt. Carlos took a step back as if he'd realized how close to chaos they'd come.

Papa turned his attention on Carlos. "All he asked for was two minutes." He kept the right amount of pleading in his voice, no censure. The Carlos she'd known had had a healthy amount of pride. Now, he seemed to have power. The two could be toxic.

"Two minutes." Carlos spun on a leather loafer. He touched Megan's shoulder, and with a squeak, she curled into him and allowed him to lead her out.

Papa's jaw clenched and he averted his gaze. When the

door slammed shut, he said, "Carlos has helped her a lot in her recovery." As if he was justifying to himself how close the two were.

"She's sleeping with him, then. Because that's what Carlos does."

The flash of anger in Papa's eyes was brief. She didn't know if it was directed at her comment, or the situation between Megan and Carlos. "I had my chance with a mate already. My sync is gone. Megan is free to be with whom she pleases."

Was it his unwillingness to commit again? Or that, like Tosca, he had nowhere else to go if he challenged either Megan or Carlos and lost? No matter the answer, the outcome for her was the same. "I can talk to Bronx outside."

"I'll give you two a moment." Papa turned his attention to Bronx. "We aren't here because we had good experiences in Numen. Your presence brings back a lot of the trauma and the fear that we're trying to heal from."

Bronx dipped his head, but he didn't readily placate Papa. "As long as this commune has nothing to do with the corruption in Numen, I have no business with any of you."

Confusion lit Papa's gaze. "Warriors hunt demons."

"Exactly," Bronx said, offering no other explanation.

With a small sigh, Papa left them alone.

Bronx turned to her. "Interesting place. Figures Carlos would be here."

Her curiosity got the better of her. They only had a couple of minutes, and she didn't want to spend it talking about Carlos, but she couldn't help it. "You know him?"

"He was a male who wanted to put in the least amount of effort to get all the reward."

She huffed out a laugh. "Sounds like him."

"You need to come with me."

In any other life, she might've relished those words coming from his lips and aimed at her. But even before she'd woken up next to a dead body, she would've refused him. She'd been burned by a playboy once already. Maybe Bronx gave his all as a warrior. Maybe he'd earned all the respect his team showed him. But as a male, he reminded her too much of Carlos. Sleek and brimming with false promises. She had the urge to please him, to do what he wanted, and that was the most dangerous feeling of all. She wouldn't go back there.

And as a fugitive, she couldn't drop everything and trust him just because he said so. "I'm staying here."

"Tosca, I'm trying to help you."

"You're trying to help your team. Whatever happened to me is connected to what you have been working on. You want answers, not to help me. I'm willing to work with you. I'm not willing to sit and drink wine with you."

Shadows darkened his eyes. He didn't like being compared to the senator, but she couldn't pivot from being suspicious of him for months to being dependent on him.

He tilted his head back and blew out a breath, his frustration apparent. Of all the body parts to pay attention to on a male, she hadn't thought a corded neck would be one of them. If she put her lips on his warm skin, would she feel his pulse?

She blinked out of her stupor when he spoke. "I get that you don't trust anyone in Numen—"

"I don't trust anyone here either. Perhaps Papa. But I do trust that they fear and dislike Numen enough to keep me a secret."

He studied her for a few moments, then nodded. "Do you have a phone?"

The commune probably had a variety of the newest smartphones. "Not that I have access to."

"Here." He dug his phone out of one of his cargo pockets and tapped around before handing it to her. It was warm from being against his body and she dropped it in her pocket before she could do something like cradle it against her chest. "Urban's waiting for me. His number's in there. I wiped out my password so you can set your own. Sierra will get me a new one."

Alarm jolted through her. Sierra. She had lost her wings. A fallen. Tosca had suspected the former warrior wasn't as former as the realm thought she was.

Bronx winced like he realized what he'd said. "She's no longer a part of Numen, but she still helps us. Looks like you have a secret of mine to keep."

"One of the hardest and firmest rules of our realm is to pretend like the fallen have never been a part of our lives. We're supposed to forget about them, ignore them. Do you know how many people in this commune are here because they couldn't stand to live in their home while their loved one lost their wings and was suffering somewhere on Earth?"

"Sierra was exploited for the benefit of a corrupt few. She dedicated her life to the realm, and she paid for it." He started for the door, dismissing the subject.

"Good thing she wasn't like the rest," Tosca said sarcastically. She had nothing against Sierra. The other female had seemed diligent and committed to her work the few times Tosca had interacted with her. So why was she so cranky about the news that Sierra's fall had turned into nothing but an inconvenience? It just seemed . . . so easy for others to bend the laws.

Bronx stopped at the door. "No, she wasn't like the rest. She was a lot like you."

When he was gone, she sank into her seat. He'd nailed the reason why the mention of Sierra had upset her. A

female with secrets who'd been alone and unable to help
herself. The only difference between them was that Tosca
still had her wings.

∾

AFTER A LONG DRIVE, after arriving in the middle of
nowhere with a single bag and no notice, after letting the
farmers know that she had nowhere else to stay, Dionna
had been welcomed by the couple who owned and ran the
palm oil farm, Afi and Zuri Mensah.

Zuri had answered the door in a green collared dress
with a white apron over it. When Dionna had introduced
herself as Charles's wife, she'd been pulled in for a giant
hug and showered with accolades about her mate.

Zuri was a lovely, energetic woman with grown
children who also worked the farm. She immediately led
Dionna to the bedroom Charles was using. Dionna
changed out of the gorgeous dress she'd just bought and
put on her more functional dress. She'd come thinking
she'd woo back her mate, but he was legitimately working.
And she refused to treat his job as if it wasn't important
to him.

She stepped out of the room and came face-to-face
with her two daughters coming out of the bedroom they
were sharing. They, too, had left Accra to help Charles
with the irrigation project, but none of them had informed
her.

Delight crossed Stella's face, but she smothered it.
"Mother? How did you find us?"

Courtney crossed her arms. They were dressed like her.
She'd made the right decision changing her clothes. She
was a fish out of water around her family as it was. She
didn't need to stick out on the farm.

"I have my ways," Dionna joked.

"Only when you want." Sadness touched Courtney's words, and she walked down the hall toward the main part of the house.

Dionna let her go. Some battles had been fought too many times for there to be a winner. She smiled at Stella. "Where is your father?"

"In the field. You can see the group if you go out the back door by the kitchen. That's the one everyone else uses."

She had an ally, if only while Courtney and her stronger personality weren't around. "Thank you."

"I'm glad you're here. It means a lot, it's just . . ."

"I understand."

"Daniel will be here soon, and they're waiting to start until he arrives." Stella rewarded her mother with a small smile before leaving in the direction of her older sister.

Daniel. The young human male was eager to intern for Charles in the irrigation project. The oil palm farm used natural watering methods but needed the stability irrigation would provide. Charles was renowned in his work, having learned much "at his father's feet."

Charles and the male everyone thought was his father were one and the same. And in twenty years, he'd go to another country with another name and talk about how he'd taken over for "Charles." When no one remembered the earlier ancestors, he could start over.

The girls were in their twenties and they looked it. Dionna and Charles could pass for a young fifty, though most people assumed they were in their thirties until one of them said otherwise. If asked, they said they had married young and had kids fast. Would it have been better if that had been the case, if she and Charles hadn't had so much time to themselves before they'd met and mated?

Outside, she walked under the fronds of the trees, some low enough to brush the top of her head. The plants resembled large pineapples that had decided they were now trees.

Up ahead, Charles talked excitedly with two local farmers. He stuttered over words when he saw her approach but otherwise didn't acknowledge her existence.

The man Charles addressed more than the others was Zuri's husband. He'd married into the family but kept the farm going, adding maize to grow with the oil palm. Afi smiled and made room in the circle for her.

Dionna waited patiently as Charles outlined his plan, stretching his arms wide and using his whole body to show where pipes would go, and how gravity would be a driving force behind the system.

Her mate had trimmed his curly black hair nearly to the scalp, preparing for long hours under the sun. The way he spread his arms accentuated his barrel chest. She missed his slate-gray wings and how they lifted and twitched as much as his hands when he talked.

She picked at a loose strand of her dress. Her angel fire vial was tucked between her breasts and her knives were strapped to her thighs. Charles would surely disapprove. She always made sure they were hidden away in her folded clothing before she crawled into bed with him.

At a break in the conversation, she spoke up.

"Charles." She adopted the same accent as him. She had heard the story he gave the locals and strangers he came in contact with. Always vague about exactly where he'd been born, he spoke of growing up in Accra and moving around the country, a large enough place to get lost in.

Angels could go anywhere on Earth for humanitarian efforts, but Africa, specifically Ghana, had attracted

Charles, and he was more at home here than he had ever been in Numen. She could see that now.

He felt useful here. In Numen, he was either waiting on her to return home, or he was on Earth without her. Might as well leave the realm and make friends while he was at it.

Her girls were less restrained than they had been growing up. There was a freedom on Earth that was missing in Numen.

Dionna hadn't noticed, thanks to her job. She came and went from her realm more often than most other angels. The cloying environment of the senators and their attitudes, and sometimes the attitudes of their families, was why she hadn't fought Charles when he'd insisted on moving him and their children to the human realm.

He had called her selfish for dedicating so much time to her job, and she'd thought he was selfish for leaving. But the move hadn't been selfish. He hadn't done it solely for him. Stella and Courtney were happy on Earth. They enjoyed helping their dad, and the cost of keeping wings morphed was small compared to the personal freedom they experienced.

Still, it didn't excuse Charles's sheer rudeness at the moment.

He continued talking.

"*Charles.*" With that tone, she'd have every warrior within earshot at attention.

He paused and almost looked her way, then resumed speaking, his hands flailing in the air. She used to be charmed by the way he talked with his hands.

Charm was nowhere to be found. She was annoyed. "Charles!" she barked.

He flashed his most winsome smile at the two men he'd been speaking to. That smile had won her over. His joy became her joy whenever he aimed his grin her way. But she hadn't seen it in years, and right now, it was fake. "Excuse me," he said to the men before turning on her and leading her away from the group, several trees down.

There was no sign of the smile when he turned to her. "You did not need to worry yourself with coming here, Dionna."

"I am not giving up on us, but if you're going to, then perhaps you should say something." Her throat grew thick and she had a tough time swallowing. What if he did say something?

His expression softened, revealing the pain he hid from her. Pain she'd caused.

Her phone buzzed. His gaze flattened, dipping to the pocket it was nestled in. "Sounds like work is calling."

She ground her teeth together and willed her muscles to remain still. She would not answer.

But it was probably work. She never had to worry about reception or signal with her natural energy powering technology. Explaining why she got better service than anyone else could get tricky, but answering her phone right now would only make it look like her mate was justified with how he was acting.

Her phone buzzed again. She held in her groan. "How long are you staying here?"

And another buzz. These were the moments she wished she swore as fruitfully as the rest of her teammates.

"Until the job is done."

The annoying vibration continued in her pocket until it blended in with the sounds of insects around them. "And how long is that?"

"An irrigation system for these crops could take weeks."

That was a generic answer, but she couldn't argue. An irrigation system was no simple plumbing job, and Charles would make sure the pipes were set correctly and working before he left. He was renowned for a reason, and not just because he'd found a reason to make his work nearly free.

Her spark of pride would never die, but it was being smothered in frustration. "Then I will stay here for weeks. I can help."

Anything other than sitting around and being ignored by those she loved the most in the world.

"Dionna," he scoffed. "We both know you can't stay away from work so long. Answer your phone and go do what you're called to do."

He returned to the men. She didn't have to see his face to know the smile was back in place, and he was likely apologizing for her interruption.

Her chest burned. At some point she would get tired of him dismissing her, but she had never been one to give up on a mission.

Except that she knew the purpose of most of the missions she went on. What was her purpose here? She wanted to reconcile with her mate and daughters. She wanted them to understand how much they meant to her, but that it was unfair for them to ask her to sacrifice human lives to be with them.

The hurt she had briefly glimpsed in his eyes was branded on her brain. She'd been dismissing her family's feelings as thoroughly as Charles had been turning his back on her.

The real question was whether Charles was still invested in their relationship or if he had truly given up.

Her phone started up again. With one last look at her mate's broad back in his navy-and-white-striped polo shirt, she ducked next to a tree to answer.

It was Director Vale. "Dionna, we have a situation. I wanted to keep you updated."

A beat of relief passed through her, and she briefly

closed her eyes. She wasn't being called to carry out a task. After her interaction with Charles and her claims of wanting to help, leaving might be the final nail in the coffin of their bond. "Go ahead."

Director Vale was blissfully intolerant of small talk. He got straight to the point and didn't ask her about how things were going in her private life. He cared, but he wasn't a talker or a sharer. And neither was she. "Tosca, one of the enforcers on Odessa's bodyguard detail?"

"I remember."

"She was framed for Jean Luc Colbert's murder."

Shock chased off a few degrees of the heat crowding around her. Would the treachery in the realm never end? "You know for sure she was framed?"

"Confident enough. It makes a lot more bloody sense that Senator Colbert is up to her elbows in treason."

Dionna stayed as far away from senators' business as she could, and she had never liked Senator Colbert. The female was just another high-society snob who flaunted her power in front of those she thought were below her, which was nearly everyone. Those types were never trustworthy.

"Tosca escaped before she was arrested," Director Vale continued. "Bronx tracked her down, got some information, but his access to her is limited."

Bronx had gotten to Tosca, but he couldn't be around her? Dionna had missed out on some events. Restlessness made her shift her stance and roll her shoulders. She'd been doing a whole lot of nothing, making no progress with Charles or her girls, and there were others who could use her help.

Frustration gnawed at her belly. "Call me if you need me?"

"That's why I filled you in. Urban's on top of things for

now, unless he draws too much attention coming and going. With Sierra off the grid, and Harlowe and Sandeen keeping a low profile after their upheaval with the senate, I have you and Ransom as Bronx's backups. With Felicia being a senator, there are too many eyes on Jagger."

"Understood. Where is Tosca?"

A raspy, humorless chuckle came over the line. "She's with a lot of people you and I would remember but others have completely forgotten. They've set up some sort of commune in Florida."

"And the senate tolerates that?" She'd missed a lot, but nothing about demons. Those bastards were always involved.

His raspy chuckle came over the line again. "Isn't that the question of the day? They ran Bronx out. I told him to keep the peace, to work with them as much as possible. I don't want to scare Tosca off. Whoever did this to her is up to something, and I'm sure it's tied in with all the shit we've been dealing with for the last few years."

"Keep me posted." She disconnected the call and stared at her mate and the other two men walking through the field. Charles was gesturing in all directions, probably explaining flow rates and how he used solar panels to power the system.

She might be willing to help, but they didn't need her. Not yet. She took the same path back to the house, crossing the lawn. An entrance in the back opened near the kitchen and dining room. Most of the family used that entrance, likely to keep the more formal sitting room clean. The door accessed the hallway that led to the guest rooms.

The back seating area, patio chairs and a table for tea, looked clear. She could walk through and nurse her wounds in the privacy of her room before she sought out Zuri.

Courtney stepped out the door near the kitchen and spotted her. Her oldest daughter watched her with shrewd brown eyes so much like her father's. Courtney was as tall as Dionna, and could wield a hard look that would cleave a lesser being at their knees. But her attitude was all Charles too.

Courtney arched a dark brow. "You're getting into humanitarian work now? I thought being a warrior was the *most* noble profession."

Dionna tried not to bristle at her daughter. She'd saved the souls of countless humans, freed them from demons, and kept the underworld creatures from interfering with their lives. "I will help where I can."

A tall man stepped out of the entrance Dionna had been aiming for. His gaze instantly went to Courtney, and infatuation filled his expression. He rubbed his hands together like talking to her daughter would be the highlight of his year. "Hello, Courtney. Did you bring another worker with you?"

Charles, Courtney, and Stella functioned as a family-owned irrigation company that charged reasonable rates. She doubted her name was attached to the company at all.

"Yes, I'm willing to dig some trenches," Dionna answered before Courtney could make an excuse for why Dionna had to leave. Otherwise it would be awkward when she insisted on staying.

"Perfect." He grinned. "Are you familiar with irrigation systems, or an intern like me?"

She almost laughed. She was over two hundred years old. It'd been a long time since she'd interned. "Charles is my husband. I'm Dionna."

Surprise crossed the man's face, and his gaze jumped to

Courtney. Dionna's stomach bottomed out. What had her daughter told him?

Courtney frowned, confusion in her eyes. "I'm sorry, Daniel. Did you think my mother had passed when I said she wasn't around?"

Dionna's sharp inhale sliced the air.

Daniel's eyes widened a moment before his nervous laugh. "I'm so sorry. My mistake."

Courtney chuckled with him, but she avoided Dionna's gaze. Her daughter hadn't told anyone she'd died, but Courtney hadn't said enough about her to make them think she was alive either.

The path to her bedroom and much-needed privacy extended five times longer than before.

As Daniel rejoiced in her unneeded resurrection, Dionna's thoughts returned to the trouble with the enforcer. No matter what was going on in her life, her mind kept swinging back to work. If she wasn't careful, her body would follow. It was natural to go somewhere you were wanted, and she was starting to fear that her family would never want her around again.

CHAPTER 6

"She'll call," Urban said.

Bronx tapped his fingers on the countertop of the booth he sat in with Urban. Both were dressed in basketball shorts and plain T-shirts, their weapons secured under the loose clothing. The AC was running full tilt and he wasn't in a hurry to go back outside. But he was frothing at the mouth, waiting for Tosca to call.

This safe house was one of the nicer ones he'd stayed in. It was two stories, along with the other houses in the area. Suburbs could be tricky to set up shop in, but the place was for rent and had come fully furnished. He and Urban had spent the first day setting up the security system Sierra had told them to purchase. They had full view of the street to each side and the cypress-tree-crowded lawn behind the house.

For the last two days, they'd sat around, prepared to extract Tosca. The neighborhood wasn't the shortest drive away from the commune, which was why they picked random diners and restaurants to hang out in halfway between.

He continued the steady drum of his fingers. "Farmers' market?"

Urban's mouth quirked as he thought about it. "From just a few gardens? For that many people?"

Bronx had described Forgotten Peace and the layout to Urban. The small cabins with worn wooden floors and creaky doors but fucking gold-lined plates. The clothing Carlos wore hadn't come from a department store. The gold watch on his wrist repelled nickel and he acted like a male who only knew the best.

And Bronx hadn't liked the proprietary way Carlos had eyed Tosca. He'd looked at Megan like she was one of the herd. But anger and ownership had mingled in his expression when he watched Tosca.

But back to how the commune paid for what they had. Several acres close to a large city, surrounded by trees? That didn't come cheap. Angels familiar with the human world, and who'd been around long enough, had learned to invest and grow money for their playtime on Earth. But that many cabins and a main building, with water and electricity, would need steady financial support. Did enough Numen leave the realm and donate their wealth?

"They don't ranch or farm," he grumbled as he looked at his new phone for the millionth time. Tosca didn't have his number, but Urban had demanded he quit asking if she'd checked in.

"Maybe they donate plasma."

That was a fuckload of plasma. "They pay for it somehow and I think the answer is going to surprise us."

"A wellness retreat for humans? They could charge thousands for that shit."

It'd be profitable, but Bronx hadn't seen any signs of humans. It'd be too risky for a community that wanted to stay off Numen's radar.

Urban took a drink of his fifth refill. The server was eying them like she was about to tell them they'd overstayed their welcome. He kept his voice low. "Who do you think polices them? It's not the enforcers, because Malin didn't say a word." At Bronx's raised eyebrow, he grunted. "Trust me. She said a lot of words. Talked nonstop for hours. I think she has a thing for the guy we saw hanging out the window when Tosca transcended. If they knew where Tosca was, she would have said. But anyway, enforcers don't leave the realm, and warriors only deal with demons. Human police won't be effective."

All Urban had gotten from Malin was confirmation that Tosca had seemed groggy to the two guys who'd found her. And she'd been naked and in bed with Jean Luc. Naked. That thought made Bronx's skin too tight. "That's for the senate to decide, and it seems at least some on the senate know about the commune."

"Then that place serves their purpose somehow and they can't be policed." Urban sat back and slung an arm over the edge of the booth. He glanced out the window and his gaze turned hard.

Bronx discreetly peered in the same direction. Two symasters clung to the back of a young couple walking their dog on the busy street. The girl kept stumbling, and if she wasn't careful, she'd tumble into traffic. "Shit."

"We can keep ourselves busy while waiting for Tosca to call."

"If she doesn't, I'm going in after her. We aren't figuring shit out in separate places."

Odessa was researching the senator and her dead mate. Felicia, her sister and a senator, was nosing around, trying to find information on Carlos.

"Agreed. But we can't ignore them."

No. If the couple survived the symasters' invisible tampering, they'd end up possessed.

Tosca was in trouble, but he and Urban were warriors first.

Two warriors without a team, making it more difficult to conceal their identity from humans, keep innocent parties from getting hurt, and kill the demons without mortally wounding themselves or worse.

Urban lifted his chin. "They're coming in."

"That'll make it easier." But it didn't help the Tosca situation. "Can you just message her?"

"Dude. You made me send her a message yesterday."

He had. And the day before that. And before that, when he hadn't had his own phone.

The couple entered the restaurant on a wave of swear words and insults.

"Stupid fucker."

"You owe me a sandwich, bitch."

The good news was that they took the server's attention off Bronx and Urban. But nothing could be done until they had some privacy. The humans in the diner couldn't know anything was different about him or Urban. And they certainly couldn't see him or Urban disappear when they yanked the demons into the Mist. The foggy realm-between-realms was the only place they were allowed to fight demons. Humans couldn't enter.

He took a drink of his ice water. Two half-melted ice cubes were left.

"Fuck off!" The young woman stomped past them on a wave of menthol cigarette smoke. She was going in the direction of the bathroom.

"I ain't fucking off anywhere." The man marched after her, adjusting the zipper of his baggy jeans. "That's your job."

"I'll take the girl. I'm gonna risk looking like a perv." Bronx slid out and followed them through the maze of tables, checking his phone like he hadn't noticed the couple arguing in front of him.

Urban slid out behind him and made a show of stretching and tossing money for the meal and tip on the table.

The girl disappeared into the bathroom nook and a door squeaked open. Perfect. Bronx slowed his steps until the guy veered into the men's room, then he charged into the women's bathroom.

The girl was about to shut the stall door when he pushed through, palming one of his daggers. "Oh, excuse me. I'm in the wrong—"

He snatched an arm of the little demon piggybacking on her and yanked as he muttered the incantation to get them both to the Mist. The girl's eyes unfocused and she blinked, confused, as Bronx disappeared.

As soon as the cool droplets of the Mist caressed his skin, he sank his knife into the bony body of the four-foot-tall demon. It snarled and twisted, but Bronx withdrew his knife, tossed the demon to the ground, and ran his blade across the thing's neck. Over and over until he wrenched the head away.

He wiped his blade on the grass and rose, barely breathing harder than when he'd entered the bathroom. Urban wasn't in sight, but geography in the Mist didn't work like usual.

He'd have to transcend to the privacy nook they'd made outside their safe house. Urban would do the same, and they'd have to call a car to come and pick up their ride.

Unless Tosca called. And if she didn't, he was going after her.

SHE WAS WORKING in the garden when she sensed the presence next to her. Based on the lack of tingles or an instant surge of defensiveness, it wasn't Bronx. He'd made good on his agreement to stay out of the commune.

Beside her, Papa stood with a pensive expression and his hands shoved into the pockets of his linen pants. She straightened, biting back a wince. The constant morph of her wings was taking its toll on her muscles. Cramps in her shoulders had woken her several times the previous night.

She shielded her eyes from the sun. "Is everything all right?"

He glanced furtively around before he walked carefully between the rows of carrots and turnips. He stooped to tug at a couple of carrot tops. She followed his lead and did the same.

He set a wad of cash on the ground by her bare foot. "You need to leave."

She nearly straightened again, but he was being secretive for a reason. She shifted up a row to the radishes. "How soon?"

There was no point in asking what was going on. *She* was what was going on. The last three days, no one had come near Papa's cabin. No one. Megan hadn't returned, and each time Tosca stepped outside, the already humid air thickened. People were talking about her. Deciding. And Papa must've caught wind that what they had decided wouldn't benefit her.

Cordelia was no longer in charge. Carlos was. Tosca's history with him didn't make her think she was immune to his power trip. Right before she'd left, he'd proven what was most important to her wasn't to him.

"As soon as you can without being too obvious," he

replied, giving a radish a tug. "They'll know I told you, but hopefully you'll be gone before anyone from the realm gets here."

"I would think they'd be happy to see me go."

"That's the problem. After you were gone, I watched Carlos turn into everything you said he was. He's selfish. His mother was too, but he's on a different level, and I don't trust him. But no one else sees it."

"No one else sees how decked out Peacequarters has become while every cabin takes on a little more wear every year?" She didn't wait for his reply before gathering a handful of radish greens to conceal the money she picked up. "I'll put these by the waterspout to wash them off, then I'll go for a walk."

His hands were full of carrots when he faced her. The sadness and regret in his eyes said he knew how long of a walk she was going on. "I'm sorry."

"Don't be. Thank you for your help."

A ghost of a sad smile crossed his lips. "I'm honored you came to me when you most needed help."

"I'm grateful for the time we had together." Turning before her eyes misted over for him and anyone watching from a distance to see, she dropped her vegetables by the water spigot. Before she reached the bathroom, she detoured out the back door to the shower stack. And she kept going, straight into the trees. It was broad daylight, but it'd look more suspicious if she was seen sneaking toward the trees.

She sent a message to Bronx describing where she'd be waiting, hoping he hadn't given up on her after so many days. Looking back, pride was the only reason for the wait. She'd needed time for her shock to wear off and she'd had Papa to catch up with. He'd asked about Numen and some of the people in it. She'd updated him on the various scandals. And he'd discussed the changes he'd been through. Cordelia's sudden passing. She'd gone back to Numen and walked into the fire after claiming Carlos as her replacement. Since she'd been the founder, no one could argue. Democratic process wasn't exactly built into the commune.

Things seemed good under Carlos, but the older angels like Papa had their concerns, though they kept quiet. The one male who'd spoken up a decade ago had disappeared a year later. Not soon enough to be coincidental, but odd nonetheless.

She couldn't do this alone and she should've called Bronx earlier. Her one-eighty in the trust department when it came to him disturbed her. It was against everything she'd experienced—with Carlos, with Juliette, and even with him. But she trusted him, and now was the time to admit it. She had heard enough about Bronx and his team to know that they took their jobs as warriors seriously, dedicating their lives to rescuing humans from demon influence.

"Tosca."

She nearly barked out a startled yelp, the muscles in her shoulders cramping, but her training kicked in. This wasn't her first time alone in the woods with a male. She kept a relaxed stance as she turned to face Carlos. Today he was dressed like he'd come straight from yoga—black fitted pants that showed off his lean frame and a black athletic shirt. Unlike her sandals, he had a pair of Nikes on. Probably stolen.

Her borrowed clothing was turning into stolen clothing, so she'd give him that leeway.

Had he been monitoring the cabin? She lifted her chin. "I don't have anything to say to you."

"You can tell yourself that."

She wanted to claw the arrogant smirk off his face. "Carlos, I'm going for a walk. Can we talk when I get back?"

"Where you going?" He stepped toward her.

She held up a hand. "You'd better stop, or we're going to have an issue. The trees aren't off-limits, are they?" She played up the indignation welling up inside her. Better than letting the anxiety that he was trying to stop her show on her face.

The change that came over him was instant. His expression darkened and the charming smile he used to cajole others was gone, replaced by desire and a come-hither curl of his lips. "You never had a problem with me getting close before," he purred in a more seductive voice than he'd ever used on her in the past. And he'd tried to get her to do stuff she hadn't been ready to do.

"I'm a lot pickier now about who I let get close to me." She cocked her head, trying to unnerve him. "But we both know you aren't."

Annoyance rippled over his face. "I wanted to see where you're going. Is everything okay?"

Change of tactics. He used to be more subtle than that. "No, Carlos, it's not. I'm going for a walk to clear my mind."

A cocky brow ticked up. "A walk through the crowded woods where there are chiggers and mosquitoes?"

Her ankles itched with just the mention. "I'm trying to figure out why you would care." She had made it sound flippant, but the question was very real in her mind. Why the hell did he care that she had disappeared into the woods? The rest of the commune was likely glad to see her gone.

"I've never quit caring about you, Tosca."

Typical Carlos. He could spin the truth in a way to keep

from lying. He had the looks of an angel, but his mind was as deceitful as a demon's.

"This helps with clearing my mind." She continued striding through the underbrush. If he followed, then she had a problem.

His footsteps rustled the plants and snapped twigs, growing closer.

Well, that was her answer. She spun. "Cut the crap. Why are you following me?"

"You killed someone, Tosca. I can't let you move around our home unobserved."

Her eyes narrowed but she wasn't solely focused on him. She listened for others following them and scanned the trees. She didn't sense anyone else. What was Carlos up to? And did anyone else know about it?

"What if I told you I was leaving?" She watched him carefully. The hair on the back of her neck was raised and turning her back on him earlier had felt too close to plastering her body with targets.

He was up to something.

"I can't let you do that. You're a wanted female. I have this place to think about, and the people in it."

"Wouldn't it be better if I was gone?" There was still something about his story that didn't fit the puzzle. These people weren't in the middle of a Florida wilderness because they followed Numen law to the letter.

"It would be better if you were in custody."

She sucked in a breath. He was working with someone in Numen. She didn't care about his motivations. Whatever they were, they were incompatible with hers.

"I'm innocent." It was just the two of them. She didn't want trouble, but she would kick his ass to get out of here.

That arrogant tilt was back. "If you could prove it, you wouldn't be here."

Proving her innocence would be difficult enough in a fair situation, but she wouldn't get the chance to prove her innocence. And he knew it.

A calculating gleam entered his eyes. The subtle tense of his muscles didn't escape her notice. He was going to charge her.

"Don't do this. It's not going to turn out how you want." She could turn and run, or she could use the training that had been worthless to her since she had woken up covered in blood.

Her confidence ruffled him. Uncertainty wavered in his eyes before his attention narrowed further. Then he lunged toward her.

She crouched and barreled into him, abruptly stopping his momentum and reversing it until he toppled backward. She fell with him, rolled, and hit her back against a tree trunk. A branch snapped against her hair.

He was quick to right himself, but not as quick as the enforcers she'd trained with.

She didn't jump up. Planting her hands against the ground, she swept her legs out, tripping him. He fell backward and his shoulder barreled into another tree, but the branches slowed his fall.

She stomped him in the stomach and took off running. She could continue to pummel him—she was tiny but trained. He'd been the cock of the walk in his minuscule little world for too long to realize that he didn't stand a chance against her. But it would be inviting trouble, and there was no need to add to her perceived crimes.

She ducked through limbs. Branches tangled in her hair, but she kept running. She needed to get as far away from the commune as fast as she could. The only thing saving her was that whoever he was in contact with hadn't been here before.

She had so many questions. About the commune. About Carlos. Fears for her papa. But the answers would come later.

Her breath sawed in and out of her lungs. She glanced behind her. Carlos staggered and stumbled after her, but she was increasing the distance between them.

Minutes passed, and when she looked again, he was gaining on her. She should've nailed him again like she'd wanted.

A break in the trees was up ahead. The road. She would make it there and take off down the highway.

The crashing behind her grew uncomfortably close. She put on as much speed as she could and broke through the tree line. As soon as her feet hit the pavement, she ran as fast as she could.

Unfortunately, when it came to sprinting, her shorter legs and sandals were a detriment. Carlos wouldn't have a problem catching up with her. She was winded and tired, and fighting him would be harder than it would've been earlier.

A car appeared around the curve, slamming on its brakes as soon as the driver saw her. She didn't care who was driving, she was getting in. As she raced toward the red Corolla, Bronx's incredulous expression became visible. The pop of the locks disengaging sounded as her hand landed on the handle.

"Go!" She jumped into the seat, closing the door too quickly. She slammed it on her leg and yelped. Pulling all her limbs inside, she got the door shut just as hands slammed on the hood. At the front of the car, an outraged Carlos glared at them.

Bronx inched the vehicle forward. Disbelief marred Carlos's handsome features as he was pushed backward.

Bronx increased the speed until Carlos tried to

scramble onto the hood. Turning the wheel side to side kept him from getting a good handhold. He stumbled backward and the car bumped and lurched as Bronx drove over his legs.

"Oh my god." She hadn't seen anyone run over before, and she momentarily forgot that Carlos would recover. Ten more vehicles could drive over him and he'd still heal. Most likely, anyway, depending on how heavy the vehicles were. She twisted in her seat to look behind them.

Carlos was crawling off the pavement. He would be pissed she'd gotten away from him again.

"Worried?" Bronx drove like he hit and ran over pedestrians every day.

She was still catching her breath, but she gawked at him. "Not about him."

She peered at the road. How had he been coming around the corner when she'd needed him? His shirt was black with neon-yellow piping. A more affordable brand of athletic shirt than what Carlos had worn.

The material might be moisture repellent, but it didn't repel the dried black blood on the sleeve. "How did you get here so fast?"

"I killed a demon and got tired of waiting. I was coming to extract you." He glanced over, his gaze tracking down her body. She was in the same clothing he'd seen her in last time, only she was dirtier from working in the garden and fleeing Carlos. "Looks like your boyfriend turned on you."

"He hasn't been my boyfriend for a long time."

"But he was?"

She flopped against her seat and glowered out the window. "Once upon a time, I trusted another deceitful prick who only wanted to use me."

CHAPTER 7

*T*osca sat restless in the passenger seat, repeatedly glancing into the rearview mirror. Periodically, she'd crane her neck and arch her back.

Had she relaxed her morph or was that forbidden at the compound?

She checked the rearview mirror again.

"No one's following us." It didn't seem like the commune had access to much for vehicles, though Bronx wouldn't be surprised if they had a beat-up VW bus hidden somewhere. Or maybe Carlos and whoever else lived in that big building had a Lexus.

"It's not that." She rolled her shoulders. The scratches on her face were already healing, leaving flakes of dried blood behind.

He waited, but she didn't elaborate. Three days, she'd kept them waiting. He'd been worried, dammit. "Care to share what it is, then?"

Her gaze flicked to him, stubbornness in the depths of her blue eyes. She didn't respond.

"I thought we established that you have to talk to me."

"Are you going to get tired of mentioning that?"

"Absolutely not. You've been a cute little pain in my ass for months. But I need to know if you're worried about something that might affect your case."

"Did you really just call me a cute little pain in the ass?"

"I said *my* ass."

Her lips quirked, making them extra kissable. Now wasn't the time to determine how kissable she looked.

"If you must know, I'm a little worried that Carlos will use the accident to get you in trouble somehow, kinda like how I was framed, but without the murder."

She was worried about him? The day he couldn't take a self-absorbed, inexperienced peacock like Carlos was the day he should lose his warrior status. "He'd have to prove he wasn't attacking me—or you—and that was sure as hell what it looked like."

"It would be his word against ours."

"There's two of us and one of him, and I haven't abandoned the realm. I don't think he'll make trouble."

She hunched in on herself and stared out the passenger window.

"Seriously, Tosca. I'm not worried about Carlos."

"He wanted to keep me there. I think he's working with someone in the realm. Why else would he insist on holding me prisoner?"

He hadn't connected Carlos pursuing her with the commune's shunning of all things Numen. Carlos should've been shoving her into the car. "What's your history with him?"

She chewed the inside of her cheek. "When he arrived, it was like Cordelia had prophesied his arrival. And we all bought it."

"They didn't know Carlos hated warrior training but his father wouldn't allow him to do anything else."

"Exactly. We were close in age, and I was tasked with showing him the ropes."

"Which were?"

She rolled her gaze to him. "They lie, cheat, and steal everything. We eat meat—but only if we can steal a cow."

"How does one steal a— Never mind. Let me guess, you all steal and everything gets funneled through that big, fancy building."

"Bingo."

"What did you do?" This wasn't an answer he needed to know. Curiosity took over. This side of Tosca shocked him. The intrepid rule follower had conned people? But from the guilt and shame running rampant in her expression, yes, she had.

"I learned to shoplift before I was eight. I picked pockets by the time I was eleven. When I was a teen, I could boost cars, but the larger the item, the more risk." She went silent, her body tight and her arms hugged around herself. "So when I was old enough, I was trained to get to know rich men, take whatever they gave me, and steal the rest."

"What the fuck? Who the hell—"

"It's not as seedy as it sounds." Her tone wasn't defensive. More forlorn. "I had limits and I thought Carlos did too. We'd hit up clubs, we'd come on to people, and when it came time to fulfill all the promises the guy thought I'd made, I'd roofie him and steal his money and car. That went on for a few years before I realized Carlos wasn't drugging his targets."

"He'd fuck 'em?"

"Yep."

"But you were with him?"

"Not like he wanted."

Carlos hadn't controlled Tosca. Males like that didn't

get rebuffed by females often. That kind of simmering resentment would've surged when she showed back up at the commune. Maybe he was in contact with Numen, but he might just be an asshole who wanted to get back at the one female who hadn't fallen for his shit. "We'll worry about Carlos when we get back to the safe house."

"Do warriors have houses all over the world?"

"Yes."

"Are we moving somewhere else? Tampa's a little close to the commune."

"I'll talk to the director. Pass along what you said."

Alarm flared in her eyes. "Are you going to tell him about—"

"Yes," he said gently, wishing he could reassure her. "But I won't go into the details. If Carlos isn't just a scorned lover, then we have to know why he was so intent on keeping you there. We have to know how far this conspiracy has spread."

"He wasn't my lover," she muttered and went back to staring out the passenger window.

The supreme satisfaction he got from those words was more than he'd gotten running the asshole over.

When he turned off the highway, she perked up, studying the passing gas stations, banks, and restaurants. "Lakeland? That's too close to Forgotten Peace."

"We had to pick a place close enough to you, but don't worry. We can go into the city to run errands so you aren't seen."

She didn't relax. Her arms were still hugged around her and her fingertips were white from digging into her flesh.

He turned off the main road and weaved through a residential area to get to the safe house. Palm trees lined the boulevards and trimmed hedges bordered several of the yards.

He usually avoided neighborhoods like this where neighbors knew each other, but the house they'd rented came with everything they needed and hopefully neighbors who didn't want to get to know them. "When I show you the bedroom you'll be using, you can let your wings out."

She swallowed hard, as if he was telling her he'd strip search her when they arrived. "Why would I let my wings out?"

She'd grown up like she had and balked at letting her wings out on Earth? "Because I'm going to snap a picture and send it to the senate in case Jean Luc Colbert's murder isn't enough to cost you your wings." He gave her a pointed look. "I know what it's like to keep your wings morphed for long periods of time. It's uncomfortable, and until you're used to it, you can let them out for a few minutes here and there. The house is secure."

She shook her head. "I'll be fine. I grew up keeping them morphed."

"And for the last how many years, you haven't morphed them once, have you?"

Those plush lips were back in a militant line. "I'll be fine."

She would be fine, but she would be in pain. First the muscles would ache, then cramps would be next, but he suspected she already suffered from those. The tan two-story house with a little peaked roof came into view.

"Suit yourself." He pulled into the garage. "Urban ran back to the realm to get some supplies while I had the car. Let me show you your room, then we'll figure out how to get you clothing."

～

Tosca rubbed both sides of her neck, wishing she could knead the muscles farther down her spine. She squared her shoulders and stood in the door frame of the bathroom. The guys had given her the master bedroom, on the second floor. She didn't look too hard into their decision. She was already in debt to them up to her eyeballs. She didn't have to start liking them on top of it.

Too late. The candid talk in the car, the one that had revealed Bronx had a serious side and wasn't just a playboy warrior, had made her drop her guard. She hadn't told him too much. Honestly, there wasn't much more to say.

But the truth of her existence was out there and she no longer felt like a low-key fugitive because of it.

She butted her back against the door frame and swayed side to side, using the wooden grooves to do what she couldn't and massage hard-to-reach muscles. It wasn't enough. Her shoulder blades were on fire, and she fantasized about releasing her wings.

It had been so long since she'd morphed, she had forgotten that it was an exercise. But morphing the last few days was like holding a wall squat without a break. Her back muscles had had enough and were protesting.

The room was dark. She'd left the lights off, and the blinds were drawn. They were the thick kind that didn't let any light through during the day. She would be safe to let out her wings, but pride was like a wall she'd have to headbutt through.

Bending over, she let her arms hang to the floor and relaxed her neck as much as possible. Her back seized, dropping her to her knees. A cry ripped out of her mouth before she could stop it.

She squeezed her eyelids shut to keep her tears at bay, then against the shock of light from the hallway as her bedroom door slammed open. Bronx. He had a dagger in one hand and was crouched and ready to strike.

"I'm fine," she wheezed. She wasn't fine. Excruciating pain burned down her back, and she was afraid she couldn't unlock her wings. She wasn't sure she could get off the floor.

His mouth tightened. A sympathetic *I told you so* registered in his brown eyes, but he crossed to her and dropped to his knees. "Can you release the morph?"

Her body was rigid, and she was shaking. "I haven't tried." She was afraid to try. How much would it hurt when the weight of her wings hung off her clenched back muscles?

He must've sensed her resistance wasn't out of sheer stubbornness. He scooted behind her and helped her crawl away from the wall. When her body wouldn't budge an inch, he grabbed her hips and dragged her on her knees until they were both clear of the doorway to the bathroom. Then he tucked his hands under her shirt.

She barked out a cry, more from the shock of his warm hands on her body than the pain caused by moving.

"Sorry." His thumbs massaged small circles at the base of her spine.

She jerked and lightning ripped under her skin.

"I'm going to give you a down and dirty massage so you can release the morph. All you need to do is relax as much as possible."

Relaxing when his hands were on her didn't seem like an option, but she wasn't in a position to argue.

He worked his way up her spine, bordering each side of her spine with his hands. Alternating pressure side to side, he worked into the knots until the pain was the *hurt so good* type rather than pure agony.

The muscles on the rest of her body started to unlock.

Her back was still on fire, but his touch was like a hose, putting out the blaze a little at a time.

"What I'm going to say next is going to make you tense up worse."

She tried to look over her shoulder, but had to settle with glancing to the side. Her neck muscles were still too tight. "Okay?"

His magical hands continued their work. What would his touch be like when it wasn't functional? When it was passionate?

The heat that flooded her body chased away some of the tension. But the realization that she wanted to know threatened to lock her up again.

"Relax," he murmured, thankfully interpreting her new rigidity as resistance to his words. "I worked with a couple warriors who held their morph way longer than their bodies were meant to. I know what you need to do, but you need to trust me."

He'd given others the same attention? His hands all over their body? Jealousy ignited a hot ball in her gut. How had she gotten herself in this position?

Abiding by the strict morphing rules of the commune had been automatic. She had been treading on thin ice, and she hadn't wanted to risk being seen with her wings out.

"What do I do?" She sounded cranky, and he would think she was irritated with him for helping her, and that was for the best right now.

He increased the pressure with each hand, pressing each fingertip deeper, and the new sound that emanated from her was more like a moan. It was a good thing her back was to him. Her face flushed hot.

"You need to take your shirt off before you can unmorph your wings."

"What?" Her body locked up again, and she groaned.

"Relax." He redoubled his efforts and another moan came out of her before she could stop it. The male was *good* with his hands, and if she weren't in so much pain, she'd be a helpless puddle. "You don't want any restriction. Your brain will want to snap the morphed wings back in place and your back will tighten up again. So you want to take your top off before you try."

When she'd returned to Numen after being away most of her life, she hadn't gone through this much pain. Unfurling her wings had been more of a relief from an ache she'd learned to ignore. She'd had to build her muscles to keep from dragging them on the floor, but nothing like this.

She'd been alone though. No undressing in front of a male. She hadn't been nude with a male in a long time. She might not have given everything to Carlos, but they'd messed around. And she'd used some of her wiles to entrap her human targets.

But that was ages ago and this was Bronx. The interest he'd initially shown her when she'd first met him hadn't made a reappearance, replaced with dedication to his work.

Had she thought she was special once again?

She tugged her shirt over her head, ignoring her protesting muscles.

She almost crammed it back on when his hands returned. Instead, she dropped the shirt and braced her hands on her knees.

"Imagine your wings slowly unfurling." He had moved his hands down to just below her shoulder blades, right under where her wing joints would be.

She tried to do what he asked. But her wings flapped out of their morph. He grunted, probably getting smacked in the face with bony wings, but his hands caught her around the waist.

"Sorry." Pain rippled through her back, but as fast as she cramped, he massaged.

"No problem. I've taken enough hits to know how it is. Just let them hang. Don't use your back muscles to lift them."

"What about standing?" Painful relief flooded her body. Exhaustion infused her muscle fibers. She wasn't sure she could stand if she tried. She inched her fingers forward on the carpet to snag the shirt she had dropped. Self-consciousness took over as she clutched the material to cover her breasts.

"Sit as long as you need to. We're not going anywhere." His pressure increased and he broadened his strokes along her skin.

A long groan left her. She should be ashamed, but she was powerless to stop it. "That feels so good."

His movements stalled, and he cleared his throat. "I, um, did this to myself on my first assignment."

To cover the sudden awkwardness that sprang between them, she latched on to the information. "And someone did this for you?"

It was probably as satisfying to stroke his broad muscular back as it was to be on the receiving end of his massage.

"No. I phoned in that I was recovering from a demon fight and stayed in bed for three days before I could morph my wings and get home."

"And you were alone the whole time?" She was used to being alone, but she hadn't recovered from any grave injuries. Not that this was an injury, but it was nearly as incapacitating, especially if it had happened to him alone on Earth.

"My parents don't come to the realm anymore, and I didn't want to worry them. So I watch the new warriors closely and try to help out if they get themselves into the same bind."

"Why isn't this talked about more?" Some of her coworkers descended to Earth on their time off, and others took longer vacations. She would've thought there would've been stories passed around.

"We're a proud people." His answer said it all.

She had grown up under some of the proudest. "I kept my wings in a morph until I moved back to Numen."

"That's a long time."

"That's probably why I thought I should be able to handle it now."

"I hear humans comment about that a lot—finding things more difficult that used to be so easy when they were younger."

She arched her back, seeking more of his touch.

He stroked his hands around her wing joints, his fingers brushing her ribs. A shiver traced down her spine, and she didn't care about hiding it. After the excruciating pain she had just been in, she wasn't running from the pleasure.

He cleared his throat. Had she gone too far? "After what you described, I can see why you're such a stickler for the rules."

"I've always been like that. Things that seemed of no consequence to the people I grew up trusting bothered me." His strokes were becoming rhythmic enough she could rock into him. "Stealing other people's cattle didn't seem right. Otherwise, why would the cows be fenced in? I used to ask that of Papa all the time, and he'd give vague answers until I was old enough to understand. Before that,

I used to ask, if I was supposed to have the money, why was it hidden in a purse or wallet?"

"Good questions to ask." Was his voice gruffer, or was it her imagination?

"I have a habit of trusting the wrong people, if you hadn't noticed."

"You can trust me, Tosca."

She let out a slow breath. The fog of pain had lifted and her sense of self-preservation was returning. "I trust you, Bronx, but ultimately, you're only helping me to serve your own needs."

He withdrew his hands, and it was like he sucked all the heat out of the room with him. "That's the difference between you and me. My needs are protecting the realm, and you're part of the realm. It's my duty. You're my duty. But you grew up around people who only cared about themselves. They couldn't bear the discomfort of living in a realm that served others. You left me waiting for days and called me when you didn't have another option. So who's the one serving their own needs now?"

Then he was gone, and she was alone in the dark room.

Bronx didn't move as Urban opened the car door and peered at him. "What the hell's going on? Tosca's half draped over the bed, passed out with no shirt on, and I find you in a dark garage staring out the windshield of a car that isn't running."

Thankfully, the painful erection he'd been fighting the entire time he'd been helping Tosca was gone.

When he had gone to rescue her, he hadn't thought the end result would be his hands on her bare skin. She had the softest skin he'd ever felt. Muscles defined her shoulders and back and she'd melted under his fingertips. He wanted to experience that again. Without the pain next time. He had other ways to get her to soften for him.

His buddy didn't know it, but he had answered his own question. Tosca was draped over a bed with no shirt on. "I needed some space from her."

A dark brow kicked up. "She's been that annoying?"

The last thing she had been was annoying. She'd been vulnerable, open, and her sexiness had only grown. He'd only seen her bare back, and it was enough to haunt his dreams for *years*. "She kept her wings morphed too long. I helped her through the pain."

"And it drove you into the garage? Instead of making a sandwich and going to your own room?"

He shot Urban a dirty look. "It was a lot, okay?"

"I can see that. The director wants to talk to you."

Getting his mind back to business would be sweet relief. "I'll just call in from here." His bedroom was across the hall from Tosca's. It was why he'd heard her cry out in pain. She might be sleeping now, but he didn't want her to wake up and overhear this conversation. Since it would be about her.

He had gone from evading her to arranging his world around her, and he wasn't going to ask himself which one he preferred.

Urban left him alone and he called his boss.

"She at the safe house?" Director Vale answered in lieu of a greeting.

"She is. One of the males at the compound tried to apprehend her. He did not want her to leave."

"Not enough females?"

"No, it's not that." He'd updated the director about what he'd seen when he'd gone to the commune. He needed to tell the director about Tosca's history with Carlos, but that didn't stop the words from burning like acid on his tongue. "Carlos and Tosca used to have a thing, but he cheated on her. So over twenty years go by, and they don't talk, but he chases her through the woods and gets himself run over to keep her from leaving."

"How did Carlos get himself run over?"

"If he insists on climbing the hood of a moving car, he has to learn what happens when he can't hang on."

Director Vale's gravelly chuckle brought Bronx back to the old days, when the director had been their team leader.

He made a good director, but Bronx missed the simplicity of the old days. When it had been easier to tell who the bad guys were because they were demons. Now instead of hunting down an archmaster possessing some unsuspecting human soul, he was rescuing an enforcer and investigating angels.

"You think there's more than his ego at play?" the director asked.

"It might be ego, but I don't know if it has to do with Tosca herself, or with what whoever framed her wants from her. Did Urban tell you about our demon hunt?"

"Yeah. I don't believe in coincidences. Not with demons."

"My thought exactly. I think we should stay here a little longer. Keep close to the commune, but see if there's any unusual demon activity in the area." An entire community of angels should make even the densest demon think twice before tampering in the vicinity.

"Agreed. If Senator Colbert is the one who framed her —and we all know she bloody well did—then she chose Tosca for a reason. She knew Tosca didn't have much for family, or she knew exactly where her remaining family was. And that leads to more questions, like how and why she'd know."

"You think she has a connection in the commune?"

"It's worth checking out."

He had no damn clue how. Tosca's father was willing to help her, but Bronx doubted a male who'd lived in the commune for almost thirty years would help a warrior. He had no other contacts. "I'll figure out what I can do."

He disconnected with his boss but didn't get out of the car and go inside the house. He glowered out the windshield.

There was so much about the situation that got under

his wings and chafed. Tosca had been a good enforcer. Damn good. And the realm had lost her. Add a whole commune of angels that the realm chose to ignore to an unsolved murder, and life just kept getting more complicated. His job description rewrote itself daily.

But enough with feeling sorry for himself. He loved his job, and eventually he'd get back to good old demon fighting. Then he'd be back to his bachelor ways—him and Urban fucking around town when they weren't fighting.

Those were the days.

He rubbed the middle of his chest.

When he'd had his hands on Tosca, a sneaky thought had swirled through his mind. What would it be like to have a place like this? To live a life like his parents and have someone with him?

Except that wasn't what he wanted. His parents' dream wasn't his, no matter how much they wanted it for him. If he didn't want it for himself, then his decision was simple.

THE ROOM WAS dark when Tosca woke. How long had she been out?

Pressing her hands into the mattress, she pushed up, then flopped back into the bedding.

Where's my shirt?

She spread her wings over her body, covering her sides, until she could orient herself. Okay, she was wearing the sweatpants she'd been living in for days. The bedroom was unfamiliar, but at least she wasn't completely naked.

Memories flooded back. The pain. Her wings out, not in Numen.

Bronx's hands on her.

She rolled to the side of the bed until she was in a

sitting position. Panic almost had her morphing her wings, but she waited and gathered her thoughts. She couldn't get herself in the same predicament Bronx had found her in.

She rose, checked that the door was locked, and then stood between the bed and the dresser, where there was the most room.

Relaxing her back, she let her wings hang. Then she lifted them high until the feathers couldn't touch the floor. Rotating through a few sets of lift exercises, she took stock of her situation.

She was in a safe house outside of the commune in Lakeland. Bronx and Urban knew where she was. She could assume the rest of their team did too.

Was Papa safe? He had to be. Otherwise Carlos would have to explain why Papa was in trouble for letting her go in the first place.

She closed her eyes and concentrated on morphing her wings. Her muscles cramped, but she kept her breathing steady. When nothing but cool air brushed across her back, she rolled her shoulders backward five times. Then forward. She would hold this morph for a day or two, then ease her wings out—as long as she still had the privacy of this room.

She hated flirting with risk. Papa had always joked she was a mama's girl. She'd loved hearing it as much as it had inspired sadness.

Clothing. Her top was still on the floor where she'd left it. She recalled crawling to the bed and collapsing on it. How much time had passed?

She searched the dresser drawers. Empty. The closet was also empty. She grabbed her top off the floor and shrugged into it before stepping into the hallway. The house was quiet. No lights were on.

Was it the middle of the night, or almost morning?

She padded down the hall. The house was nothing like Papa's cabin. White-painted walls with molding. A hardwood floor smoother than the cabin's rough planks. And so much space.

The bedroom she had been in was half the size of Papa's cabin. In Numen, she had lived in a small house close to the center of the realm. Her place was near enforcer headquarters and that was all she'd cared about at the time.

Downstairs, she stared at the kitchen for several moments. Even with the lights off inside the house and ambient light coming through the window from streetlights, she could tell this kitchen was nothing like any she had used before.

Her job had required her to enter people's houses at times, though she had been more intent on why she'd been there than on their structures and layouts. And after work, she always grabbed fresh food from the market to eat. She didn't make elaborate meals. She kept it simple, like the food she'd eaten growing up.

The appliances were stainless steel. The time blinked on the oven. It was four in the morning. She had slept for over twelve hours.

She crossed to the fridge and looked inside. Please let there be something she didn't have to cook.

"There's some sandwiches left over from last night."

She jumped and bit her lip to keep from crying out. He out-stealthed her training. "Bronx, you scared me."

"Always be prepared, even in your own home."

She shot him a quick scowl and dug out the food. The sandwiches were piled high with meat and veggies. Her stomach rumbled.

"Hungry?"

Since he sounded more amused than sarcastic, she

nodded. "Not to sound ungrateful, but a diet of nothing but eggs and vegetables for the last three days has left me with some cravings."

She didn't look at him as she slid onto a barstool at the island. When she'd last seen him, he'd been touching her in all the right ways—and she'd wanted so much more. But she'd upset him. So she settled for peeking at him out of the corner of her eye.

He was up before the crack of dawn, yet his hair was slicked back like he was ready to hit up the clubs. She would think that was where he had come from if it weren't for the black T-shirt and black-and-green flannel pajama pants he wore. The shirt he wore demanded way too much of her attention. She'd known he was leanly muscled, but the shirt practically outlined every muscle fiber.

An orange bag of chips plopped on the island in front of her. This time, she did lift her gaze, but only to cover her visceral reaction to him with annoyance. "What's that?"

Bronx frowned. "Cheetos. Urban loves those things."

"I don't know if my body can handle the shock of going from carrots and radishes to that." She peeled the clear plastic film off the sandwiches. "Besides, Carlos used to love those things."

He grabbed the chips and tossed the bag behind them onto the counter. "Fuck Cheetos."

She bit back a smile and took a bite of the sandwich. It was all she could do not to roll her eyes and groan. She didn't mind the food at Papa's. She enjoyed vegetables fresh from the garden; it was what she had grown up on. But she had a soft spot for processed meat and simple carbs.

Bronx propped his hands on the counter across from her. She studied the sandwich as if she was going to give every layer a grade when she was done. But he was looming over her and . . . she didn't mind.

"In a few hours," he said, his voice gruff like it had been in the bedroom, "we'll run to town and get some clothes. Urban's going to use the nook in the back we made to transcend without being seen. It would gather too much attention if the neighbors saw two of us coming and going and one of you."

She swallowed her mouthful. "I thought humans had grown less prudish."

"Doesn't mean they don't like to speculate and gossip. We need to look like an ordinary couple."

How would that be possible? He looked like he'd walked off a Hollywood set. There was nothing ordinary about him. He was considered handsome in every realm, and she'd heard too many stories about his popularity with human women.

"What's that look for?" He hadn't moved. Still looming.

Well, he'd asked. "It's going to be hard to be an ordinary couple when some of our neighbors are going to want to sleep with you."

Shock passed through his face. "Why would you think that?"

"Humans aren't the only ones that like speculation and gossip."

His surprise changed to consternation. "What if our neighbors want to sleep with you?"

"I blend in better than you. I'm just average." Was that why she'd glowed inside when he called her a cute little pain in his ass?

She took another bite and chewed, studying the tile pattern of the island. When he didn't reply, she glanced up.

He was staring at her, incredulity in his eyes. "You think you're just average?"

"Yeah," she said around her mouthful. She finished chewing before she explained. "When I first approached the enforcers, I was told I might be too small for the position. They didn't think I could throw around unruly angels if I needed to. They said I should talk to the warriors. Since I was plain enough to blend in on Earth."

She could recite the story now that it had been so long. But coming off the heels of Carlos's betrayal, the comment had stung like a six-foot bee ramming its stinger into her gut.

"Who the fuck said that?"

"Stede I know, I know. He had his own issues, but he wasn't wrong. I had to steal so much makeup to vamp myself up and catfish. And I never got asked out in Numen." She grimaced, remembering Dan the Man, a tragic stereotype in an angel's body. She refused to count Dan. He'd mount a mule if he weren't supervised. "Anyway, I shouldn't go shopping unless you hit up the really cheap places."

"Why only cheap? Doesn't Forgotten Peace need the essentials?"

"True. I can give you a list."

"No, I could use your insight."

She paused with the sandwich halfway to her mouth. "On what?"

His jaw clenched, but she didn't sense it was about the question. Something else was on his mind. "If the activity in the closest human population to Forgotten Peace is normal or abnormal."

"What kind of activity?"

"Anything. Mostly demon. Urban and I took out two sylphs. And if you kept a low profile at the commune, other Numen from there shouldn't recognize you, but if they do, their reaction will tell us a lot. I've got an extra T-shirt and shorts you can wear."

He was nearly a foot taller than her. She might be less noticeable wearing the dirty flowing top and sweatpants. But she didn't have many other options. "At least you won't ask me to steal anything."

"But I'm going to have to ask you to lie."

"What?" Who would she lie to? She'd just fled everyone she knew, and she wasn't going to Numen.

"Our cover story. When we're in a safe house for an indeterminate length of time, we come up with cover stories. In places where the neighbors actually give a shit."

That made sense. Lying to humans was like the one loophole in an angel's life. They weren't supposed to lie otherwise, but as Tosca unfortunately knew, her kind lied all the time. "So what's our story?"

"You and I have been married for a few years." She made a choking sound and started coughing. He reached into the fridge and got her a bottle of water. She sucked a gulp of cold liquid down as he continued.

"Three years. Our anniversary is in the fall—October if they ask for a month. If they're super nosy. The nineteenth."

"Why that date?"

He gave her a perplexed look. "I just came up with it. We met at Universal Studios and fell in love. We're both from Florida. Just say Orlando or something. The bigger the city, the fewer details you have to come up with."

She ducked her head, remembering all the times she had confronted him about his work. He had talked around the truth but never outright lied. Yet now false details spilled freely from his lips for their cover story.

She had tracked him based on Juliette's word, and all it had done was show her how wrong she had been.

"Our last name is Hansen with an *e* because we need to be generic but not too generic. Pick a first name."

She blinked. *Pick a name.* She'd been named after her mother. Her father had left the realm with nothing but her, and now she had nothing but the stolen clothing on her body. "I . . . can't."

His dark brows drew together. "Why?"

"My mother . . ." Tears burned the backs of her eyes and she tried to swallow the welling emotion down. She shouldn't get this emotional over a simple alias. She blamed the upheaval from yesterday. "Sorry. I've used fake names before, but I still had a life then."

"How about Tasha?" he suggested gently. He gave his head a shake and stared at the wall. "No, that's too close."

Her brain was coming back online. Bronx didn't have to do all the work. "Julie. It's close enough to Juliette and they would never expect me to go by a name so similar to hers."

His approving nod sent a swirl through her belly. "Julie and Brandon Hansen."

"The *e* makes all the difference."

When he let out a laugh, all the seriousness drained out of him and what was left was nothing like the fake charisma he'd tried to use on her when they'd first met. For a heartbeat, she saw the real Bronx. He was a carefree, happy male.

She dropped her gaze to the water bottle. "Brandon and Julie Hansen. Married for three years, October. What do we do for a living?"

"We both work from home. It's an easy way to justify our random comings and goings. In this type of neighborhood, people keep track of that stuff."

So no different than Numen. "What do I do for a living?"

"I'm transitioning between selling life insurance policies to health insurance. And you're an interior design consultant."

"What do I know about interior design?"

"You'll have to bluff your way through. Hopefully, we won't get stuck talking to anyone long enough to explain."

"I guess it's good enough. I'll resurrect the skills of my youth and BS my way through a conversation."

He tipped his head. "That's my girl."

Heat licked up her neck and into her cheeks. She didn't need his approval.

Then why did it feel so good?

It was too early in the morning for this. She slid off her stool and put her plate by the sink. Clutching her water bottle, she gave him a tight smile. "I'll go clean up. Mind leaving that clothing outside my door?"

"It's already lying in front of it."

He was good. One of those guys who was good at everything. Those were dangerous to a female's heart. And when it came to Bronx, he was the most dangerous of all.

CHAPTER 9

$\mathcal{B}$ronx waited for Tosca, scrolling through his phone. When he heard flip-flops smacking the ceramic tiles of the floor, he glanced up. Laughter sputtered from his lips.

Her militant glare didn't help him stop snickering. His shirt swamped her. She had tied a knot in the side, but all that did was show that the basketball shorts he had loaned her made the ugliest skirt in the world.

Her eyes narrowed. "You can quit laughing anytime."

"I should make you stay here. You're going to stand out in people's memories."

She flipped her short hair and marched toward the door to the garage. He followed.

Trying not to pay attention to her while he was driving proved harder than the last time they'd ridden in the car together. Her arms were folded across her stomach, and her fingers tapped her arms.

"Nervous?"

"No." She frowned. "Yes. I can't stop planning how to

lift what we're picking up. Old habits and all. It's messed up."

This was her first real outing on Earth without being tied to the commune. "We'll get what we need. Sierra can order some additional things for us."

"I know you won't tell me much about her, but she's . . . adjusting?"

Did Tosca think she would spend her life on the run or lose her wings too? His team would figure out what had really happened. They had to. Her stormy-gray wings were too lovely to hack off. "Look, I know I compared you two before, but you swindled humans, and while that's wrong, it's not something our realm considers worth a fall. We'll prove your innocence."

"Why do you believe me? After finding out about my past, why wouldn't you think I have it in me?"

"You're asking me why I don't think you were having a torrid affair with Jean Luc when I learned you picked a few pockets and roofied some guys so you wouldn't have to fuck them like Carlos did with his targets?"

She pursed her lips. "Okay, I get it."

He pulled into the department store parking lot. It was early yet, and there weren't many cars. He killed the engine and waited for a minute, scanning the lot.

"What are you looking for?" She craned her neck around, mimicking him.

"Demons."

"I have no idea what to do if I see one."

He considered her. Short hair feathered around her face. Baggy clothing. "You've seriously never seen one?"

She shook her head.

"Well, you don't have to do anything. But I'm a warrior. I need to be ready for them."

"How do you know what to look for?"

He snorted. "They don't exactly look like kittens."

Concern crossed her face and he realized his error. She was like one of his newbies. Just like the wing situation. Angels who hadn't come to Earth before needed to be trained in how to spot demons. To see the little sylphs that skittered among humans, causing just enough chaos to disrupt a person's life and make them cranky and run down and open to the seductive whispers of the archmasters. Sylphs were in the open, but none of the demons were corporeal.

As prominent as it felt like demons were in the world, it was only because Bronx actively sought them out. Earth was a big place, over seven billion people for demons to mess with. Not all environments were ideal. He hoped that proved true for Lakeland, and that the sylphs he and Urban had vanquished were a fluke.

He launched into an impromptu lesson. "So the sylphs are obvious. They're small, they're ugly, and they look like a demon." She nodded, her detached professionalism starting to kick in. "Symasters ride around like the grossest damn backpack you've ever seen. Sometimes they'll sit on a human's shoulder, on top of their head, or attached to their back like an underworld piggyback ride. They're ugly. Archmasters are the hardest. They're ugly too, but they can possess a host and be hard to see."

"It's so weird. I've heard my coworkers mention these types of demons over the years, almost in an ironic way. Like name-calling. I was almost lulled into thinking they weren't real. Even though I know better."

"Then that means warriors are doing their job. The way we teach new warriors to spot a possessed host is to walk around like they're dazed. Relax your vision as if you're looking through everyone to the horizon. Then you'll focus less on features and more on the general image.

That's when you'll be able to make out the demon's features underneath."

"What if I run into one?"

"Pretend you don't see it and let me know." He leaned over the console, intent on getting his point across. This close, he could see the ring around her irises, a stormy gray like her wings. "It's critical that you pretend you don't see them. Only Numen can see them, and they'll know what you are."

She nodded, her wide gaze clashing with his. He was inches from her mouth. The cab closed in on them. His gaze dipped to the bow her pink mouth formed.

"Tosca?" Her lips parted, and just a little closer— A clash of carts outside the car snapped some sense into him. "Ready to go?"

Blinking, she scrambled out of the car. He followed. For a moment, he was tempted to fall a few steps behind her and watch her ass cheeks work against the material of the shorts. He'd almost kissed her. What the hell was he thinking?

She was the kind of female a guy gave everything up for. He ground his teeth together and glared at the entrance.

Inside the store, he followed her lead. She circled through the women's area, tossing the cheapest underwear, socks, and bras into the cart he pushed. When it came to clothing, she was more discerning. He didn't know shit about fabric, but she seemed to choose the ones that appeared more expensive. Tops and bottoms that could be considered casual wear were carefully set in the cart.

"I suppose I need everyday clothes." She tossed in linen shorts that would make her long legs look delectable. A shirt with cartoon characters, hopefully looser so he couldn't see her tits straining against the fabric.

Fuck. The almost kiss was bad enough.

A couple pajama pants were tossed in and he was stuck on hoping he'd get to see her ass in those too.

She looked over her haul. "That should do it."

They were about to clear the last rack of clothing when she stopped. He came a few millimeters from ramming the butt he'd been thinking about all morning with the cart.

He spotted what was wrong before he had to ask. Two sylphs danced down the aisle, their target a harried mom with a baby screaming in the car seat and a crying toddler hanging from her hand.

Tosca looked at him, her eyes pleading for him to do something. Under normal circumstances, this would be a tricky situation. But just him, in a public place? Impossible.

"We need to pay," he said softly.

The disappointment in her eyes made him feel like a failure, but he couldn't explain the nuances of his job in the middle of a public space. People filled the checkout lines, shopped around them, and ambled up and down the main aisle.

"Go to the checkout, Julie."

Her expression hardened, and she stomped toward the checkout with the shortest line. The cashier didn't try to talk to them, no doubt assuming they were in a lover's quarrel. He paid for the items and led Tosca back to the car.

When he dumped the bags in the trunk and got behind the wheel, Tosca was glaring out the windshield. A one-eighty from how she had acted before going into the store.

"Tosca."

"No. It's not my business. I'm just an enforcer."

He twisted in his seat. "Department stores are some of the hardest places to deal with demons. They're some of the best places to find them, but I can't exactly dive onto something no human can see while chanting words they don't understand and then disappear in front of their eyes."

The tension eked out of her, and she sighed. "You don't have to explain."

"But I do. I feel for that mom, I really do. She's stressed and those sylphs are going to keep messing with her until her thoughts turn dark. She's a target and she deserves to be saved." He rubbed his temples. He couldn't call other warriors to the area because no one was supposed to know where he was, and definitely not where Tosca was. And by the time more warriors arrived, the mom would be gone.

The human was helpless. She'd have no idea she was being pushed toward a dangerous path that would open her up for possession. "Fuck it. Here's what we're going to do."

TOSCA WANDERED through the pet food aisle, her heart slamming against her ribs. To anyone else, she would look like she was intent on only the best food for her cat.

She'd never thought she would be on Earth, aiding a warrior in a demon hunt. But the thrill shooting through her chased away some of the stress of the last few days. She could still be beneficial to others and not just a drain on the resources of her realm because she had naively trusted the wrong person.

The mom was ahead of her, the gleeful sylphs at her feet and oblivious to Tosca, too focused on their target.

"Mama!" the toddler shrieked as the sylph skittered by her legs. Humans couldn't see the little beasts, but Bronx had said sylphs could focus small bursts of energy to make objects drop or turn their bony little projections tangible enough to poke the delicate skin of a small child.

"I said quiet, Katie. How many fucking times . . ." The overwrought mom inhaled a shuddering breath. The second sylph danced over the edge of the cart, curling its body into a ball and rolling over the baby.

A piercing shriek filled the air. A sob left the mom and she clutched the handle of her cart with both hands. Her body shook as she tried to gather herself. When she glanced over her shoulder and noticed Tosca, she hastily swiped a hand under each eye.

Tosca gave her an understanding smile. "What can I help you with? It looks like you have your hands full."

The woman's expression turned suspicious and she tugged the girl closer to her. Tosca didn't try to get closer. She didn't have to be a mom to understand mama-bear instincts.

The sylphs went still and scrutinized her, but Tosca ignored them. *It's harder for them to tell what you are than it is for us to tell what they are.*

Bronx's quick training from the car scrolled through her mind. She'd gone from wanting to strangle him with his own tongue to hanging on his every word in a short amount of time. Pretty much since she'd woken up next to a dead guy and realized her assumptions about everyone were backward.

"No, we're fine," the mom snapped and pushed the cart around the end of the aisle.

Tosca fell back and spun the opposite direction. Bronx was waiting by the office supplies two aisles down. He slipped his hand in hers and she jolted.

"We're married," he murmured.

"I don't have a ring," she hissed, the first thing that came to mind.

"We're one of those progressive couples that don't need to prove our love to the world."

She gave him a *Seriously?* look. To retaliate, he swiped the inside of her palm with his thumb. Shivers tracked down her body, and she was tempted to smother the cocky expression off his face. Only the method she wanted to use wasn't appropriate in public. She needed to focus. "She's not gonna let me closer."

"Potty!" the toddler yelled.

Bronx glanced at the mom and her kids out of the corner of his eye and cocked a brow. "Just found your plan *B*."

Enforcers had procedures and policies. Every situation that had been encountered in the past had generated a procedure for how an enforcer should deal with it. Warriors were much more fluid. They had more independently moving parts in their scenarios than an enforcer ever would. It was as fascinating as it was nerve racking and exhausting.

Warriors worked in teams of seven, but here it was just Bronx and her, an untrained fugitive. Yet she was determined to save this woman and her children. If her name was never cleared, at least her time on Earth would not be in vain.

The mom pushed her rattling cart past them toward the bathrooms behind the electronics department.

Bronx let go of Tosca's hand and wound his arm around her waist. She went stiff. A lot more of her was touching him than a simple handhold, and she was shocked at how badly she wanted to turn into his embrace.

He spoke as if he didn't notice her reaction. "We're going to risk looking like we're following her. We have to time this right. As soon as she disappears into the bathroom, I need to get the sylphs into the Mist before they follow her, or we'll draw too much attention. You need to be my lookout. If anyone can see me disappear, you have to tell me no."

He'd have to abort the mission. She nodded. "I'm ready." Her pulse kicked up and she might've inched just a little bit closer to his strong body.

He kept his arm around her as he maneuvered through the aisles toward the electronics department. The mom was disappearing into the vestibule that contained the doors to the restrooms. Just as she turned to the left, Bronx put on a burst of speed.

He closed the distance just as the mom was dragging the toddler into the bathroom. He had less than a moment to intercept the sylphs without barreling into the bathroom and terrifying the woman and her kids.

Tosca spun around, her back to the bathroom entrances. Shoppers were minding their own business. "Clear."

There was a scuffle behind her, a grunt, and nothing. She glanced over her shoulder, and relief calmed her heart rate. The vestibule was empty.

Would Bronx be okay? It was just two sylphs. Of course he would be fine. Two shoppers, a kid and an older man wandered into the electronics area, but they ignored her.

She tapped the toe of her flip-flop. No wonder the mom hadn't trusted her. Her outfit was erratic, her hair was finger combed, and she probably had an uncertain look in her eye.

Still, it had stung. She'd been able to trick men out of their watches, empty their wallets, and one time, she'd even been gifted a car. But add a few demons and she'd fallen off the horse. A woman's life was in danger, her kids too, and Tosca hadn't been able to perform.

Bronx should be back any second. But it was still two against one. If one got away, Bronx would have to track it down. Tosca hadn't experienced the Mist, but she'd heard enough to know that someone like her could get lost and wander forever, but Bronx knew his way around.

The bathroom door squeaked open. "Come on." The exhausted mom rounded the corner. Too late, Tosca realized she was waiting right next to the woman's cart.

The baby carrier swung from the mom's bent arm as her hostile glare speared Tosca. "Are you following me? Are you planning to abduct my kids or turn me into CPS?"

The woman thought Tosca would hurt her. That was even worse. "N-no, I just wanted to help."

"Why? Do I look pathetic?" Tears poured down the distraught woman's face.

It was time to dust off those skills. She wasn't dressed the part, but there'd been a time when that hadn't been critical to her success. "Strong women only look pathetic to those who are weaker." She gave a silly curtsy. "Call me underestimated, but people think I'm a hot mess inside and out. I was actually a cop once. Truly, I only meant to help."

Her words were genuine and the woman's stance relaxed. She loosened her hold on the toddler, who clung to the woman's leg. "You were a cop?"

Tosca nodded just as Bronx stepped out of the vestibule. "Isn't that right, honey? He blames the uniform for why I have no fashion sense."

A smile played over the woman's lips.

Bronx once again slid his strong arm around Tosca's waist and pressed a kiss to her forehead. The touch of his lips was brief, but her eyelids drifted shut, and she soaked up the feeling. "Sorry to keep you waiting, babe. Hey," Bronx said in a low, soothing voice. He squatted down but didn't get closer to the little girl. "I bet you're a big help to your mama. Do you help her take care of the little baby?"

The little girl blossomed under Bronx's attention. She

beamed and nodded enthusiastically. The mom was as mesmerized as her daughter.

Tosca too.

He tapped the floor in front of the girl's shoes, and she skittered back, but gave him a toothy grin like it was a game.

The rumble of his deep chuckle went right through her. The mom too. His chiseled good looks and easy smile had made her forget her suspicions. The lack of demons helped.

Bronx straightened and stepped back, sliding an arm back around Tosca. For an act, it felt so natural.

"Well, I hope you and your littles have a good rest of the day." Bronx's smile told the woman it was going to get better no matter what.

The woman nodded, her expression dumbfounded, like she believed him and had no idea why.

Bronx steered Tosca away and through the store. It wasn't until they got back to the car that he let her go. The cocoon of his arm vanished and she was left reeling.

What the hell was that?

"What else do you need?" His tone was almost bored, as if having her tucked against him hadn't affected him at all. Kind of like the back massage. And the kiss on her forehead.

Why was she looking for more where she'd only get hurt? Some things never changed.

CHAPTER 10

Bronx relaxed on the couch with his feet kicked up on the coffee table. He tapped out a message to the director about the sylphs in the department store. At the very least, the suburbs around Forgotten Peace had demons feeling it out. Were they testing the waters, or had they struck a deal with the angels in the area to look the other way?

When they had returned to the safe house, Tosca had gone upstairs to let her wings out. He had stayed on the opposite end of the house, fighting the urge to ask if she needed another massage. Twice, he'd stood up to go check on her. His hands ached for the soft slide of her warm skin under his. But he didn't care to explain why he was sitting in the car in the garage if she came out of her room early, so the couch it was.

As much as he needed a distraction, the dong of the doorbell wasn't welcome. Visitors at the safe house were usually the last thing he and his team wanted to deal with, but he needed something to stop the constant replay of Tosca nestled into his side.

She'd branded his side. She fit perfectly, dammit.

On the other side of the peephole, a nondescript guy in a ball cap shoved his hands into the pockets of his cargo shorts. The view was warped, but it looked like one of the guys from the neighborhood. According to Sierra's notes, his name was Stephen Lopez. His wife was Katy, and they owned their own business. Stephen flipped houses and Katy ran the admin side.

And Tosca was going to hate her interior-design backstory.

He plastered a smile on his face and opened the door.

Stephen lifted his chin like they were bros who hadn't seen each other in a few weeks. "Hey, how you doing?"

"Not bad, man. What's going on?" Bronx rested an arm on the door frame and leaned out, like it was any other Saturday. Or was it Friday? He had a hard time keeping track of the days. It wasn't like he got weekends off.

"Oh, pretty good. I'm Stephen. Stephen Lopez." He stuck his hand out for Bronx to shake. His grip was strong, but not obnoxious.

"Brandon Hansen. My wife is Julie."

Stephen's gaze flickered. "You look like that guy on that show on TV."

"Daniel Henney. I get that a lot." It'd change. In thirty or forty years, he'd look like another guy on TV.

Stephen rubbed his hands together like he was going to ask to borrow twenty grand. "My wife, Katy, sent me over. We wanted to invite you to our barbecue tomorrow. It's a small, little neighborhood thing, and since you two are new, it'd be a good way to get to know everyone."

Translation: they were nosy as hell and wanted the 411 on him and Tosca.

Getting to know everyone was the last thing he wanted to do. "When?" How odd would it be to skip the party? Yet it could be an opportunity to check out the neighborhood, like the director wanted. If the demon infestation had gone unchecked for years, with no one like Tosca around to ask hard questions, they might have spread to the suburbs, bringing their chaos from the hustle and bustle of the city.

"This weekend. Saturday. Seven?"

"Sure. What should we bring?" He'd need to figure out a different backstory for Tosca. Julie couldn't be an interior designer around a guy who flipped houses.

"We'll have drinks, but bring what you prefer."

"Sounds good." Stephen tossed him a wave and meandered back down the walk, giving the house's property a not-so-subtle once-over.

Bronx closed and locked the door and stared at it. What the hell was he going to bring to a neighborhood party? Small talk for hours without disclosing anything. Having to remember what they said for future chitchat. He spent a lot of time around humans and among them, but not with them, not for long periods. And he'd never pretended to be married either.

"Who was that? Is something wrong?"

He spun. Tosca stood at the bottom of the stairs. Her wings were morphed and she had on some of the new clothing she'd bought. The linen shorts he'd thought would make her legs look temptingly lickable did just that. She'd paired them with a white T-shirt with a cartoon character emblazoned across the front. She had a bra on, but the shirt still hugged her curves and made her breasts pop.

She tucked her hair behind her right ear and let the other side hang free. He could see exactly why Senator Colbert had latched on to her, and why the commune had used her to con. People didn't look at Tosca and think she was up to no good.

It was absurd that the entire realm thought she was a

scorned lover. She was too discerning. He hadn't heard of her hooking up with a male in the realm. Other than Carlos, and she'd said—

She touched the side of her face like she was self-conscious. "What? Is there something . . ."

He'd been staring, stroking her face with his gaze, like he wanted to do to her body. "No, uh. We're meeting the neighbors. On Saturday. Seven. Bringing drinks."

Why was he suddenly looking forward to going out with her? Seeing her dressed up and laughing?

He was more like his parents than he'd thought. Except he loved his job.

Her brows lifted and she propped her hands on her hips. The material of that damn shirt pulled tighter across her tits. She should've gotten a bigger size. "A party? With a bunch of humans?"

He nodded. "It's either that or find a new safe house on short notice."

"Because if we don't go there, they'll watch us even more?"

"Weird neighbors get more attention. The most pressing problem is figuring out what drinks to bring."

It was like a switch flipped. She went from confused to calculating. "We're a couple who just moved into our first house. I'm in my mid-to-late twenties—wine or seltzer. Maybe both? You're the same age. Raised in the city. You're going to want a middle-shelf liquor or a trendy craft beer. Yeah, that's it. Local craft brew, but not too stout. You're kind of a lightweight."

"The fuck I am."

She rolled her eyes. "Brandon Hansen is a lightweight. Let's see what you have."

"We don't keep alcohol in the house."

She spun on a heel. "Can Sierra arrange that delivery with more clothing?"

"More clothing?"

"I'll need to wear name brand. Nothing high end, but I will have to wear my nicest summer casual to the party. Because Julie is an interior designer after all."

"You can change the backstory. It's not too late."

She shook her head and flopped on the couch, stretching those curvy legs of hers onto the coffee table. She produced the phone he'd given her and tapped the screen. "Nah. I have a few days. I've been researching my profession. Julie is an eclectic chic interior designer who specializes in harmony and rhythm." She inhaled a deep breath and closed her eyes like she was namaste-ing. "I feel what my clients want and create an aesthetic unique to them."

"Holy shit, Tosca. *I'm* going to hire you before the party's done."

The corner of her mouth lifted before something shy drew over her expression. "It's nice to use my powers for good."

He settled on the couch next to her. Too close to be considered appropriate, but he needed some part of his flesh to touch hers. "You did that as soon as you became an enforcer. Part of that was an act."

She frowned. "A long con?"

"You were committed." Was he leaning closer?

Her gaze caught his. She'd noticed too. "Bronx?"

"Yeah?" He swayed a little closer. Her blossom scent filled his nose.

"I'm not some girl on one of your missions that you can fuck around with."

He pulled back. "What?"

"We're pretending to be married, but I can only carry

the act so far. Like you said, I commit. To an act. To people. But this is fake."

Fake. She thought what he felt for her was fake.

He scooted farther back on the couch. Of course it was fake. He didn't commit to anything but his job. What was coursing through him was good old lust. Nothing more. "You don't fuck around. I get it."

The tension didn't leave her body. "Right. So, um, the design. Is Sierra making a fake website for me?"

He answered her questions, trying to ignore how her rejection got to him.

CHARLES HAD MANAGED to stay away from the main house every day in the week she'd been at the farm. Dionna wanted to help with irrigation, but Charles wouldn't put her to work. He'd order everyone else around but her. Standing in the middle of a field surrounded by humans who thought of her as more of a guest didn't help either. If Charles wasn't going to put her to work, they certainly wouldn't.

At least Zuri had no issues putting her to work, as if she recognized Dionna's need to be doing something. So Dionna helped prepare each meal. Breakfast was always served at the house before Afi, Charles, and the workers went to the field. The midday meal was split between the dining table and packed lunches for the workers. The evening meal was served close to seven and everyone was back at the table to relax and talk about the day.

In between meals, Dionna had gotten a whirlwind education on chicken rearing. The work was saved for the younger generations of Mensahs, but Dionna was allowed to participate since they thought she enjoyed it.

And she did. Clucking and humming around chickens as she gathered eggs each morning reduced her stress almost better than afternoon tea. The chickens hadn't been used to her at first, but after a few days they'd gotten to know her, and while they clucked and ran in different directions around her, they were no longer frenzied.

Too bad her family hadn't grown as used to her presence.

It was afternoon now, and she wandered into the breezeway where Zuri's mother, Nana, was pouring tea.

"Is Zuri in the field?" Dionna asked.

Nana's face crinkled as she smiled. "Yes. She can't stay inside for long without going stir-crazy. The same goes for Afi if he has to step foot in the kitchen."

Dionna chuckled as she sat in the weathered chair. She'd grown fond of Nana's afternoon tea. It didn't matter who could join the women, she prepared a large pot and poured at least one extra glass. Sometimes one other person would join her, sometimes four or five. Today looked to be a two-person tea.

Dionna sipped the chai, gentle spices rolling over her tongue. She let out a contented sigh after she set the cup down.

Nana beamed but took her attention away as if she knew Dionna would grow uncomfortable. Warriors didn't let out contented sighs.

"Courtney and Stella aren't joining us today?"

The contentment from seconds ago died. Stella loved learning about the business and working in the field. She was gone all day like Charles. Courtney had sat through one tea with Dionna and never returned. "No, Stella is with Charles, and Courtney's with Daniel."

"Those two have a thing, yes?"

Only if her daughter was as brazen as Dionna feared.

Leading the poor boy on was cruel, but if Courtney fell for him, it'd put her in danger. Hard to explain to a human mate why she wasn't aging. She couldn't tell Daniel the truth without putting her wings at risk. And if she did, there was no telling if she'd survive the fall. Fallen weren't dumped anywhere they'd been before. Losing all previous connections was one of the punishments of losing your wings. "I don't know. I don't know what Courtney's thinking." It was too easy to answer honestly around Nana.

The woman was understanding, and that was why talking to her freely came naturally. Dionna's parents were long gone, and as a warrior, she didn't hang around other females and talk about the trials and tribulations of motherhood. But Nana knew. Keeping this farm going through climate change, political change, and technological change had kept her sharp and determined, all while raising four kids.

"You don't approve of Daniel?" Nana asked with no judgment in her voice.

Dionna would approve—if Daniel were Numen. "Daniel's a nice boy, but Courtney's not planning to stay here. She's not staying in Ghana, and I don't think Daniel plans to leave."

"Daniel's a wanderer. He may go where she does."

"Then he will be disappointed when he wakes up one day and she's gone." Preferably before he started to wonder why Courtney still looked twenty-eight after twenty years had passed.

"So, it's like that." Nana nodded and stared into the distance at the large fronds of the oil palm trees.

"Yes. And I'm afraid the more I remind Courtney she's like that, the more determined she will be to let Daniel think there's long-term promise between them."

"You don't get along? Even as adults?" Nana aimed

another relaxed smile her way. Some people might find her questions too forward, but they were refreshing. Numen talked in circles like they had all the time in the world, and in a lot of ways, they did. Dionna preferred to be direct and it hadn't won her any friends in a realm full of egotistical beings.

She thought about her answer instead of finding a way to circumvent it. It was just her and Nana, and she wanted to talk.

She'd been lonely for a long time.

"I work a lot," Dionna finally said. "She feels I wasn't present. They all feel I wasn't present."

"And what do you feel?"

"That I tried my hardest." She gripped her tea to give her suddenly shaking hands something to do. "But perhaps . . . I wasn't around as much as I should've been. That perhaps if I gave my family as much dedication as I gave my work, they wouldn't have moved to a different realm—uh, country, and I wouldn't have had to take a sabbatical to find them."

She stared into her cup. Realms? She never made slips around humans. But who else could she talk to? For decades, she'd been the only mated one on her team. Only recently had her teammates started finding mates. What would they know about the trials and tribulations of old mated couples?

"If we could go back in time, the world would be perfect today." Nana squinted into the distance. "But we have to keep moving forward. It's clear you love them. It's clear they're giving you the cold shoulder. If I were you, I'd kick Charles into the ocean with one paddle and a half-inflated life preserver."

Dionna coughed trying to sip her tea. "You would?"

"You're dedicated to your family. And you realize that

things could have been different. That as important as the security work you do is, you don't think it's more important than your family. They'll see it, and they'll realize that they're holding you to standards they can't attain themselves."

Nana's words washed through her like a cleansing rain. All the important pieces were still there, but the mess of her emotions wasn't clouding her view.

"You're doing the right thing, Dionna." She inhaled, then let out a slow, contented breath. "That man looks at you like you're his world."

Dionna snorted. "I don't know how you think that. He doesn't look at me at all."

Nana's mouth quirked. "People let their guard down around old women. Charles is no different."

Dionna took a sip of her tea, a thread of hope winding around her heart.

"Oh, speaking of." Nana rose, looking behind Dionna. "Charles. You can have my seat."

Charles was here? He was always in the field as long as possible. A perfect reason to avoid their shared bed.

"No, Nana," said Charles. "You must stay. I need to clean up anyway."

Nana pointed to the sky. "I'm not getting caught outside." She scurried away, dropping awkwardness in her wake.

Dionna twisted in her seat. "Is it supposed to rain?"

The knees of Charles's pants were dirty and his polo shirt was just as bad. He wiped his forehead with the arm of his shirt and the green material came away dirtier. "No. I think that was her way of getting us alone."

"Why don't you have a seat? Want some tea?"

He flopped in Nana's vacated chair. The overhang of the porch kept the sun off them. "That sounds good."

She poured him a cup in the glass Zuri usually used. When he reached for it, his fingers wrapped around hers.

Nearly fumbling the cup, he cleared his throat. "Thank you."

She had to draw her hand away or she'd spill his drink and risk breaking Zuri's cup. "You're welcome."

He sipped quietly and they each stared into the distance at the fronds lining the field.

He switched his gaze to the liquid left in his cup. "I'm sorry I didn't tell you we were leaving."

She wasn't ready to accept his apology. The hurt of being abandoned by everyone was too fresh.

"It wasn't supposed to be until next week, but Daniel needed to get his internship started to qualify for jobs in the wet season." He met her gaze, his expression determined. "And I'm not used to having to check with you."

"Like you said, I've done it enough."

"But you've never just left. It was wrong, and it was bad for the girls to see." He squinted at the clouds gathering in the horizon. "I never wanted to drive them away from you."

"I accept my role in that."

"Dionna, I . . ." He let out a long breath. "I like it on Earth. I like having the freedom to set down roots, however temporary, where I want. The girls like it here. I know they're adults, but they're not ready to be on their own, nor do they want to be."

"I never had a problem with you living on Earth, but you know it's harder for me."

"Your place is not here."

"My place is where I'm needed and that includes with family. But I'd like a place where I can be *me*. Charles, I can't be the only one making concessions."

His face clouded over, as dark as the gathering rain in the distance. Nana had been right. "We haven't asked you to change."

"Exactly. I get pointed comments. Barbs and insinuations. But you haven't discussed your issues with me."

A frustrated huff left him as he stood. "I've got work to do."

She carefully set her cup down and rose, cutting off his departure. They were face-to-face. They'd been having sex over the years, quick joinings in the dark, but it'd been ages since they'd faced each other like this. Face-to-face in the light of day.

She cupped his face. "Can we talk long enough to get somewhere?" Touching him often deescalated arguments, or at the very least redirected them. It was how they ended up having more sex than deep conversations.

He worked his jaw under her hands like he was chewing over words he couldn't say. "Talking was never what we were good at."

Heat crashed through her body like it did whenever he was close and she was touching him. They were estranged every way but physically. "We're good at sex because we took the time to get to know each other. We haven't done the same out of bed."

Energy rushed out of him until she thought he'd deflate. Fatigue entered his eyes and he took her hands in his, giving them the briefest squeeze before releasing. "I'm afraid it might be too little too late, my dear. I will work on helping the girls resurrect their relationship with you. You're important to them, and they're hurt and angry."

"And you?" She didn't scare easily, but his answer terrified her. This was the first time they'd scratched beneath the surface of their bitterness. She didn't like what they'd uncovered. Instead of the passionate mate she'd hoped to find, she faced a male who'd moved on.

"You're important to me. You always will be. We have our bond, like you said at the flat. But you have your work, I have mine, and the girls are adults. Perhaps . . . more isn't as necessary as we want to believe."

He circled around and she let him go. He didn't believe more was vital. She wanted him. She wanted her family, not a bond as empty as their home in Numen. But she couldn't make him want the same things. The next time he walked away from her might be the last.

CHAPTER 11

Tosca was on. She oozed more charm than a season of *The Bachelor*. She'd had Stephen and Katy laughing within minutes. She'd learned the names and sports of Greg and Tomas's kids, and she'd complimented Gloria and Jack on the level pruning of their boxwood shrubs by the curb. And she'd gushed to Stephen about the tile work around the pool.

Within five minutes, everyone loved her. Hell, Bronx would've turned over his wallet.

And to think she'd learned it all when he was still in school trying to figure out how to get into a female's robes. He almost shook his head. But like everyone else, he was riveted.

Her laughter tinkled like a magical bell that could grant listeners their greatest wishes. "And then Brandon kept looping through the cul-de-sac and said we must've taken a wrong turn."

He nearly choked on his drink as everyone laughed. Stephen had offered him some sort of local brew that was extra hoppy and too warm to enjoy. Exactly what Tosca said he'd drink. As Tosca told them all how he'd supposedly met her parents, laughter rang around the back patio—*with impeccable stonework around the fire pit. Love the slate!*

Bronx had to keep from gawking when Tosca grinned and tilted her head to the side. It was like she was flirting with everyone at the party. And it was working.

He clenched his teeth. They were supposed to fly under the radar. Be forgettable. He didn't need Stephen and Katy flashing their selfies with Tosca over eight different social media networks.

He'd have to ask Sierra how much she could scrub from the internet after tonight.

As if Tosca sensed his consternation, she eyed the tennis bracelet on Katy's wrist. "Oh my, that's gorgeous. Where did you get it?"

Katy beamed as she held her arm out like she'd been waiting for someone to notice the ring of diamonds around her wrist. "Stephen got it for me. Our fifth anniversary."

Tosca gushed and peppered them with questions about how they'd met until Katy was the one telling stories, effectively taking the focus off them until Katy's phone dinged.

"Oh!" She spun, waving her phone in the air. "Gena and Bennie are here."

Bronx sifted through the info Sierra had gathered on the neighborhood. Gena and Bennie Duncan lived two houses down from the safe house. They'd been gone since Bronx and Tosca had been there.

Tosca crossed one leg over the other. Her golden sandals were "a steal" from an online retailer he'd never heard of, but when she'd peeped out the window a few days ago, she'd noticed Katy wore this brand. And those damn shoes were like a marquee for the quickie DIY pedicure she'd given herself because "trust me, they're all going to have their fingers and toes done."

She wasn't wrong.

Bronx had walked out with his standard finger comb, which girls had never seemed to have a problem with before, but Tosca had marched up to him and ruffled his strands. Then the look of concentration she'd adopted had sent dread pooling in his gut as she'd teased and puffed his hair into a rough peak that she insisted wasn't a fauxhawk. But his hair was styled.

Stephen had his the same way, only Bronx doubted Katy had done it for him.

Tosca leaned into him. They had to pretend to be a young couple in love, but he swayed closer to her before consciously thinking about it. Underneath the styling product she'd used in her hair and the scented lotion she'd made sure Sierra ordered, he inhaled the smell of his shampoo on her, mingling with her natural blossom scent.

Relief washed away rising concern. She may have taken her act as far as the styling products she used, but if she continued using his shampoo and body wash under all the hundred-dollar shit that had been shipped to the house, then she was still his Tosca, the Tosca he knew from Numen. Not the con artist from south Florida who laughed like a silver bell and made her blue eyes twinkle on demand.

She could have had all the jewelry from this place in her pockets by now if she'd wanted.

Gena rounded the side of the house and strolled toward the patio, her hips swaying and bracelets jangling on her wrists.

Stephen's gaze tracked her like she was the winning fantasy football combination. "Gena."

"Stephen." Her voice was melted caramel and her gaze was just as warm. When she hugged Stephen, Tosca stiffened. Riding tall and proud on Gena's bare shoulder was a wrinkled symaster, a nude female with bony wings and a crotch that looked like it should cough smoke.

He brushed a kiss along Tosca's ear, murmuring, "Don't look directly at it."

A shiver raced down her body, but her slight nod made her hair tickle his nose.

Stephen draped an overly familiar arm around Gena's shoulders. The symaster perched like a hologram over Stephen's hand. "Julie, Brandon, this is Gena."

As they murmured greetings, a man came from the same direction as Gena. Bennie. A squat archmaster stared through his eyes.

Shit.

Too many demons in too short of a time. This zip code had a problem. Next, they'd have to figure out the origin. Daemon acting on their own? Or Numen making deals?

Sour acid churned his stomach. He was afraid he knew the answer.

Tosca played it cool as she glanced over Gena's shoulder through the demon. "And you must be Bennie. Nice to finally meet you both."

"We just got back from our second honeymoon," Gena gushed. "Bennie had a good sales quarter and we went to St. Croix. Again."

"Nice." Bronx stood as he shook Bennie's cold hand. The demon scrutinized him, but Bronx acted like Bennie was just another dude to have a dick measuring contest with. "It's nice this time of year. I was telling Julie we need to go back to Saint-Tropez again. In France." How would they react?

Annoyance flickered across Gena's face. That was how

the demon was getting in. The grass was always greener on the other side, and she wanted the whole damn lawn. "Bennie's job is so demanding, it's hard for him to get away. Maybe Saint-Tropez next year. Right, honey?"

Bennie didn't look like he gave a shit as a human but the way the demon's eyes dilated when he looked at Stephen's arm around Gena's shoulders, he was all about the woman.

To most demons, who Gena fucked—or wanted to fuck—wouldn't have mattered. Demons wanted to wreak havoc on their host's life and on the realm. The typical archmaster would have trashed the woman's body and then sicced his sylphs on someone else. But some demons were smarter, more patient, had goals, and preserved their hosts. This one was obsessed with Gena.

Tosca had returned to her seat, probably uncomfortable being so close to a demon, but he was standing next to Bennie in case the demon charged Stephen. It was his duty to stop the demon, but maybe Stephen could suffer just a little before he was saved. The guy was married.

Katy sashayed back to the porch, but instead of stopping next to her husband, she planted herself by Bronx. She was as close to him as Stephen was to Gena, but she didn't have her arm around him. Yet.

He glanced around. Had he missed the upside-down pineapple symbol of a swinger's house? He didn't get the impression the other two couples messed around, and there were no decals in the windows. The welcome mats were pineapple-free.

On another mission, Bronx might have let a swinger scenario carry so far—in the name of the job. But he had no desire to seduce Katy. And if Stephen touched Tosca, he'd knee Stephen's balls and risk his wings yanking the demon to the Mist in front of human witnesses.

No. There'd be no playing along if these humans wanted to swing, swap, or orgy. It was a ménage-a-no for him.

Leaving Stephen to his fate if he didn't take his hands off Gena, Bronx shifted backward to his spot. He sat, propped one leg over the other, and laid his hand passively on Tosca's bare leg. She paused midsip of her wine, and her gaze dropped to where he touched her.

Katy's mouth pursed into a puckered smile. "Aren't you two cute." It was the wistfulness that got him. She had stood close to him, hoping to capture some of the attention Stephen was draping around Gena's shoulder. And it hadn't worked.

He adopted a winning grin, like he was oblivious to the tension and the two uninvited demons. "Thanks. I'm dedicated to this woman. She's my angel, but she's certainly a little bit wicked."

BRONX *DID NOT* JUST SAY that.

She'd been back on her game, dusting her old skills off like they hadn't been buried for decades. How easy it had come back—lying and deflecting.

Then the demons had walked in. The guy's face. A nightmare hologram. How had she avoided seeing demons in the human realm until now? She'd been all over the nearby communities, running her scams, stealing and hocking, and she'd never seen one demon.

The sylphs haunting the young mom. Then the birdlike one perched on this woman's shoulder. Did Gena have any idea? Her soul was in grave danger. Bennie's was worse.

Tosca would've been fine if she'd never seen an archmaster in person. The gleaming shrewdness. The air of cruelty hanging over Bennie's head. Meeting Bennie's gaze was like looking into the darkness while the darkness looked back.

She didn't have to ask herself how they'd gotten their demon problem. The insecurities these two had, insecurities demons could exploit, were painfully obvious. It was more than half of the seven sins. Pride, greed, lust, envy—and wrath if Stephen didn't back off Gena.

Poor Katy. Bronx might not have seen her vulnerability when she'd tried to cuddle up to him, but Tosca had. The woman knew her husband was a player, but she wanted to be a part of this crowd. The tennis bracelet. The Range Rover parked in the driveway and not the garage while all the neighbors were over. This life with its status symbols—Katy wanted it but hadn't anticipated losing her husband to it.

And the demons were probably taking notes. Stephen and Katy could be next, and sylphs wouldn't even be needed.

Bennie yanked Gena toward him. She stumbled and almost fell.

"Whoa there, big guy," Stephen half laughed. The enjoyment of getting to Bennie made the greed in Stephen's eyes shine brighter. No possession necessary for him to be a dick. "You're going to hurt her."

"I only hurt her in the bedroom—when she asks for it," Bennie sneered.

Gena's nervous chuckle sent uncomfortable prickles over Tosca's skin. Katy's awkward laughter matched.

Was there anything Tosca could do? Run down Bennie? But he was human. And the victim. She had none of Bronx's abilities with demon hunting or killing.

Bronx's fingers tightened on her leg. "Feeling okay, angel?"

Was he purposely flaunting what they were? Or was he being so obvious because then the demons would never suspect they were Numen?

He narrowed his eyes like he was inspecting her for signs of fever or illness, but she knew what he was really doing. He was giving her an out.

"Yeah," she sighed, adding a little drama. "I knew I shouldn't have had wine."

"Gas?"

She'd make him pay for that. "Tannins." Her tone was flat. She never slipped character, but she was out of practice. And she'd never had anyone mess with her like he did. "They give me a headache."

"Oh, no!" Gena sounded perfectly scandalized.

Tosca waved her hand over the top of the glass. "I know. I had a bad experience with wine once, but I keep trying. I like it *so* much, but I don't think it'll ever be the same."

"Yes," Bronx added in a grave tone, and Tosca just knew she wouldn't like the rest of his contribution to the conversation. "It was like she'd been drugged. Not herself at all." He slapped his thighs and rose. "I'd better get her home so I can accost her before the headache sets in."

Everyone laughed at his joke. The delighted gleam in Bennie's eyes when Bronx said *accost* nearly made Tosca run out of the house. She'd dealt with perverts in her time on Earth and as an enforcer, but she hadn't had the added sense of being slimed.

Bronx tangled his fingers in hers. They said their goodbyes and walked to the safe house hand in hand. She clung to him a little harder than before. She was leaving demons behind. This wasn't like the young mother. Gena and Bennie could be dead by morning. And Bronx had cracked jokes—at her expense.

Once they were in the safety of the house, she jerked her fingers from his grasp, instantly missing the warmth of his grip. "Calling me angel wasn't funny."

"It was kind of funny."

"Bronx."

He stuffed his hands in his pockets and shrugged. "The demon wasn't suspicious. It was exactly what he needed to see and hear from us."

"What about the other demon?"

"The symaster? They're not as intelligent. The archmaster is my main concern. He's obsessed with Gena, so he'll preserve Bennie—as long as there's no showdown with Stephen tonight, but I doubt it. Some archmasters play a long game with their host, and I think that's what he's doing so he can keep Gena."

She shuddered. Gena had no idea what she went to bed next to every night. Had sex with. Went on vacation with.

Tosca had barely been keeping it together, and she'd thought Bronx wasn't taking it seriously, just giving her a hard time for her ignorance about demons. But he'd been studying and laying groundwork. The archmaster didn't think they were anything more than a human couple. "Sorry. In a matter of days, I've seen all classes of Daemon, and they're sleeping two houses down."

"We have our confirmation that there's a widespread issue in the area that hasn't been brought to Director Vale's attention. We need to find out why."

"Right?" She ruffled a hand through her hair without thinking. Dammit. She'd so diligently blown it out and curled it into waves, she hated to ruin it. "How?"

"The archmaster. He ranks high enough to have some answers. I just have to talk to Director Vale and see how he wants us to approach it. It'll take more than me and Urban."

More than them and what little she could contribute. Reaching down, she tugged off her sandals and flexed her toes. Peering at the backs of her ankles, she scowled. "Ugh. I'd better not get blisters."

Her feet would be healed in a few hours, but the hot spots were annoying. She had demons to deal with, dang it. Blisters shouldn't take more brain space.

"Sit on the couch." Bronx toed out of his OluKai boat shoes—the same style Greg and Tomas had each worn. She hadn't lost her touch.

The shoes were wiped out of her mind when she realized what he'd told her to do. "Why?"

"So I can rub your feet."

She drew in a sharp breath. The memory of how he'd massaged her back stayed fresh in her head no matter how many days had passed. But her legs moved before she'd made a conscious decision.

His hands on her feet sounded divine and she wouldn't mind if he rubbed away the ickiness the demons had left behind.

She flopped on the couch and stretched her legs out. Bronx sank into the other end. They were turned toward each other, and she swung a foot onto his lap. When his big, warm hands closed around her skin and squeezed, a long moan escaped her.

Embarrassment heated her face, but she didn't stop him. Her eyelids drifted shut and she tipped her head back. It'd been ages since she'd worn anything but comfortable boots and walked on soft-as-velvet Numen grass. Even the marble pathways in the realm weren't as hard as the concrete sidewalks and stone patios on Earth.

When the heat from his hands crept up her legs and swirled around her core, she scrambled for something to talk about.

"Is it normal to get that feeling around demons?" Popping her head up and opening her eyes, she caught Bronx watching, his expression hungry, his eyes fathomless.

In a heartbeat, he was back to aloof Bronx. His touch lightened. "What feeling?"

"Like I just walked through an oil slick full of evil."

"Some angels are more sensitive than others. Demons come from a place of power and control." He concentrated on his massage, his gaze caressing her toes. "Maybe that's why the demons are attracted to Bennie. He's got a competitive spirit, only he has more freedom on Earth than the demons ever have in Daemon."

"You really think there's a connection?" She switched feet and bit back a groan when he kneaded the ball of her other foot. The guy was talented with his hands. She'd suspected it. It was worse knowing. Made her want more.

"Too much of a coincidence when we take into account how Carlos didn't want you to leave."

"How high are the chances there's a link between Forgotten Peace and Senator Colbert?"

"I'd guess she was involved with trafficking the females, and her son and husband were her tools." His grip tightened with his anger.

Despite the gravity of the topic, she was melting into the couch. And she wanted to pull Bronx on top of her and have his magical hands on the rest of her.

She sat up, removing her foot from his grip. Satisfaction seeped into her bones when disappointment turned his lips down. Her fingers tingled. She wanted to touch him. And this was twice now he'd helped with a massage.

"Give me a foot." She crooked her fingers at him.

"What?"

"Your turn."

He stared at her for a moment. "You're going to massage my feet?"

She didn't think he'd do it. Appealing to his competitive nature should work. "What guys can do, girls can do better."

He rolled his eyes and swung his leg on the couch. His heel landed close to her crotch. She wasn't into foot kink, but her belly flipped anyway. Digging into him midfoot, she earned a groan and he leaned his head back like she'd been doing a minute ago.

Strength vibrated through her hands. His calves and thighs flexed and relaxed like she was short-circuiting his body. A heady experience. This guy had been with plenty of females who were capable of twisting males into knots, but her little foot rub was making him twitch.

Delight lit through her body, threatening to morph into desire. No. She couldn't handle getting turned on while he was on the other end of the couch and she was touching him.

"You know what I'm grateful for?" Other than having something else to distract her mind and hopefully her body. "That my situation uncovered a bigger plot than Juliette being a conniving bitch."

"Connected or not, she's dirty as hell."

His muscles rippled under her hands. Feet weren't supposed to be manly, yet elegant. Strong, but beautiful. They were feet. But they were attached to muscular calves. He had nice legs. He wore Lululemon shorts for men; they didn't wear him. *Think about something other than his body!* "I want to catch her, and I want to get to the bottom of the demon infestation around here. I was rusty tonight, but I'll get better."

He cracked an eye open. "If that was you rusty . . . Fuck, Tosca. That commune doesn't stand a chance."

A sudden rush of anger made her irrational, and she dumped his foot off her lap. "You need to quit being like that!"

His eyes widened, abject confusion lightening the brown of his irises. "Like what?"

"Nice. Understanding. Compassionate. God. You can't be a player, someone who fucks around like he doesn't care about anyone's feelings, and then turn into"—she waved her hand like she was clearing smoke—"you."

"This *is* me, Tosca. And I don't fuck with females' feelings." He shifted fast, right over the cushions of the couch separating them.

She shrank back, but the effect lengthened her out under him.

"I've fucked around, Tosca. Why does that piss you off? Why does it make you angry that I have a lot of sexual experience? I'm not Carlos. I'm not leading anyone on or making promises I don't intend to keep."

Her back was flattened over the armrest of the couch and he hovered over her, barely touching her. Shadows kissed along his jaw and under his cheekbones. An avenging angel turning her languid body molten.

"Answer me, Tosca."

"I . . ." The answer left her too raw. Too vulnerable. Instead, she laced her hands around the back of his neck and dragged his head down until their mouths clashed.

When she opened for him, she tasted the craft brew on his tongue. She didn't know she'd widened her legs to fit him between her thighs until the hard ridge of his erection pressed into her belly.

She wanted to see it. To feel it. Was it long and

beautiful? Elegant? Veins lining his length like he was carved from marble?

She curled her hands into his shirt and tugged it up before the courage to go farther south than his abs left her. When the fabric came free of his shorts, she pressed her palms against his stomach. He clenched his muscles under her hands and his kiss deepened. He liked what she was doing.

Not caring how horribly unpracticed she was at kissing after so many years, she stroked up and down his defined torso. Ridged abdominal muscles. Chiseled pecs.

He lowered more weight onto her, caressing her sides and bunching the material of her shirt up until her belly was bare. He feathered his fingers up her side to cup a breast over her bra.

She wanted more. This male was potent. Intoxicating. And worse—she trusted him. Her life was in his hands and he hadn't failed her. She wanted to put more in his hands. And she was tired of restraint. So dang tired.

She was also tired of pretending she was something she wasn't. Worldly and resistant to his charm. She was neither, and she had to quit pretending she was.

Creeping her hands up his chest, she danced her fingers over the bunched fabric of his shirt and cupped his chin. She broke the kiss and licked her lips. His gaze tracked the path of her tongue.

"I . . . um . . ."

"Yeah?" His voice was gruff and he held himself so rigidly, waiting for her to speak, his body trembled.

Just get it out. He might not understand. He might look at her like she had oversized oval eyes and antennae. "I haven't done this before. And that's why you intimidate me." The rest spilled out, like the wall damming in her thoughts had been obliterated. "I was saving myself for Carlos—or maybe I wasn't and that's why I didn't sleep with him. But I wanted one thing in my life to be real. I wanted an authentic experience and I knew—I *knew*—that if I slept with Carlos, or anyone, then that part of myself would become just another tool."

His brows pinched together as horrific comprehension dawned across his face.

A virgin.

Her lack of experience shocked him, and her embarrassment smothered her.

The sliding door in the dining room cracked open. Bronx flew off her, his ass hitting the armrest on the other side. He slid down and adopted a casual pose in less than a second. She burrowed into the corner of the couch, drawing her legs up, and wished she could sink into the cushions and never come up again.

CHAPTER 12

Urban stepped through the sliding door, rolling his shoulders. Bronx did the same thing when adjusting to a new morph of his wings, but right now, he needed to roll more than his shoulders. His entire body was tight, and pretending to be chill was painful.

He swallowed hard. There was no way his buddy wouldn't know something was up. Tosca's face flamed red. Bronx had an erection that was one shift of his hips away from exploding, and Tosca's admission rang in his ears.

It wasn't that he didn't think virgin Numen over the age of twenty-five existed, but he was too old to run across any. He'd waited until he was old enough to be a warrior before he'd had sex, then he'd embraced the life. Warriors liked to fuck around. At any moment they could get grievously injured in the line of duty and be assigned a sync mate to help them heal. Someone they might not have even met yet. Eternal monogamy with a stranger. So before warriors had to settle down, they played.

He'd played with the best of them. And they'd played right back. His partners had been experienced.

How could Tosca be— No, she'd explained it. She'd protected herself.

Urban's gaze jumped back and forth. "Everything okay?"

"The neighbors are possessed," Tosca said, her tone almost petulant, like the demons had ruined the party.

What was going through her head? Was she worried how he'd take the information? It was a shock. There was no doubt about that. And, yeah, he needed time to process. He hadn't had to consider that his partner had never had sex before.

She'd saved herself for *decades*.

She'd done it out of self-preservation. But what about when she'd lived in Numen? He hadn't thought she dated a lot, but never? Hadn't she met anyone she wanted to be with, or was trust too hard to come by? Too hard to explain?

Urban perched on the edge of the recliner. "Are you guys finding the demons, or are they finding you?"

"We're definitely finding them," he answered. As he reoriented his thoughts, blood slowly drained from his erection. And as long as he didn't look at Tosca, didn't inhale too deeply and draw in her blossom scent, he was safe from sporting another hard-on. "There's someone behind this. Some reason why they're so plentiful but a warrior team hasn't been assigned to the area."

Urban nodded, his concerned gaze darting to Tosca and back to him. "Have you notified Director Vale?"

"No." Bronx tried to study Tosca from the corner of his eye. She was scrutinizing the wood pattern on the end table. "I was going to call it in the morning."

Tosca jumped off the couch. "I'm sure it has something to do with the commune. I'll let you two talk about it."

"Good night," Urban said with a wave.

"Night," Bronx murmured without looking at her. Just hearing her voice was enough to reroute his blood flow.

"Night," she mumbled as she circled behind the couch to take the stairs to her bedroom, not once passing through his line of vision.

When the door upstairs opened and closed, Urban smacked his lips. "I walked in on something, didn't I?"

Bronx wanted to tell him everything. He usually did. But this was Tosca's privacy. "Yeah."

"Was it going south before I got here?"

"It was going somewhere." He rubbed his hands over his face. "I'll talk to her after I figure out what I'm going to say."

"Well, that tells me nothing." He straightened and slapped Bronx's shoulder. "But it tells me a whole damn lot too."

"What's that mean?"

Urban gestured to him, then in the direction of Tosca's bedroom. "You talk about everything and everyone. But with her? You have nothing to bitch at her about and now you have nothing to tell me. You're falling for her."

"No." It was an automatic reply. He never fell for anyone. His buddy's dubious look forced more words out. "She's always gotten under my skin with her rule following. And then seeing her on her game tonight, but terrified of the demons—it's a lot to wrap my head around." And her admission had made his head spin.

"Okay. Why don't I talk to the director? You can talk to Tosca."

He wanted to do more than talk to her, but the mission came first, otherwise she wasn't safe. "We have to deal with the neighbors. An archmaster has the husband, and I think he's obsessed with the wife, who's got a symaster riding around with her."

"Think the archmaster wants the wife possessed, or just under his control?"

"I don't want to find out, but we should have backup before we deal with it."

Urban nodded. "Let me see what Director Vale says. Maybe we can get Dionna or Harlowe here."

"Thanks, man."

"You got it. Just FYI, I'm not coming back until late morning." Urban slipped out the way he'd come.

Bronx let out a long breath and stared at the stairs. How did he feel about what Tosca had said? She hadn't been warning him off or telling him to go slow. She'd been answering a question. His question.

She'd been frustrated because he'd been nice instead of the ass she expected an overly confident male to be. He wasn't like Carlos, and she didn't know what to do when she couldn't hate a male, and she was attracted to him.

Bronx didn't know what to do with a Tosca who was attracted to him. But he knew what he'd like to do. No matter what, they had to clear the air between them. She'd left on an awkward note that could easily become a misunderstanding. There was a lot of work to do, and they needed open communication.

He was in front of her bedroom door in moments, knocking lightly.

"Yeah?"

"We need to talk."

A minute ticked by. Would she blow him off?

The door creaked open. She wore the T-shirt and shorts she'd borrowed from him. Her face had been scrubbed free of the little makeup she'd worn. He'd never be able to see her as the intrepid enforcer again. The strict, by-the-book female. She was his age and jaded from her past, but also young and innocent.

"About what you said—"

She huffed out a breath and planted her gaze on the ceiling. "Can we go back in time and forget it?"

"I'd rather not."

She crossed her arms in a way that made it obvious she wasn't wearing a bra. He forced his gaze to her face, and thankfully, she brought her chin down to meet his gaze or he'd be thinking about kissing along her slender neck. "You're not the virgin." Her gaze was as flat as her tone.

"I haven't been for a long time. But"—he put his hand on his heart and bent forward—"I'd like to think I am a good listener, cherry or no."

She kicked a blond brow up. "I kinda wish you weren't right now."

"You waited to be with someone you could trust. But no one's come along in all those years. Until me." He didn't take his eyes off her as she rolled her lips in like she was trying to stifle her agreement. "But you know I'm not looking to settle down. Is that why you're upset with me?"

She didn't immediately reply. She kept her arms crossed with her boobs rounded over the curve of her arm. "I'm not looking to settle down either."

Why did that news fill him with dismay? She was a female some guy would be fucking lucky to spend eternity with.

He wasn't the guy. He had too much to do.

She sniffed. "I'd like to get rid of it."

"Get rid of it? Like it's a mole?"

"Yes. For decades, I've worked with males who thought they could seduce my intelligence away when I called them on their BS. Yet all the time, I felt like, You know what? They know something I don't. They do know how to seduce someone. They've had actual sex before. I was trained to get guys to *think* I would sleep with them, then steal something."

He narrowed his eyes, trying to follow her logic. Enforcers under Stede's rule had been arrogant and not that concerned about right or wrong. They were still that way, since it seemed Senator Colbert held a lot more power than previously thought. Tosca had been a square peg trying to fit in a round hole with the enforcers.

Or she'd been a round peg who'd whittled herself square. Then when she'd been stuffed into the hole, she still hadn't fit in.

"I'm missing out," she said. "And I want to know what I'm missing out on."

"You want to do it because you're curious?" There were worse reasons, but he wanted more for her.

"Yeah, that's about it. And I trust you're not going to make me use sex as a tool. I'm ready."

The world spun behind her. She was the steady center of a storm, but he was caught in the maelstrom. She wanted to have sex with him? She wanted him to be her first?

He squared his shoulders as he thought about that. Of all the reasons females had said they wanted to be with him, he'd never heard trust. He knew he looked good. Human women crawled all over him. He had muscles, was intentionally mysterious, looked like a TV actor, and dressed like he had money. Numen females liked that he was a warrior. That was all he needed in his realm, though he preferred humans for the likelihood that he wouldn't see them again in their lifetime.

"So . . ." He wasn't sure how his next words would go over, but he had to make sure they were on the same page. "You wanna do it?" Leaning closer, he had to verify the most important detail. "No strings attached?"

She tapped the fingers of one hand against her folded arm. "Yeah, I do. It's not like it gets more precious with age."

"Not that I don't want your first time to be spectacular, but you shouldn't be treated like a jewel only until you do it for the first time."

"Jeez, Bronx. There you go again." She fisted her hands in his shirt and dragged him into the room.

He kicked the door closed behind him and picked her up. She twined her legs around his waist. She wouldn't fall, but he pressed his hands into her ass. No need to miss an opportunity. He'd had enough dreams about her butt.

Their mouths were smashed together again, and it might've been less than a half hour, but it felt like an eternity since he'd tasted her. Thank fuck Urban had left when he had.

Bronx walked them to her bed and carefully laid her down in the middle. She sprawled across the sheets, the covers thrown back from when she'd been in bed when he'd knocked.

Nerves fired in his gut. It was easy to talk a good game, and he had confidence in his abilities, but performance anxiety was sinking in. He couldn't just strip her down and go to town. "What have you done before?"

Pink dusted across her cheeks. "Um . . . I'd rather not . . ."

Not much. That was the answer if she wasn't willing to talk about it when she'd been so candid up to this point. He didn't want her to wonder what he was going to do next, so he laid it out. "I'm going to undress you, and since I've been fantasizing about your tits and your ass and those legs wrapped around me, I'm going to play for a while. I'm going to put my mouth wherever you'll let me until I settle between those thighs of yours. They

could crush my skull and damn if that doesn't turn
me on."

Her lips parted and her pupils dilated. But she didn't
back away. She didn't skitter across the bed to get away
from him. She sucked her lower lip between her teeth and
dropped her gaze to his crotch.

He resisted the urge to palm himself. His dick was
getting mighty uncomfortable caged in his shorts. He
flicked open the button and zipper and shoved his shorts
down. Her gaze dropped to his erection.

Was he a self-centered bastard because he liked the awe
in her eyes? Who cared? He shed his shirt. Her gaze
stroked up his abdomen like light kisses along his skin. His
muscles tightened. She looked ready to prowl across the
bed to devour him.

"We'll get there, Tosca. The first time is all about you."

"The first time?"

He nearly groaned. "Your first time with sex. But I'll be
getting you off way more than that." Wait. "Have you
orgasmed before?"

Her expression closed off but she nodded.

"With anyone but yourself?"

She scowled and shook her head.

"All right." He was tempted to crack his knuckles and
roll his neck. "Let's change that."

HE DESCENDED ON HER. For a moment, Tosca worried she'd
combat roll right off the bed. But the sight of him stalking
her, climbing onto the bed and stretching over her—she
wasn't going anywhere.

Her body was on fire, one big electrical current traveling

under her skin. She didn't know if she should scissor her legs or stroke herself to stop the throb between her thighs, but Bronx settled between them, making the decision for her.

He gave her a long, lingering kiss before tugging her bottom lip between his teeth and releasing it to kiss his way down her neck. Thanks to the earlier massages, she didn't flinch when his warm fingers brushed her abdomen and rolled her shirt up. Until cool air breezed across her taut nipples.

She tensed as he drew the top over her head—until she saw the way he was looking at her. Hungry. Greedy. Focused on her pebbled pink nipples. And he made good on his promise. He dipped his head and caught one nipple between his lips.

She groaned, her legs opening wider. He settled more of his weight on her. Back and forth he went between her breasts. Licking and nibbling. Blowing across one wet tip, then the other. She writhed under him, but his weight pinned her in place.

Her belly clenched, then flipped, her nerves threatening to ruin the moment. Already he'd blown past what she'd experienced with Carlos and her targets. They hadn't looked at her like Bronx did. They hadn't touched her like he did. And they definitely hadn't been as handsome as him.

"These," he growled as he licked a circle around one peak, "are the sweetest tits I've ever tasted."

Just when she thought she was going to come from nipple stimulation alone, he trailed down her stomach. His fingers hooked over the waistband of her shorts—what used to be his shorts, but she wasn't going to give them back.

The material drew down, his head a breath above her

skin as he pulled them all the way off. "Fuck yeah, this is what I've been dreaming about."

He'd said something like that before. It was enough to pull her out of her lust stupor. "Have you really fantasized about this? With me?"

"Since you first showed up at Odessa's mansion ready for guard duty."

That was when they'd first met. She'd thought he was everything she should stay away from, and she'd resisted the late-night fantasies as long as possible. "I knew you were dangerous then."

"Nah, Tosca." His hot breath wafted over her most sensitive skin. "I'll never be dangerous to you." He settled his shoulders between her legs and placed a kiss on her right thigh and then her left. Then he kissed closer.

With each touch of his lips, she fought a battle between scooting away from his encroaching mouth and sinking her hands into his glossy hair and tugging him closer.

Then he placed a kiss right on her seam. She jerked. This wasn't her first time doing this, but her anxiety that Carlos would ask her to do it with a target hadn't left her then, and she hadn't been able to orgasm. That worry was gone now. Bronx was one of the good guys. She trusted him.

So when he licked through her seam and lapped over her clit, she lost any residual tension. She was in the moment.

"That's it. Relax and let me make you feel good."

She already felt spectacular. What else was coming?

He showed her. As he tested what she was the most responsive to, she climbed closer to her peak. And when he settled into a rhythm, he pushed her higher, then pulled back. The explosion was going to be an out-of-body experience. It was going to be even more than that.

But as her body coiled tighter, readying for the impending peak, she panted his name and fisted his hair. "I don't think I can—this is too much."

He growled. *Growled*. And she loved it.

Then he inserted a finger, as slowly and carefully as he'd licked her, considerate even now. And she detonated. The fullness combined with the strokes of his tongue—she was gone.

She bucked, her body racked with tremors as soul-stealing ecstasy coursed through her veins, her nerves, electrocuting every inch of her skin.

And then the naughty male threaded another finger in her, pushing her rapture higher until she screamed. She didn't know if his name or anything coherent came out of her mouth.

And when she crashed to the bed not having left it at all, he slowed to a stop and kissed each thigh again.

"Damn, Tosca. That was the most beautiful thing I've ever seen."

She released his head to push a hand through her own tangles, which had landed on her face while she'd been thrashing. "Oh my gosh. That's nothing like what I can do for myself."

His low chuckle was like sprinkling lighter fluid on a dying flame. Just like that, heat was flooding back into places it had just been released from.

He was over her and gazing down into her eyes. "You ready?"

"Bronx." *Yes*. She couldn't get the word out, but she sensed he wouldn't move until she explicitly agreed. "I think I'll die if you get me off like that again." Understanding filled his eyes and he nodded, pulling back. She held him in place. "But dang, what a way to go. I can't wait."

His grin was breathtaking and he claimed her mouth once more. Her flavor mingled with his. New and unique. All their own. She rolled her hips, like she was encouraging him to just get on with it. But this was Bronx. He wasn't shoving inside. The returning heat in her body burned hot until she could compete with the sun. He used his legs to wedge her knees farther apart.

The broad tip of his erection was at her entrance. Just as she was about to tense, he swept his tongue inside to meet hers. The way he invaded her mouth, mimicking the way he'd thrust inside of her, made her open for him like a blossom in the middle of June.

Pushing in, he took it slow, reading her better than she could ever read herself. If she'd missed decades of mediocre sex just for this moment, then she couldn't summon one ounce of regret. She'd missed nothing. Her intuition told her that there was nothing like being with Bronx.

And her brain told her there never would be.

Tension crept back in, and his talented fingers were at her breast, kneading and massaging.

As he was entering her, filling her, stretching her until she wasn't sure if she'd accommodate him or splinter apart, she realized that she wouldn't want to be with anyone else. That even if a sync brand stamped her wrist, she would refuse her mate if it wasn't Bronx.

She struggled for air. He'd said no strings attached.

He broke the kiss and stopped his forward push. "Are you all right?"

He was holding himself as rigidly as he had on the couch. He'd wanted her then and they'd only been kissing. His reaction was from her.

The last of her resistance wavered. Maybe she should back out.

No. No strings attached. She could separate sex from feelings, she just had to stay strong. Doing it together didn't mean staying together forever.

Even if that might be what she wanted.

"I'm in my head." For such an awkward moment, she wasn't cringing. He was a few inches inside of her, and her legs were spread with her knees up, but the tenderness in his face washed away her fears. They were for another time. This moment was for her. "Keep going. Please."

"Aw, my little enforcer. You never have to beg." He caught her lips again and pushed forward. Stretching and the faintest threat of a pinch were crowded out by the sensation of fullness. Of rightness.

Fully seated, he broke the kiss again and brushed the backs of his fingers down one side of her face. "You good?" His voice was gruff and heavy with need.

"Yeah." Hers was breathless. She rocked her hips, and he dropped his forehead to hers.

"Fuck, Tosca. You feel like heaven wrapped in a blanket of sin."

And then he moved. In and out he thrust, varying the speed and power like he was testing her. And like before, she didn't care what the heck he did, she couldn't get enough.

"Bronx," she panted. "I need more."

"I'll give you more, but you're not ready yet."

What did he mean—

He wedged a hand between them and touched her oversensitive clit.

"Oh my god," she groaned and arched her back, trying to get away from his finger and closer at the same time.

He didn't have to move his hand. He rested it between them and the force of their bodies did the rest.

The energy was back, coursing through her and

exposing every nook and cranny she'd hidden away from the world, from herself, from him. She was exposed. And when the climax ripped through her, she clung to Bronx, afraid she'd fly through the ceiling.

"Fuck, Tosca." He grunted as heat flooded between them. "So fucking tight—" he roared, throwing his head back. He pumped his hips and she took him, took all of him, until he sagged over her.

She caught him, wrapping her arms and legs around him, and they lay still for several moments, catching their breath.

When his breathing slowed, he brushed a hand over her leg and hip and up her side. "Give me a moment to recover, and then we're doing it again."

"I hate to be the naive virgin, but how many times can you do it in a night?"

The grin he flashed was all Bronx. The swaggering warrior. "There are no virgins here, and as many times as you'll let me."

CHAPTER 13

"When did he say he was going to be here?" Tosca asked between pants.

"Later this morning." He wanted to be done before Urban walked in on his thrusting ass. "But if you can still talk, I'm not fucking you hard enough." He had her bent over the sink, watching her tits sway with each thrust in the mirror.

This was round number . . . He'd lost track. All he knew was that he'd never fucked this much before at one time. Tosca was ravenous. Insatiable, but he could satiate her very well. Really fucking well, thank you very much. But by the time he'd recovered, so had she.

She was a naturally sexual female. She was fucking perfect.

And didn't that make him stop and look at himself in the mirror. Strain and lust carved into his expression. One hand on her shoulder and one on her hip to hold her in place and keep from face-planting her into the mirror.

"Bronx?" She wiggled that ass and he automatically started pumping. But his mind wasn't back in the game.

"I like watching you get off." It was the truth even if it wasn't what he was concentrating on.

"You like watching me watch myself get off."

His grin was lopsided and quick because he had to refocus on hitting her sweet spot. "Fuck yeah, I do."

She bowed her back and put her elbows on the counter, sticking her ass into him. There it was. He pumped right where he knew it'd drive her the craziest.

This time, his name came out on a groan. *"Bronx."*

Her walls were clenching around him, milking him in a way that would haunt his dreams. If he ever needed to masturbate against the clock, it was this feeling he'd recall, and he'd be off in seconds.

"So fucking tight, Tosca." He could fuck her a hundred thousand times and never get enough.

As he released, he tried to escape the thought dogging him.

He'd never get enough of her.

He wanted her so bad he wasn't going to want anyone else.

God, was he ready to mate after one night of sex? Was he ready to give it all up for good—mind-blowing—sex?

He finished coming, their cries echoing across the tiles of the bathroom. He draped himself over her back, careful to prop most of his weight on his hands. She laid her head in her arms.

Could he give it all up? He'd seen so many bonds tested when a warrior didn't leave their assignment. Dionna was a resounding example. She hadn't told them anything, but he could read into her sabbatical. Her mate had moved away from the realm long ago. She wouldn't be gone now if everything was great between them.

Director Vale had left his position. Sierra had fallen, but Jagger and Harlowe were both migrating out of their warrior roles. Their bonds would likely stay strong because of it. Like his parents' had.

Only he didn't want to quit being a warrior. Would Tosca even want to live back in the realm if they could clear her name?

And that was his buffer, the wall he could build between his heart and a night of losing himself in her body. Her future was a giant unknown, therefore it definitely didn't include mating.

She drew in a long breath like she was finally coming up for air after being in an underwater sexfest for hours. "I should get cleaned up before Urban gets here."

"Me too." He pulled out of her and stroked a hand over the rounded flesh of her butt. She had a phenomenal ass. "I'll grab my clothes and use the other bathroom."

He said it as casually as possible when his emotions were all over the place. He left her in the bathroom, picked up his clothing, and went down the hall to the other bathroom.

The shower was one of the fastest he'd ever taken. By the time he was downstairs and digging out bagels, cheese, and fruit spread, Urban walked in the sliding door. His buddy's gaze went from him to the upper level.

"Everything good?"

No. It was messier than before. "Yeah, we're good."

Urban cast another glance in the direction of Tosca's room, as if he didn't know how to interpret Bronx's answer, and slid onto a stool at the island. "What are you making me for breakfast?"

"Didn't you eat?"

"No. I went to the market, but Persephone was patrolling."

Bronx snorted and cut into a block of gouda. "Are you sure she wasn't there for her own food?"

"Not when she's following me asking what I do on Earth and why my sidekick isn't with me."

He paused the knife. "She doesn't realize you're the sidekick?"

"Ha ha, fucker. She called me her hero." Urban got up to grab a water out of the fridge. "She's coming on real strong, and believe me, I put her in her place. But I can't figure out why she was even interested."

Urban didn't put anyone in their place, especially a senator's daughter.

"Persephone Nassim?" Tosca appeared at the bottom of the stairs.

Tosca rolled her shoulders. Was she stretching stiff muscles, or had she let her wings out for a few minutes?

He wouldn't mind massaging her back again.

"That's the one." Urban slid back into his stool and snagged a piece of cheese from the tray. "Know her?"

"I've seen her talking to Juliette. She has major mommy issues, so I wouldn't doubt Senator Colbert is using her for something."

Bronx traded looks with Urban. Hadn't they wondered the same thing? "Ever catch what they were talking about?"

Tosca shook her head, all business. He admired the way she could mask her emotions. He couldn't be the only one left reeling from last night—and this morning. "No. But the senator always looked super concerned and maternal, and Persephone hung on it. At the time, I thought it was legit. I should've known better."

The water bottle in Urban's hand squeaked under the pressure of his grip. "She's lucky she didn't end up on the missing angels list."

Bronx spun the cheese toward them and shoved the bagels and fruit spread across the table. "Should we warn her?"

"Maybe the director should talk to her parents," Urban said.

"You should if you have any sort of rapport with her." Tosca slid into her seat. "Persephone has a catty reputation for a reason, but no one really thinks about why. Her parents are well respected, but they don't give her their time. So if they warn her off Juliette, it's only going to make Persephone more desperate to please the senator."

"I don't have a rapport with her," Urban said. "We're not even friends. I've always been a dumb grunt to her, like warriors are to most of the senators' kids."

Tosca lifted a shoulder and grabbed a bagel. "Then you should use it."

He nodded and Bronx asked, "What did the director say?"

"Keep gathering information and he'll send Harlowe and Ransom. Dionna's still got some shit going on with her family. I am officially your college bro who's staying with you for a few days."

"It's almost like we're back to being a warrior team." Bronx's chest squeezed. Fuck, he missed the hunt. He didn't want a human to be possessed, but he'd nearly cheered when he'd seen the archmaster in Bennie.

"There'll be five of us if we count Tosca," Urban said. "Almost six since Sierra's monitoring the outside cameras, spying on your neighbors as much as they're spying on you."

"Two short of a full team, but damn, it feels good to hunt demons again." Energy flooded his veins. Plans ran through his head—reasons to drop by Gena and Bennie's place, how to get inside, how to get the archmaster and symaster when the two humans were in separate rooms and wouldn't know what was happening to the other.

Tosca set the knife down she was using to spread jam

on her bagel. "I guess if I'm going to be acting like a warrior while I'm in hiding, you two need to give me lessons on what to do."

Ideas were clicking into place. "Honestly, except for the demon-fighting part, you're perfect for the job."

THE WALK WAS Bronx's idea. They were hand in hand like a couple in love. Startling how much easier it was to slip into a lovey-dovey persona after they'd spent the night together.

She no longer tensed each time he touched her. She wanted to lean into him. Which, fair, that was what she'd wanted before. But this time she had an excuse to tuck herself into his side as they walked through the neighborhood.

"Shit, don't look," he said under his breath.

Instead, she looked up at the way the palm trees canopied overhead. This was a gorgeous neighborhood. A less ostentatious version of the area in Numen where the senators lived. The houses weren't as affluent, but the lots were large, and with plenty of cypress trees separating the properties, they were almost as secluded.

Resisting the urge to glance toward Gena and Bennie's house, she directed her gaze back on the pavement.

"Gargoyles are now part of their flower bed decor," Bronx murmured.

Gargoyles. Another thing she'd learned about but had no real experience with. The little underworld spies couldn't roam the realm like sylphs. They had to reside in garden gnomes, where they could stand higher, stay in place for a long time, and look innocent enough to be put anywhere.

She finally brushed her gaze over the house, a two-level place like the safe house. The flower bed bordered either side of the door and followed the path to the driveway. She counted at least three red gnome statues. "Daemon's version of security cameras?"

"Only no Sierra on the other end."

"Gena doesn't look like a garden gnome aficionado."

"My thoughts exactly, but with a symaster whispering in her ear, she's probably doing a lot of things she normally wouldn't."

They continued their stroll past the Smiths' house to the Lopezes'. Katy was outside, lounging on her front porch with Gena. Stephen was nowhere to be seen and the two women appeared more comfortable around each other than they had at the get-together.

"Hey, neighbors!" Katy called. "Come on over."

Bronx gave Tosca's fingers a squeeze, and they veered off the quiet street up the driveway and to the front porch. This was it. They were on.

Gena's shoulder was still the symaster's perch. The demon glared at them as Gena aimed her grin at Tosca. "You look better today."

No, she didn't. Since this wasn't a leisurely walk, she'd put on her bohemian flats—which were hell on her little toe—her print knit shorts, and an off-the-shoulder pink top. She was summer chic all the way, but she hadn't done herself up like she had last night.

"Thank you." She grinned as if she knew a secret they didn't and rolled her eyes toward Bronx. "He took care of me."

"I'll bet he did," Katy muttered, but with half the energy she'd used the previous evening when Stephen could witness. It helped when he wasn't draped over another woman. "Come, join us. I have more sweet tea."

Tosca's taste buds watered. Sweet tea had been like a delicacy at the commune, what with a five-pound pack of sugar being difficult to steal. "I'd love some."

Katy disappeared inside for a few glasses. Tosca leaned against the railing next to Bronx. He propped his arm behind her.

Part of her wished this wasn't for show. And part of her was thrilled she could do what she'd grown up doing, what she was good at, to help others and not for profit.

"Where's Bennie and Stephen?" Bronx asked.

Gena's eyes pinched at the corner when she smiled. The symaster picked at its crotch. "Bennie's been passed out in bed all day. I swear, he's gotten his hours switched around, and when he has a day off, I can't get him up."

It had to be hard to recover from a possession. Some demons couldn't hold the soul at bay for long periods of time and instead treated the host like a pet rock. "I hope he's feeling okay."

She nodded, but her reassuring smile didn't reach her eyes. "I'm sure he will be. He goes through phases like this. High-pressure job and all." She turned up the wattage on her grin. "Not all of us can work from home."

That was an opening she needed to jump on. They needed a good idea of the layout of the Smiths' house, and they'd discussed several ways to get it. The walk had been a general approach. They could determine where the kitchen and living room were, and from there, they could guess at the layout of the bedrooms, but they wouldn't truly know without peeping in the windows.

Security cameras and gnomes made that difficult.

Katy banged out the door with two glasses of sweet tea. Tosca accepted one and sipped, letting out a little approving moan when the lemony sweetness hit her tongue. Bronx held the glass. A security measure just in case something was added to the tea. They hadn't discussed it ahead of time. Tosca was willing to be the guinea pig.

She set her glass on the railing. "I'm finding it a hard adjustment. Our bedroom is on the top floor and the office is across from it." It wasn't. That was Bronx's room. "And it makes it *so* hard when I can look up from my desk and see my bed."

Katy sat and crossed her legs. "What did I miss?"

Bronx answered first, casual as ever. "How the layouts of homes make it hard to work from home. I set up at the island, but the afternoon sun hits my laptop like a bitch and I have to move. But we only have one office and my lady gets that."

Katy scrunched her nose. "I know, right? Stephen's always going on about how he wants to work from home, but we only have two bedrooms and we want one to be a nursery someday." Her smile was shy, while Gena's horrified expression said she was either not planning for kids or glad that Bennie didn't want to work from home.

It'd be odd if Tosca asked her about the layout of her house, but she willed the woman to tell them something. Even if they knew the layout of only one of the rooms, it'd help when they planned their attack on the demons.

"Our master bedroom is downstairs and we have two rooms upstairs." Gena sucked her teeth against her lips. "Neither of which will be a nursery."

Katy tilted her head. "I didn't know you don't like kids." She glanced around as if she was wondering why they'd moved to a family neighborhood.

"No. With Bennie's hours, I'd have no break. And we have no family, and just . . . no."

Bronx took another pretend sip from his drink. "You

must have to hang a Do Not Disturb sign when Bennie gets home so late."

Was he digging to see if they slept in the same room?

Gena chuckled. "Sometimes I fall asleep on the couch while waiting for him. If he's schmoozing clients, then I might even sleep in the guest room." She wrinkled her nose. "He's especially persistent on those nights."

"Is that why he's so tired today? Schmoozing?"

"That's tomorrow night." The sylph on her shoulder danced to the other side. How could she not feel that? "And that'll definitely be a guest room night."

"Your next vacation will make everything worth it." Tosca's reassurance wasn't about tomorrow night. She wanted to take care of their demon problem so the couple was around for their next vacation.

After Tosca had finished her drink and discreetly sipped half of Bronx's, she tugged his hand. "I should get back to work. My client's shiplap wall isn't going to design itself."

The symaster curled its little lip and petted Gena's hair during the round of goodbyes. That was what Gena was to it. A pet who had to be watched while the master was away.

As they walked back to their house, Bronx murmured, "Sounds like tomorrow night is the best night to kill some demons."

CHAPTER 14

"I can feel your judgment, Mother," Courtney chided. Stella shook her head and continued to chop plantains for the main meal.

Daniel had popped into the kitchen minutes ago, asking if they needed help. Dionna had shooed him out before Courtney could launch into a flirtfest in front of her while they cooked. "I said nothing."

Courtney grunted and put the lid on the pot of rice for the jollof. Her brown-and-orange skirt brushed the tops of her ankles, but she'd donned an apron to keep from getting tomato juice on her dress. "Your face says it all. I swear, I don't know how you're as good as they say when your expressions are so loud."

Dionna took a measured breath. She could get upset. She could let herself be hurt. But she was wearing the yellow-and-orange wrap dress she'd bought at the market. Her girls were cooking with her instead of making excuses to be elsewhere. The mood was lighter than it'd been in months. So she chose another tactic. "My expressions say I'm a badass."

Stella let out a surprised giggle.

Courtney stared at Dionna like she'd never seen her before. "Did you make a joke?"

"What does my expression say?"

Stella chortled and shared a smile with Dionna.

Dionna's heart soared. Had she finally broken through the concrete wall her family had erected?

Courtney didn't smile. Her surprise was replaced with a frown. Dionna's stomach sank just as Daniel rushed in.

His smile was strained, his eyes pleading. "I hate to ask when you're so generously cooking for Zuri, but are we able to accommodate three extra people?"

"Absolutely," Courtney said without hesitation. Dionna nodded. They'd just started and it wouldn't be hard to adjust the amount they were making. It would force her daughters to talk to her more.

He clapped his hands, back to his typical enthusiastic self. He was joy personified. Dionna could see why he'd caught her oldest daughter's eye. She just wished Courtney's common sense would catch up with her rebellious streak.

"My mother and father have traveled a long way, and my sister . . ." His expression faltered. What was the story about the sister? "Well, she can use the getaway. A chance to get out of the city. They can't wait to see the farm."

He rushed back out. Dionna peered after him. "What's wrong with his sister?"

She hadn't been around Daniel for more than a few days, but he wasn't a worrier. Stones could rain from the sky and thrash the crops and he'd roll up his sleeves and encourage everyone to have hope.

She didn't think Courtney would answer her, but she did. "He said she's been getting into trouble. It started with talking back to their parents and it's escalated. She's even been in jail. It's heartbreaking."

"How old is she?"

"Nineteen. I haven't met her, but he talks about her all the time."

Odd for a kid so old to act out, but Dionna wasn't in Ghana, missing weeks of work, because she'd been an awesome mother, or because her old-enough-to-know-better daughters didn't lash out in their own way. "I'll rearrange the table so we can all sit."

In the dining area, a large fan lazily circled overhead. The lingering spice of Nana's chai tea hung in the air. It had rained over afternoon tea and she'd taken her drink inside.

Dionna busied herself at the table, adjusting plates and nudging chairs around to create room for three more adults. When she turned, Charles was in the doorway. His attention was riveted on the pattern of the dress. After a few moments, his deep-brown gaze lifted to hers.

"I haven't seen you wear that before." The huskiness in his voice was something she hadn't heard in years.

Her face warmed. Was she actually blushing? After all she'd seen, it was still possible. "I bought it at the market before I left. Your friend sold it to me, and . . . I don't often get to wear clothing that isn't basically a disguise."

"It's . . . stunning. The blue is . . ." His gaze dropped to her hips and heated in a way that turned her insides to butter. "Quite lovely on you."

Startled, she couldn't think of anything to say. Perhaps she should've purchased five more.

The heat in his expression died down a few degrees. A worn smile lifted his lips. "It's been nice having you here."

Her mirth from earlier returned. It seemed to have

broken the ice with Courtney and was easier to handle than hope. "I'm sorry. Who are you?"

His brows lifted, but the smile was no longer melancholy. "I should be asking you that, with that dress, but fair enough. I've put in some long days in the field." Fatigue hung on his broad shoulders. His khaki pants had quit being tan days ago, and his blue polo shirt was covered in dirt. Sweat had soaked through the material around his armpits and at the collar.

She had assumed he'd been avoiding her, coming to bed late after she'd turned in and leaving before she was up. But the male in front of her had been working his wings to the nubs. "This is a hard project, yes?"

He nodded and rubbed his neck, then brushed his thumb over his fingers as if he tired of only moving dirt around. "The nearest water source is farther away than any I've worked on before." He shook his head, concern in his eyes. "But they can't depend on rain and keep going the way they are. A combination is best, but it's backbreaking work."

"You can do it. I have faith in you." And she did. Charles had been irrigating farms all over the world for at least a century. There was no one in the three realms better than him.

He tilted his head and studied her, his gaze traveling down her dress to her sandals and back up. This time he didn't smother or hide the desire in his gaze. "You have faith in us. You've kept it when I didn't."

She shrugged and stuffed her hands in the deep pockets of her dress, not knowing what to say. She could default to her career, mention that fighting demons was worth it so humans could enjoy the blink they got for their lifetimes. So they could experience the joy she'd had when she'd first synced with Charles. But she didn't. It'd be like dunking him in seawater to revive the sting from a million little cuts.

"Can you stay?" he asked. "Just a little longer, and after this job, we'll talk. Really talk. You and me. And then you, me, and the girls."

Would she be able to resurrect their bond? Had this trip been worth it? "I'd like that."

They shared a smile, then he glanced down at himself and winced. "I hear we're having company. Afi wanted us in at a decent time tonight. I'd better shower." With one more grin, he was off, and she floated to the kitchen, happier than she'd been in a long time.

RANSOM AND HARLOWE entered the house behind Urban. All of them were dressed like Bronx. Black tactical pants and long-sleeved black shirts.

Harlowe handed a pile of black clothing to Tosca. "I picked these up from Sierra. They should fit well enough for the mission tonight."

Next, she dropped a stack of black balaclavas onto the coffee table.

Tosca hugged her clothing. "I'll go get changed." Her expression was serious, apprehensive, as she ran up to her room.

This had to be different for her. For him, tonight would be a relatively quick mission. They'd planned it after they'd returned from their walk over twenty-four hours ago and would be done before dawn—and hopefully successful. Though Tosca, too, was used to getting a call, following protocol, and immediately carrying out her duty.

Ransom cut a hand through his loose blond curls as he went to the picture window. He stood at the edge even though the lights in the safe house were off and it was well after midnight. He peered outside. "The two-story stucco with the—ah, the gnomes. Always a good indicator."

Not all gnome statues were possessed by gargoyles, but in neighborhoods like this with immaculate landscape design, they stood out. The streetlights added a layer of difficulty. They could hide from many security cameras, but gargoyles knew what to watch out for.

"The light went off in the upstairs bedroom about thirty minutes ago." He'd been watching, wishing he could lose himself in Tosca for another night instead. How quickly great sex made him want something other than a night of hunting demons with his team.

They were two short, but the director had given them the go-ahead to take out Gena's symaster and Bennie's archmaster. Maybe they'd even get some answers.

Tosca came downstairs, tucking her shirt into her pants. She had a vial of angel fire around her neck and a borrowed dagger belted around her waist. She only needed enough to protect herself. She wouldn't be fighting.

Ransom checked his phone. "Sierra knocked out the cameras next door, and when we signal her, she'll knock out the Duncans'. We can sneak through the adjacent backyard and enter the Duncans' house from the sliding door in the back. It's the only one without an electronic lock."

Urban reiterated the rest of the plan. "We get Gena's symaster first. Lie in wait for Bennie. Ransom will signal the archmaster's presence and then we'll take him out."

"After we ask him a few questions," Bronx said and Tosca nodded.

Harlowe's mouth twisted. "We can try. Are you sure you don't want me to grab Sandeen? He'd *love* to interrogate another archmaster."

Sandeen would get answers, but the director had said no. "We can't have the underworld rallying against him and trying to take over the mines. Right now, they're happy with the futons and the Cocoa Puffs he's carting into the realm. But Tosca needs to go into the Mist with the demon. She knows all the details and needs to hear the answers."

Ransom took one more look out the window. "I can't wait to stomp the gargoyles. Pesky bastards."

Bronx rose. "Let's do it."

Outside, insects buzzed as they crept through a break in the hedges between their yard and Gloria and Jack Barkley's house. Their place was silent and the cameras were dead until morning.

Sticking close to the hedges and trees, they skirted around the pool.

Urban held up a hand when he reached the edge of the Barkleys' yard. Ransom crouched to message Sierra. A minute went by, then he raised his hand and made a move motion.

Tosca stuck close to Bronx, moving as silently and swiftly as the rest of them. She wasn't a warrior, but she was trained. And when they reached the Duncans' backyard, she circled around Bronx toward the door.

The biggest obstacle in most of the missions was entry. But knocking out cameras was easier than ever thanks to wireless smart home systems. Sierra could hack them within minutes whereas before, she might've needed to enter a home to get access to the network. God bless the cloud and its hackability.

They could all pick a wafer tumbler lock, but when Tosca had demonstrated it on the sliding door of the safe house, she'd been able to do it in under thirty seconds.

The faint click and slide of the door didn't carry far and wouldn't be enough to alert the gargoyles.

Once they were in, it was a waiting game. Harlowe and Urban stood post at the guest bedroom door, and Ransom backed into the pantry. He left the door open enough to catch sight of Bennie and determine if he was possessed. If he wasn't, the team would have to abort and get out of the house, preferably without being noticed. Bronx and Tosca crept to the master bedroom and plastered themselves along the wall by the door.

He leaned close to her ear and breathed, "Doing okay?"

"My nerves are on fire, but yeah."

The wait stretched on. Tosca shifted, the fabric of her clothing rustling against the wall. She tugged at her face mask. He didn't mind this part, but she was going to vibrate out of her skin.

"Relax, my little enforcer."

He couldn't see more than her outline, but he felt her eye roll.

"This is what you guys do?" she hissed. Good thing the guest room was upstairs.

"Patience is a warrior's virtue."

Her silhouetted face screamed *Seriously?* in the dark and he stifled a chuckle.

"Shh," she said almost playfully and his body shook with repressed laughter.

The rumble of a garage carried through the house. Tosca went stiff.

"Showtime."

The door opened and a light flipped on outside the bedroom door. As long as Bennie didn't want a middle-of-the-night snack, they should be fine.

"Gena!" Was Bennie drunk?

Dammit. It'd be better if Bennie went quietly to bed.

They hadn't anticipated him looking for his wife for a drunk fuck.

His phone vibrated, and since Bennie hadn't come close to the master bedroom, Bronx checked the message.

Confirm.

The archmaster was in control of Bennie. Bronx nudged Tosca and tucked his phone away. She nodded, and he hoped she remembered to breathe while they waited.

The creak of stairs filtered to the bedroom, followed by pounding on the door. "Gena! Fuck, open up!"

His team had discussed this. Gena was supposed to sleep in another room, they had counted on it for tonight. But if she gave in to Bennie . . .

Gena didn't reply. If she was smart, she'd likely pretend to sleep through the whole thing. The symaster would probably let her. Working for an archmaster was one thing. Being front row to its boss fucking the wife was another.

"Gena!" A snarl sounded from the upper level before pounding came back down the stairs. "Fucking bitch. Gonna break down that damn door."

He stomped past the bedroom door and opened a closet at the end of the hall. Tosca swiveled her head to look at Bronx, but he shrugged. What the hell was Bennie doing?

Footsteps hit the hardwood, pounding past the door of the master bedroom. Bronx leaned out. Bennie was carrying a long stick, like a broom.

Was he seriously going to break down the door with a broom?

No matter what, the plan had changed. The team needed to improvise. He tapped Tosca and slipped past her into the hallway. She followed.

The pantry door pushed open, but Ransom didn't jump out.

Bennie stopped. "What the fuck?"

Bronx lunged forward and put one hand on Bennie's shoulder as he said the incantation and palmed a blade with the other. He was stepping into the Mist just as Bennie shouted and fell to the floor.

Harlowe and Urban would have to deal with Gena. Bronx ripped his face mask off and faced an enraged demon with short, sharpened horns, mottled skin that'd look better on a drowned corpse, and a putrid stench that would take three showers to wash off.

Tosca's sharp inhale behind him was enough for Bronx to know she'd made it.

The demon tried to backhand him, his talons flashing. Bronx jumped to the side so he didn't barrel Tosca over. "Wanna tell me who you're working for?"

The demon paused, his already twisted lips sneering. "I work for no one."

"Nice try." Tosca's voice gained in strength as she spoke. She'd rolled up her face mask until her blond hair stuck out. "She's already turned on you."

A rough bark left the demon. "I don't work for bitches. I fuck them. You'll find out soon enough, morsel."

Tosca paled but her hand hovered by her dagger. She should've drawn it, but she was used to working with angels and trying to prevent altercations. Warriors dove headfirst into them. "Yeah, but the angel you work with takes orders from a female."

The demon snapped at the air, spittle flying out of his mouth and sizzling. "You lie."

Bronx waited, wary, hating that they were taking their time. Half the battle with demons was catching them off guard. They weren't planners, but it was just him and Tosca against the archmaster. Yet he couldn't deny she was effective as hell. Bronx would've asked straightforward questions the demon wouldn't have answered.

She shook her head. "I'm an angel. I don't lie. So that means you take orders from a bitch." She added the perfect taunting note to her tone.

"My deal is with Carlos! Not a bitch!"

"Carlos answers to a bitch."

Fangs dripped with yellow spit as the demon's jaws gaped open. He flapped his craggy wings and lunged. Bronx intercepted, slashing up with his knife. Blood and spit splattered his skin, burning through his flesh.

He ducked the fangs, then the horns.

He couldn't pay attention to what Tosca was doing. He danced into the demon's reach, slicing and slashing, and darted back out. A claw grazed his chin, and another shredded the skin on his gut.

But just as the demon thought he knew exactly what Bronx would do, Bronx changed his tactics. He spun in and slashed, but with his other hand, he ripped the vial off his neck and dumped the contents. Angel fire splattered the demon at the crook of his shoulder and neck. He roared and Bronx spun away.

A talon-tipped wing caught him in the side and he went down, the demon tumbling over him. He stuffed his boots into the demon's gut to shove him off but caught a mouthful of acidic blood.

He coughed and choked, his legs giving out just as something booted the demon aside. The archmaster landed with a thud and rolled to his side. Bronx flipped to his hands and feet, spitting blood, his mouth on fire, as Tosca flew over him and onto the demon.

She stabbed over and over until the demon quit moving. The angel fire did its job, eating through the head of the demon until it rolled free. Tosca continued stabbing.

"Tosca," Bronx rasped. The word made no sense. It was nothing but a gasp, his tongue barely working. But it was enough to stop her crazed stabbing. She blinked at him, her face white behind the droplets of the Mist.

She jumped off, her gaze going from the blood covering her hand to the limp body of the demon. "Is he—is he dead?"

Bronx nodded, gasping through the agony in his mouth. He spit, tasting fresh blood with the sour acid of the archmaster.

"Are you okay?" She dropped to her knees at his side.

He nodded, but no. He wasn't okay. He'd heal though. It could've been worse. He could've gotten a mouthful of bloody angel fire.

He pulled up a handful of grass and wiped out his mouth, doing it over and over, not caring how much of his own flesh he scraped off. He'd be back to normal by morning. He just didn't want to suffer until then.

"Oh, god, Bronx. Are you sure you're going to be okay?"

He gave her a wan smile that probably looked more like a grimace. It was a grimace. Moving his lips fucking hurt. "I've had worse." His wince followed. Fuck, he'd have to wait to talk.

She cupped his face, leaning close to him. "Your lips are blistered. Oh my god, your tongue is swollen. What can I do?"

He shook his head and gripped her arms. He stared into her bright-blue eyes, then leaned just a little closer. Talking wasn't going to happen.

She nodded, drawing in a shaky breath. She released his face to help him up. When she wrapped her arm around his side, he hissed—which was like whipping the burning frenzy in his mouth into an inferno.

"I'm sorry." She withdrew her arm. "He stabbed you. And cut you. And—"

He nodded and rose to an unsteady standing position. She had a hand on his elbow like it was the only place not covered in blood. No, he doubted it was blood-free.

A blond figure approached, running. Tosca let Bronx go to stand in front of him, her dagger brandished. She relaxed when Ransom's features solidified.

Ransom looked at the archmaster. "Damn, I'm too late. I couldn't find you right away. This damn Mist. Harlowe and Urban took out the sylph as soon as Gena ran to check on Bennie." He looked over Tosca, then stepped closer to peer at Bronx. "Oof, a shower and rest for you."

"He'll be all right?"

Ransom's smile was supposed to be reassuring, but it was grim. "Part of the job, Tosca. Did you get info?"

She nodded. "Carlos has a deal with them. But we didn't learn who Carlos is taking orders from."

Ransom stepped to the other side of Bronx and put his arm around the male. "On three, we go to the safe house."

Bronx had never looked so forward to a shower and a bed. He wanted to wake up in Tosca's arms, fully healed. But he wished he could wipe the concern from her eyes. This was why bondings failed for warriors. She'd know now. This was what he did. Stab wounds and acid burns like this weren't unusual. And asking a warrior's mate to suck it up and heal him and oh, by the way, try not to worry, was a stab in the gut all on its own.

CHAPTER 15

The kitchen was bustling. Nana grabbed the jollof rice to take to the table. Zuri had just left with Stella's plantain dish.

Dionna worked with her daughters. They were three cogs whirling around each other like they had when the girls were younger, before Charles's parents had decided to walk into the fire together. The evening had only gotten better. A routine evening meal was turning into an event.

Zuri popped her head in, her expression regretful. "Our other guests have arrived. I must greet them."

"Go," Dionna said. "We'll get the rest."

Courtney smoothed a hand over her hair. "I should greet them as well."

Dionna pressed her lips together to keep from pointing out that it would only complicate matters when she had to let Daniel down. Meeting the parents separately would make it seem like she and Daniel were more than friends. Perhaps they were. One pleasant afternoon and evening cooking together wouldn't make her daughter open up to her.

As if Stella read her mind and agreed with her, she hefted two pitchers of water. "Mother and I will be behind you. I'll set these out on the way."

Courtney rolled her eyes, but walked out, smoothing her skirt and apron. Her head was down when she reached the doorway that opened into the dining room. Zuri would be greeting the new arrivals on the other side of the dining room where Charles had been standing earlier.

Stella's skirt swished as she followed her sister. Dionna fell in behind her.

Courtney stopped, a gasp strangled in her throat. She abruptly started backing up, bumping into Stella. Water sloshed over the pitchers.

"Court—"

"Shh." Courtney spun. More water spilled, splashing both girls and across the floor.

Her oldest daughter's eyes were wide, fear blazing in their brown depths. "Mother, are those demons?"

The choked terror in her voice stripped Dionna of the calm she'd found in the last few days. She cleared her mind and backed up, dragging her girls with her.

"Wait here." Gripping the pitchers, she kept her voice low. "Find something to do. Act normal. If a sylph comes in here, you don't see it. You don't look directly at it, you don't talk about it, you don't act any differently. Do you understand?"

Both girls' eyes were wide, white ringing their irises.

Dionna set a pitcher on the counter and snapped her fingers. Courtney blinked, but Stella curled into her sister's side. This wouldn't work.

"Change of plans." She shoved the remaining pitcher into Courtney's hands. The knife block was a few feet away. She flipped her apron up and stuffed a butcher knife into the pocket of her skirt. Her apron didn't cover the handle, but she adjusted it. A little off-kilter. It'd have to do. "We're going out there."

Stella squeaked, and she hadn't been the one to see the demon.

"Together," Dionna stressed. "It's imperative you act naturally. Demons panic as much as we do. Sylphs might just scatter, or they might bring back reinforcements when they learn there's a Numen family under the roof."

Courtney swallowed. "Mother, there was . . . Daniel's sister . . ." She moved her hand over her face in a circle.

Dread pooled in Dionna's gut. Numen could see demons possessing hosts, and she'd told her girls long ago how to spot one. She'd also told them what to do, like she had repeated earlier, but this was the first time they'd run across any.

And if Daniel's sister was indeed possessed by an archmaster, then it was time for Dionna to get to work. "We'll bring the water out. I'll tell them we had a little accident and need to go change. Then we'll find Charles and come up with a plan."

"A plan?" Courtney whispered.

"Yes. To save Daniel's sister."

Courtney's eyes strayed in the direction of the dining room, and she paled. "No one else can help them?"

"It's what I do. It's what we must do." Daniel's family had no one else.

Zuri bustled into the kitchen and stopped short when she spotted them huddled together. "Is something wrong?"

Dionna flashed a smile. "Just a little clumsy accident. Mind if we set the water out and then go to our room to change?"

Sympathy filled Zuri's face. "Of course, of course. What can I carry?"

Dionna lifted the pitcher off the counter and shoved it toward her. "I appreciate it."

When Zuri turned to go back to the dining room, Dionna grabbed a steak knife and hid it with the other knife. She jerked her head for the girls to follow.

Adopting the sheepishness of someone who'd had a minor mishap, Dionna ducked and wrapped her hands in her apron. It helped her hide the knives and gave her a reason to scan the room. Zuri and Afi talked with two other adults around the same age as them. Daniel was talking, his gestures almost like he was begging.

"I told you I don't like jollof," a girl snapped, and thanks to her speaking, Dionna had an excuse to look right at her. "It's garbage."

Oh . . . it was dire. The girl's curly hair puffed around her face, half of it in a haphazard bun at the back of her head. Her skin was dull and raw in places where she must've itched until she bled. The humans would be oblivious to how the demon's black eyes drowned out the girl's brown ones. The vibrant red-brown-and-yellow-patterned dress she wore hung off her as if she'd been starving herself for months.

This was a long-term possession. The demon was putting this kid through hell.

"What are you looking at?" the girl snapped.

Dionna chuckled nervously. "I love jollof. I can't believe you don't like it."

"I didn't ask for your opinion," she sneered.

Courtney gasped, but Dionna sidestepped to block her daughter. The archmaster couldn't suspect he was visible to Dionna or either daughter. He'd kill his host as he fled just for fun.

"Well, I hope Stella's plantain dish is to your liking.

You'll have to excuse us." She let out another nervous chuckle. "We had a kitchen mishap."

Stress pinched the corners of Daniel's parents' eyes, but they smiled as if they were relieved there would temporarily be fewer people to witness their daughter's outbursts.

Dionna spun and ushered the girls ahead of her. Courtney shot Daniel a sympathetic look that fit perfectly with their story. He'd think it was because they were holding up the dinner party, or his sister's behavior had scandalized them, and not because a powerful demon controlled his loved one.

They turned the corner, raced down the hall, and rounded another corner. Stella stopped and cowered against Dionna's shoulder. "Mother. That poor girl."

Charles stepped into the hallway, buttoning a fresh red polo shirt. Surprise lifted his brows, then concern dropped them. "What is wrong?"

Dionna lifted her chin to the bedroom door. Charles read the gravity in her expression and moved out of the way so they could enter first. He watched behind them as the girls and Dionna scurried inside.

Once the bedroom door was closed, Dionna kept her voice low as she explained the situation. Charles's brow furrowed deeper until she finished. "You can't save her, Dionna. You don't have your gear."

It was true. She couldn't stay with a bunch of humans and keep her weapons and angel fire on her or hidden where someone might find them. And she was in a dress. "I have a couple knives. We'll go eat, pretend everything's normal, and when the girl goes somewhere alone, you need to distract everyone while I get the demon in the Mist."

Charles rapidly shook his head. "No, you can't. You'll be in as much danger as her."

Dionna cupped his face, aware their girls were watching. "I am trained. That girl is not. Each second is hell for her, Charles. She's so close to collapsing, and that demon will run her until she drops."

He continued shaking his head. "You're not prepared." He waved his hand over her body. "A dress?"

The dress she had bought at the market before she'd left. Her worlds were no longer separate. A warrior could fight in a dress.

A heated conversation filtered down the hall. Daniel and his sister. He must've dragged her somewhere private to talk some sense into her, only feeding the demon's glee.

"We need to move now." Without waiting for his acquiescence, she breezed out the door, untying her apron behind her. "Oh, hello again, Daniel. Ejo."

Dismay crossed Daniel's face. "We did not mean to interrupt. My sister . . . uh . . ."

"You need to wash up before the meal?" Dionna continued marching toward them, plan in mind. She kept the apron bunched in her hand to hide the knife handles. Ejo eyed her approach with the sneer that had likely curled her lip since she'd been possessed.

"No."

Dionna ignored her. "Come. I'll show you."

"I said—"

"The washroom is so close. You must've missed it." She dropped the apron and put her hands on Ejo's bony shoulders and spun her. Steering her to the washroom three feet away, she glanced over her shoulder.

Daniel was shooting his sister warning glares not to make a scene. Even so, if Dionna's family didn't have her back, she'd have to abort. But the washroom was only a few feet away.

Panic flitted across Courtney's face. Stella hid behind her dad, and Charles opened his mouth, warning in his eyes.

Courtney's gaze dropped to the apron. "Go ahead, Mother. I'll grab your apron."

That stole Daniel's attention. His gaze was off Ejo and on the floor. "I'll get it." He stooped to pick it up.

Ejo twisted. "Let me go—"

Dionna shoved Ejo into the washroom, keeping the girl in her grip, and hip checked the door closed. She uttered the verses to get the demon out of Ejo and into the Mist.

Cool droplets surrounded her. A snarling archmaster faced her with jagged yellow fangs, yellowed and blistered skin, curved horns protruding from his forehead, and claw-tipped wings.

"Warrior bitch." Drool flew from his mouth as he lunged. His jaw widened as he went for her neck.

Ducking and spinning, she wrapped her hand around one of the knife handles. She tugged, but it tangled in her skirt with the movement.

The demon jutted a wing out, clipping the side of her head. She tumbled into the blanket of thick grass and rolled. One of the blades bit into her skin, but she had freed the butcher knife by the time she jumped to her feet.

The demon launched himself at her. She stabbed upward, catching him in the gut. He shrieked and snarled, snapping his jaws at her. The fangs tangled in her hair. Pain seared her scalp as he went down.

The knife handle was slick with his blood and her grip slipped. The edge cut into her hand. She hissed but tightened her hold and jerked it out as he fell.

Pulling her arm back farther than she normally would

with one of her smaller fighting blades, she prepared to slice him across the throat. But he lowered his head in line with her abdomen and lunged.

She was too close to him, too unprepared. She reeled backward but wasn't quick enough. The horns pierced through the dress into her skin. And he didn't just impale her. He shook his head.

A cry ripped from her. Adjusting the arc of her swing, she stabbed him through a wing into his back. His snarls and growls mixed with her moans. Agony tore through her until it was almost all she knew.

Only experience kept her mind going. Giving up meant death and a demon roaming the Mist. She was alone. No team to back her up if she fell. No one to save her.

With her own gear, she could've used her angel fire on him. But all she had was the butcher knife stuck in his bony back and a steak knife she couldn't reach.

He tried to leverage himself against the wet grass and shred her insides until she collapsed. She refused. Her nonslip sandals were as good as her boots.

Yanking the knife out of his back, she sliced at his neck. And kept going, slicing and stabbing at the narrow part of his body. He realized what she was doing and kept trying to rise. She kneed his face, gritting her teeth through the blinding pain.

His movements grew sluggish. She rallied her remaining energy and slammed the blade down, cleaving through what was left.

His body dropped away, and his horns pulled free of her as his head fell to the ground.

She staggered back, her hand clutching the knife so hard she wasn't sure she could peel her fingers off. Her breathing was labored, her inhales more like gasps.

Squeezing her eyes momentarily shut, she was afraid to look.

Before she could open them, she swayed and stumbled. The knife fell from her fingers. The reality of her situation sank in just as her brain was growing foggy.

So much pain. Everywhere. There wasn't an inch of her body free from agony.

The screech of ripping fabric pierced the Mist's stillness, and her dress pulled tight before it suddenly loosened to hang around her neck. She couldn't hold the morph on her wings anymore and their release was the final assault on her dress. A metaphor she didn't have the will to interpret. At least the demon was dead. She couldn't have fought him as well with her wings tangled in her clothing.

A weak laugh slipped from between her lips. *Fought well* might be an exaggeration. This wound could prove mortal. He'd gored her. She still hadn't looked at the damage. There was no point.

She either lingered in the Mist and healed, or she succumbed, one of the few angels to die without being burned or beheaded. A lone warrior with no teammates to summon her mate.

Going back so Charles could heal her meant risking someone seeing her with wings out and wounds no human could recover from. It'd mean losing her wings and possibly dragging her family with her. They'd be separated. Her girls would each be alone.

Perhaps she could make it to Numen. Someone would see her and alert Director Vale. He'd know where to find Charles.

All she had to do was take a few steps. Cross into her home realm.

She staggered to the side, weaving and unable to

maintain her balance. Her mind was too fuzzy to know where she was going, to think about where she should step into Numen.

She sagged to her knees. Cool droplets licked over her skin and surrounded her face. The chill seeped into her. The pain wasn't so strong anymore.

As she listed to her side and fell the rest of the way to the cool ground, she wished this had ended differently.

And she wished she had spent more time with her family.

She wished . . .

BRONX WAS PASSED OUT. Sometime during the day, he'd flipped onto his belly and draped an arm over her. Sleeping in the same bedroom as him signaled to the rest of the team they were more than just buds, but she'd refused to leave his side.

She'd helped him through the shower. So much blood had swirled down the drain until his wounds had begun to knit themselves together. He hadn't talked and she hadn't asked him to.

He'd fallen into a restless slumber until the majority of the healing was done. Now he was out, and she'd done little more than doze.

The Mist had been terrifying. She'd had no need to go into the eerie realm before, and she couldn't comfortably go in there again. Bronx's fight with the archmaster had been terrifying, and she'd been close to useless.

Sure, she'd gotten one detail cleared up. They knew who to target. Who to watch. And Harlowe had said she'd talk to the director, and when Bronx was awake, they'd figure out their plan.

But Tosca was over being useless. This wasn't about her. She'd been framed, yes, but it was part of a much larger plot. Forgotten Peace no longer served the purpose it had been made for. It served someone who was working with demons.

She'd gotten them into Gena and Bennie's house, but the warriors were perfectly capable of picking a lock. Her added speed hadn't been critical. She'd gotten confirmation that Carlos was behind the demon problem in the area. But they'd already suspected that.

So. If she wanted to help, she had to pony up some skills. She could break into Carlos's place and confront him. Or . . .

That wasn't the most terrible idea.

She'd had a thing for him once.

No. He'd never buy it.

Unless . . . she could sell it. She used to be good at it.

Bronx murmured and shifted, curling closer to her.

He pried an eye open and squinted at her. No light was getting in around the thick blinds. They were steeped in shadows.

"Hey," she said to let him know she was awake if he couldn't see her eyes open in the dark. "How are you feeling?"

He smacked his lips. "Better." His voice was still hoarse.

She eased out from under him and grabbed a glass of water. "Here."

He sat up and sucked it down. She handed him a bottle of orange juice next. He drank half and gave the rest to her.

"Are we the only ones here?"

"I think Harlowe and Ransom wanted to stay until you were awake. They were going to talk to the director with Urban."

He rolled his shoulders. He was nude. She was in the

shirt and shorts he'd loaned her and she wouldn't return. "I want to let my wings out."

She'd love to release her morph. The stress of the night had ratcheted her muscle fibers until they vibrated. "I will if you will."

He rolled away from her, onto his belly, and let his wings unfurl.

She slipped her shirt off and stood, doing the same.

He turned his head, his gaze stroking over her breasts, down to her belly.

"Should I take the shorts off?" She hooked her fingers over her waistband, her belly flipping. Except he didn't answer. "Oh, gosh, I'm sorry. You're still healing."

"No, Tosca, it's not that." His voice was stronger. He was fully healed.

She sat on the edge of the bed. "We need to deal with Carlos?"

"Fuck Carlos." He curved his wings around himself and rolled to a seat. "I don't want to quit being a warrior." He paused, like it was a momentous answer.

"Okay."

"You're not a fling."

She rolled her shoulders as she tried to understand, grateful for the stretching in her muscles from their weight. "I know we agreed that it would be like a fling between us, but I realize I only asked you to help me with my first time."

Embarrassment flooded her cheeks. They'd been so focused on Bennie and Gena since they'd had sex that she'd forgotten their agreement.

"No," he said again. "I'm not talking about an arrangement. I'm saying that I could do so much more with you but it wouldn't be fair."

"How so?"

"I'm a warrior, Tosca. We mess around until we're assigned that mate who's supposed to be our one true love. Only it falls apart. Dionna . . . it's none of my business, but we all know she's off trying to save her family. My teammates are drifting away from the life because they found their mates. And my parents quit the field entirely when they found each other. They didn't want to destroy what they had found."

He fell silent and she gave herself time to work through what he'd said. He simultaneously wanted to mate her while admitting he couldn't mate her. "You're saying that you're falling for me and that's not a good thing because if we end up mating, then you'll quit being a warrior?"

"Yes."

"Bronx, that seems a stretch."

"What's Forgotten Peace full of? People like your father who lost their mate in the line of duty?"

"That's not fair."

"But it's true. You'd wait around the realm for me? You'd have to drop your work to save my ass when I get injured like that again."

"One, you haven't even asked me to mate with you. This is barely a step up from a hypothetical conversation. And two, that would be my decision. The only reason it has anything to do with me depends on the amount of support you'd give me otherwise. But we've been together for a week. We slept together two nights ago. And you're already writing us off?"

"That's how much you mean to me."

"That's messed up." Still sitting, she reached down for her shirt. Rolling her shoulders, she prepared to morph.

He stilled her with a hand on her back. "I want you. That'll never change."

She fished for her shirt. "So I guess you'll get back to

me after a few centuries of fucking around and we can talk about settling down then."

"Tosca."

She rose, morphed her wings, and stuffed her head into her shirt. "Look, you've said your piece. I'm both hurt and flattered, I guess. But ultimately, there are humans in danger. We need to get to Carlos and see if he'll tell us what's going on. We shouldn't be messing around up here anyway."

She went to the door.

He jumped out of bed. A tall, lean, naked angel stalked her and she wanted to be wrapped in those wings so badly. "It doesn't feel right, you leaving like this."

He towered over her. Not too long ago, she would've gazed at him and needled him. Challenged him and that arrogance that was bred into warriors.

But his attitude was about pure dedication to his work. A job that didn't include using people. He wasn't corrupt. And once Carlos was busted and her name was cleared, she wouldn't have a reason to talk to him ever again.

Her chest ached. This was it. She'd only had to keep her heart and her head separate for two days, but something shattered inside her chest. "We both know I can't stay."

And she slipped out the door.

Bronx had folded his wings back into a morph and dressed in a new set of black tactical pants and shirt. He replaced his vial of angel fire and cleaned his weapons.

Tosca sat at the island by Harlowe. A loud and clear message that he wasn't to get close to her.

Urban and Ransom were on the couch, but Bronx paced. Tosca had just laid out her idea.

"I don't like it," he said as he traced the outer edges of the living room.

"You don't have to."

"It's a good plan," Harlowe said, flinging her long, blond braid over her back. Her gaze jumped between them. She wasn't the only one who sensed tension arcing between him and Tosca.

It was a good plan. Their best option. And he fucking hated it.

"Carlos won't buy it after you ran from him." He'd definitely carry a grudge about being run over.

"I already covered that part." Tosca's tone was bored when he knew damn well she wasn't. Their conversation had to be weighing down her insides with a hundred bowling balls like it was doing to him.

He shook his head, propping his hands on his hips. The blinds on all the windows were closed. There were too many people roaming his house. He didn't need to worry about nosy neighbors wondering how he could have guests when no cars were parked outside. "I don't like it. It's too risky. If you end up in the enforcers' hands, we can't get you out."

She slipped off her stool and turned to him. "Then you'd better find out if there's a connection between Carlos and Juliette."

They faced off like they were the only two people in the house.

"And if we can't?" he asked tightly.

"Then maybe I can find out enough. If he's not working with Juliette, he's working with someone in the realm. But we know the likelihood is low or he would've held my door open when you picked me up." She gave him a *you know I'm right* look.

Ransom rose, a peacekeeper expression on his face. "We

definitely need to run the plan past the director before Tosca goes back to Forgotten Peace."

Harlowe popped up. "I'll go with." She gave Urban a pointed look. "You're coming too."

Urban's brow furrowed. "Three of us?"

Harlowe let out a sigh. "These two have some shit to work through. How about we give them privacy?"

Ransom nodded and understanding lit Urban's gaze. Tosca's mouth tightened like she wanted to bury her face in her hands. Bronx didn't bother arguing. Harlowe was right.

Ransom drifted to the sliding door. "We'll, uh, message once we get the okay . . . before we come back."

When the three had ascended to Numen, Tosca crossed her arms. "Why are you having such a problem with this?"

"I said it already—it's too risky."

"Yeah, but someone has to risk something, and while I'm sitting nice and comfy in a safe house, there are people out there suffering. Women like Gena getting targeted by archmasters. That mom. Kids. You name it. I can help put a stop to it, and I'd much rather put myself at risk than have four warriors sitting around because of me."

He'd want the same in her position, but his feelings didn't make him stop resisting. "I don't like it."

"I don't need you to."

He tipped his head back to stare at the off-white ceiling. "I know you don't." She wasn't his mate, and even if she were, it wouldn't be like he'd check in with her about all his missions. Nor would she alert him before she stepped into a domestic dispute. Wasn't this why he'd told her they couldn't be together?

All that bugged him, but there was something else. She was going to appeal to Carlos. Get close to him. He'd seen how she won over their neighbors at the party. She'd told him why she hadn't had sex.

"I'm worried," he finally said.

"I know. So am I."

"No, not about that." He cut a hand through the air. "Yes, I mean I'm worried about your safety. It's you. You trusted me not to use you or your body like Carlos would have when you were growing up. And that's what this feels like. Like I'm agreeing to send you back to Forgotten Peace to use everything you've got against Carlos."

"I can do it without sleeping with him."

If only he had fangs like the archmaster he'd fought. If he ripped Carlos's throat out, the male couldn't take advantage of Tosca. "You shouldn't have to seduce him."

"No. I shouldn't. But that might be what it takes." She pushed off her stool and crossed the distance between them until they were only a foot apart. "And it doesn't mean I have to spread my legs for him. Before, I did everything they told me to, and I knew I'd do that too. It's not like that now. I'm in charge. Even if I get thrown into custody." She poked a finger at herself. "I'm still in charge of myself."

Not him. He stroked a finger down her soft cheek. "You'll be careful?"

She ticked up a brow as if to ask if he'd be any more careful than her in the same situation.

He tugged her toward him and murmured, "Fuck, Tosca."

She tilted her face up, and he didn't stop himself. He pressed his mouth to hers. Her hands curled into his shirt and she deepened the kiss for a few seconds before she pulled back.

"Be with me. One more time before I go."

She was asking like she might never have a chance to be

with anyone again. He was her last meal before she ventured into a place infested with demons. She could get arrested. She could die.

And she wanted to be with him.

He wanted to be with her.

He picked her up and carried her to the island. Before he set her ass on the counter, he yanked her shorts down. She whipped her top off, then dragged his over his head. He dropped his pants and kicked them away.

He planned to feast on her, to drape her legs over his shoulders and bury his face between her thighs. After she came, maybe twice, he'd take her right on the island. He needed her now.

But he wanted to be with all of her. She was putting those beautiful wings at risk, and he was selfish enough to want to have them to himself first. He wanted all of her. So he'd let himself be greedy.

He palmed his erection, and her gaze dropped to where he stroked himself. Need raged through his blood like a Category 5 hurricane. "Let your wings out."

She ripped her gaze off his dick, and it was like a cool breeze wafted across his body. She glanced at all the windows, her pink tongue darting out to lick her lips.

She shifted her shoulders, and her stormy-gray wings unfurled and hung down each side of the counter.

"So fucking beautiful." He did the same with his, liking the appreciation in her eyes when she looked at his body—all of it.

"I always thought your wings were the cockiest thing about you." She reached over his shoulder and stroked her hand over an arch. "It used to infuriate me. You'd act as if I was nothing and then you'd walk away with those steel-gray wings lifted so damn high it was like even your boots were too good to touch the ground."

She'd thought that of him? "Then I'd jack off to you all damn night." Her lips parted and he pressed her knees open. "I'd imagine doing this." He bent and nipped the inside of her thigh. She arched her back off the surface. "And this." He hooked his arms under her legs and swirled a circle around her clit.

She moaned and relaxed her legs farther apart. "Bronx, you earned the cockiness."

He'd earn it for the rest of his life. This female was his. He didn't have to test her this time. This wasn't like their first night together. He knew her body. He knew what she liked.

He licked her to a fast, hard peak. She exploded over his tongue and he kept going.

"Bronx," she gasped, her fingers tangling in his hair. "I can't—ungh." She fell back, writhing in his hold. He took her to another climax, and this time when she came down, she clamped her thighs against his head like she was forcing him away.

Fair enough. He had planned to crawl on top of the counter and take her, but she was risking her wings, dammit.

Helping her slide down, he spun her and gripped either side of her hips. "Tosca." He didn't know what he was trying to say.

He shoved inside of her and held still. He dug his fingers into her flesh but held himself still. Just a moment to savor having her to himself. He didn't have to let her go. But when they were done, she would be getting ready. She would prepare to go to Forgotten Peace and he might never see her again.

She shoved her ass into him, demanding more. This wasn't like in the bathroom. He wasn't getting off on watching her in the mirror. This was them, together. No promises. No agreements that it wouldn't be more. Just them.

He thrust and he didn't stop. He hit all the angles that drove her crazy. She gripped the edges of the counter, her wings flared in his face. His were lifted high off the floor just like she had accused him of doing, but he wasn't cocky.

Insecurity was stuffed into his crevices. Fear. Regret. He was in the hell he'd been afraid of putting his mate in. The worry. The time apart. He was doing the right thing not pursuing more with Tosca, just as he was even more certain he'd made a mistake.

Lightning raced down his spine and roped around his balls. His climax slammed into him, a thunder clap echoing between his ears. He was barely conscious enough to register Tosca rippling around him, her body gripping his as hard as his fingers were digging into her.

After he crested, he sank against her. Her front was pressed to the counter and his face was buried in her wings. Soft feathers tickled his nose.

"I don't want to let you go." A confession that wasn't just about her transcending to Forgotten Peace. He didn't want to *ever* let her go. He wanted it all.

"I know. But we both know I have to."

Everything was dark. The scent of fresh earth and cool water surrounded her. She could still smell Charles in death.

A wall of heat enveloped her.

She inhaled long and deep, like it was the first time in a long time that she'd done so. She struggled to blink.

It wasn't dark. And she wasn't dead. Was she? She was in a bedroom steeped in shadows. She blinked a few more times, as if clearing away built-up dust and dirt. This was her bedroom. In Numen.

She was home. But how?

"Ah, there she is. For an immortal, you had me worried." The wall of heat spoke behind her.

A frown pulled at her lips. "Charles?"

"Are there other mates saving you, my love?" His deep voice resonated right through her body, telling her no, she wasn't dead and neither was her sex drive.

She tried to flip over but her wings were as stiff as the rest of her body, and Charles's dusky-gray wings blanketed her. She was in a cocoon of male and feathers. And she didn't want to leave.

Her last memories slammed into her and she gasped. "The girls."

"Safe." He stroked his hand up and down her arm. She doubted she was dressed. She hoped he'd burned that dress. She was alive to buy another. "You'd have been proud of them. Courtney drew Daniel to the dining room, and Stella broke into the washroom and stayed with Ejo until she regained consciousness. I said you had gotten a sudden migraine and needed to rest. Then I went to find you."

"How much time has passed?"

"Two days."

"Two?" She jerked up, but his arm clamped over her.

"Don't worry. Between me and the girls, we spun a fairly believable family emergency that required us to leave in the middle of the night when they couldn't see you go. I promised I would return when all is well."

She relaxed into the mattress. "It's all taken care of?" She shouldn't sound so disbelieving but this was the family that hated what she did.

"It's all taken care of." He brushed his hand up her arm and kissed the top of her head. "I should be angry with you. I almost didn't find you in time and when I did—" His voice cracked.

She must've made a nightmarish picture. Gutted and bleeding, her skin ashen as her blood leaked into the thick grass of the Mist. "I'm glad you found me. I thought . . ." She had to blow out a hard breath and inhale another before she could get the word out. She'd had some close calls, but never injuries to the extent that she'd needed a mate's healing energy to stave off death. Charles had helped her heal before. Critical injuries for a mortal, but more a nuisance for her. Then as he'd stayed on Earth longer and longer, she'd been really careful.

Two days ago, she had been careful, but she'd been ill prepared.

"I thought I'd traded my life for that girl's, and you'd all hate me for it."

He pressed another kiss to her head. "Hate? No, my love. I've never been prouder, or more desperate to apologize for my behavior. I've been selfish."

"No." She put her hand over his. "I'm the one who's been selfish. I would've died regretting not spending more time with you and the girls."

"Dionna, it was easy for me, for the girls, to be upset. To think you were passing us over for your work. We didn't see the victims." He let out a quiet, humorless laugh. "We didn't even see the demons. Stella's had a hard time sleeping. But Ejo was suffering. And I wouldn't have been able to help her. The girls couldn't have helped her. We would've sat through dinner knowing she was going to die and the demon would move on to another host. We've never seen how you help humans and it's anything but selfish."

His words sank in and she closed her eyes for a moment. "Perhaps we're both right."

He kissed his way down her neck. "Yes, perhaps that's it."

A moan escaped her lips. His touch wasn't mechanical. It wasn't a deliberate shutdown of resentment and feelings. Yet she didn't want to be with him like this after all this time. "I should clean up."

"I cleaned you every day you were passed out."

Embarrassment heated her cheeks. "Charles—"

"Dionna, you mean everything to me. I need to be inside you. You warned me once that I'd turn around and you wouldn't be there. That happened, and I almost didn't find you in time. I need you now."

"I need you too." She'd needed him for so long.

He rolled her over, careful of her wings, and claimed her mouth. Their tongues swirled together as heat pumped through her body. He settled between her legs and continued claiming her mouth. His wings blanketed them, blocking out the little light the shades let in. She widened her legs to allow him closer to her. She was naked, and he was too.

This was how it should've been for the last several years, but they'd circled back. They'd reunited. They weren't mourning what was dying between them but celebrating what had come alive.

As the kiss deepened, grew needier, he lifted his hips, but he didn't thrust inside of her. Instead, he stroked his fingers through her wetness, landing on her clit. She gasped and he caught the sound, not to quiet her as he might have before, but like he wanted everything from her now, everything she had to give. They were in sync. She moaned and he kissed down her neck. She undulated her hips and he shifted to give her room to move.

Her climax hit fast and hard, but Charles caught her. She cried into his shoulder and shook in his arms.

"You're beautiful when you come." His voice was thick with need. "I dream of you. I've dreamed of you every night we've been apart."

She cupped his face. "I was so scared I'd lost you."

"Never, my love. I may get dense at times, but you'll never lose me. I am only yours."

And with that, he thrust inside. She bowed into him, her body filling as he seated himself inside. Finally, she was complete. They were connected.

He rocked in and out of her and she matched his

rhythm, pleasure traveling between them, only growing stronger. Sync mates.

His thrusts came faster and harder. Energy zipped over her skin, and when the second climatic wave crashed into her, he clamped his mouth over hers. They captured each other's cries, coming together, sharing the ecstasy until it was so strong she wasn't sure they were actually two separate people.

They might've drifted apart, but they'd never lost this connection. Anger, misunderstanding, and resentment had concealed it, but it had never broken.

He stayed inside her, and she kept him there.

"I love you, Dionna."

So simple. But it said so much. "I love you too, Charles."

A knock rattled the door. She jerked, but Charles didn't move. There was nothing to hide. There never should've been.

"Yes?" he called.

Stella answered. "Is Mother awake?"

Charles grinned at her. "Do you need more rest?"

She'd been in this bed long enough. She and Charles could lose themselves in each other for days, but she missed her kids. "Give us a couple minutes and we'll be right out," she called to the girls.

"Don't take your time," Courtney grumbled.

Charles chuckled and dropped a kiss on her mouth. "Director Vale's also been checking on you. If you need to go back to work, you'll go back with our support."

"I meant what I said. I want to spend more time with my family. My team might need me, but so do you."

"So we'll figure out how to combine our callings. I don't want you working without their backup anymore."

She feathered her fingers over his short hair. "No, I won't be working alone again if I can help it. And we owe

Zuri a new knife block." Her smile was wry. "I don't think she wants her knives back."

"Too soon, Dionna," he warned, but a smile played at his lips. Then his expression sobered. "Give us today though? Before you call the director back?"

"Absolutely."

TOSCA SAT at Papa's table. She had shown up at the cabin's back door and crept in, expecting to interrupt him at breakfast with Megan and debating how to stall the woman from running to Carlos, but Papa had been eating alone. Apparently Megan hadn't been back since Tosca was last here. That hadn't stopped Papa from hissing at her to leave or she'd get caught. But when she'd asked him for help, he'd gone quiet.

That was ten minutes ago. After a quick rundown of what she'd been up to, he'd gone quiet again, absorbing the news.

Finally, Papa's brows dropped over his eyes. "I can't believe Carlos would work with demons."

"Demons lie, but I doubt the archmaster had time to think about it."

Stress creased his face. "You actually faced one?"

"In person, in the Mist. They're everywhere outside of the trees that surround the commune. Do you know of a connection between Carlos and Juliette Colbert?"

"Cordelia used to go back to the realm regularly. She tried to hide it, but word got around. No one knew why, of course, but most of us assumed she was visiting her mate. He'd refused to let Carlos come with her to the commune."

"What about after Carlos came here?"

"I thought maybe she still missed her mate, but then she

went one day and never came back."

"Was she acting differently before her last trip?"

He shook his head. "She exuded peace and tranquility, but she lost her patience a lot more with the new arrivals. A few almost left."

"Have things changed, you know, since Carlos?"

Papa worried his chin between his thumb and forefinger. "A lot of us longtime residents don't go out much anymore. It's even discouraged for us to leave the commune."

"Do you think it's because you'd disagree with what you saw outside of the gates?"

He lifted a shoulder and rotated his coffee mug around. "It's because we don't steal or con like we used to."

"What?"

"Carlos wants to make this place less a smuggler's den and more of a refuge, like it was intended."

"But you're still able to afford so much luxury."

He gave another casual shrug. "We're learning to do without. Or to work for it. Those sweats you borrowed from Megan?" He gestured to the pile on the counter. "She bought them. At the mall. With money earned from selling extra chicken eggs."

"Why didn't you mention all this?"

"It was a gradual change. Not a sudden one. And a welcome one, for a lot of us." His forehead creased. "And I wanted you to keep hating Carlos."

"I don't think there's much concern I'm going to fall for him."

"No, I don't suppose there is. You always had your own mind. Ultimately, it's why you had to leave." He drew in a mighty breath and swept his gaze around the cabin. "We all stayed here because we resented being told what to do, but really we just wanted to be told to do something different."

The weariness of his life was etched into his features. "We didn't want to have to think about others, because that's what got us hurt."

She'd known that. Deep down, everyone here did. It was what made whatever Carlos was doing extra crappy. "What about Peacequarters? That's quite the upgrade and I haven't even been inside since I've returned. Hasn't anyone asked how he can afford all that?"

"We've talked among ourselves. He's mentioned investing. 'Growing money the proper way.' But we also thought maybe he fooled an aging heiress here and there. You might condemn us for looking the other way, but we have nowhere else to go. Carlos didn't order us, so it wasn't so bad. He hasn't demanded we lie, cheat, and steal like his mother did, and that's been enough for us. But demons? None of us would've thought they were the reason behind the wealth."

"Someone in Numen is the reason." Demons were a step removed, a tool depriving the residents of the commune reason to speak up.

"They're coming," Papa said under his breath. "I can tell by the silence."

The rest of the commune had gone quiet. "Do it just as we planned." She kept her pose casual with her elbows on the tabletop, like she was in deep conversation with Papa.

The door busted open. Two males she'd grown up with raced in. They flanked her, armed with nothing but cuffs that'd prevent her from transcending.

She pressed her back against the wall and rose. "Roscoe? What the hell are you doing?"

Carlos strode in, dressed like he had been the last time he'd entered the cabin, in a crisp white shirt and charcoal slacks straight from a high-rise office. "Jack, put the cuffs on her."

Papa rose. "Carlos! What in the hell—"

Carlos held up his hand, but his gaze pinned her. "You want to make this harder on him?"

She was breathing hard, striking a balance between fake and real. Too far in either direction and he wouldn't buy it. Three males faced her and she so badly wanted to take them all. But Papa would get involved. "I only came to tell him goodbye. You can just let me leave—like you did back then. No one will blame you. I'm more trouble than it's worth."

Irritation flashed across Carlos's handsome features. "Cuff her."

"Carlos, come on." She let out a nervous laugh. "You can't be upset about earlier. I just want to go. You know I didn't do anything."

The level of guilt in his face didn't make sense, but he covered it quickly enough.

Jack approached her. She tried to skirt along the wall toward the door. Roscoe blocked her. She darted between Carlos and the table. Papa jumped back against the wall.

Carlos caught her by the arm and spun her around. She could've throat punched him, and when he dropped, she'd have kneed him in the face or the junk, whichever was accessible. But she whipped her arm like she was going to try to fling him off, and when it didn't work, she pulled a move she knew he could dodge, dropping down and kicking her leg out.

Carlos danced backward and Jack put her in a headlock, tossing the cuffs to Roscoe. Cold steel snapped around her wrists.

Papa held his hands out like the pacifist he'd turned into. "This is unnecessary. We are a safe haven."

Carlos barely cast her a glance. "A safe haven she's abandoned once."

"She abandoned you." Papa adopted a fatherly tone. "Are you sure that isn't what this is about?"

A flush crept past Carlos's collar. "This is about Forgotten Peace and our safety. The safety of everyone here. We can't be caught harboring a fugitive."

"She's innocent," Papa scoffed.

"That's not for us to judge. I'll take her to Peacequarters and notify my aunt. You got your goodbye. Be happy with that."

His aunt? Papa met her questioning gaze and shook his head. To the others, it'd look like he was distraught, didn't know what to do. But really he was answering her unspoken question. He didn't know who Carlos's aunt was either.

Jack loosened his hold on her and jerked her to her feet.

"I'm sorry, Papa," she said as she was dragged out the door.

Papa stumbled out of the cabin after them. People from camp stared. She tripped and argued with Jack and Roscoe that she could walk, but really she was monitoring reactions and expressions.

No reactions she wouldn't expect. Surprise. Horror, like they couldn't believe a fugitive was in their presence. Stunned ignorance from those who didn't know who she was and hadn't paid attention to earlier gossip about her first visit.

Was Carlos acting alone?

She didn't bother to ask Carlos any questions while there were witnesses. Papa would note the same reactions and pass the information to her team when tonight's hubbub died down.

Peacequarters loomed in front of them. Peaked roof, large windows that reflected the surrounding environment.

The rest of the commune was quiet, but equipment whirred around Peacequarters. When Carlos breezed through the door, a blast of air-conditioning hit her in the face.

"Since when does Peacequarters have AC?"

Carlos didn't turn to look at her. He continued striding across the meeting area that now had a massive TV that could double as a movie theater screen. The bench seats were gone, replaced by individual plush chairs and even a few couches.

"You must've scored a big payday."

Carlos's wide shoulders stiffened, but he continued down a long hallway. A door at the end hung open. The office that used to be Cordelia's wasn't the same twenty-four years later. They might as well be in a Manhattan skyscraper.

But Jack kept pushing her through the modern-industrial-meets-wellness-retreat space, toward a door Carlos was unlocking. She light-fingered the key for the cuffs and slipped it into her shorts pocket.

Jack and his brute hands had never been as good as her at picking pockets.

"What's that? I don't remember your mother having a private room off her office."

He didn't answer again. She was shoved into a square room with a cage in the corner.

"What—"

Hinges squeaked as he opened the door. Roscoe blocked the doorway to the office, Carlos held the iron bars, and Jack pushed her past the threshold. She tried to duck and run, but Carlos was quick with the door. An iron slat nailed her in the face.

Pain exploded across her face and she staggered backward. The cell door clicked shut.

She blinked the agony away, her vision clearing. The three males stared at her.

"Carlos." She touched her nose to make sure it wasn't bleeding. She strove to sound as incensed yet breathless as possible. "Don't do this."

"For fuck's sake, Tosca. What the hell are you playing at?"

She had to give him credit. He was genuinely upset that he had to deal with her. Did that mean what he had to do next wouldn't be palatable?

She scrambled for a new plan before he had Numen pick her up—or worse. She hadn't counted on a *cage*.

He was supposed to just take her to his office, then dismiss Jack and Roscoe. Then they'd be alone. He wouldn't drop his guard around the other two males, but she couldn't let him just leave her here. Not yet.

"What about you?" She gestured to the door. "Peacequarters has certainly changed. Hedge funds? Email scams? A small island of lonely heiresses?"

He worked his jaw. "I've gotten smarter at business."

His statement was almost reluctant. A lie, but not really.

"She was dying, wasn't she?" She edged closer to the bars and dropped her voice, adding a heap of sympathy. "Those are the biggest paydays. You must've *really* made her love you."

He jerked his head toward the door. It must've been a signal because the other two males left. As she'd suspected, whatever was going on, Carlos was hiding the specifics from Jack and Roscoe.

"We don't live the way we used to."

She adopted an appreciative look. "Maybe I would've come back earlier."

"No. You wouldn't have. You're a good girl. You always were. You hated how my mother ran things."

"I'm sorry, by the way. I heard she walked into the fire."

Consternation crossed his face. "Why do you care?"

"I didn't become an enforcer because I don't care. I just didn't agree with how she funded this place." She disagreed even more with how Carlos funded his lavish lifestyle within the commune now, but she left out all hint of insinuation from her voice.

"She took too many risks, and when the cops came calling after a con gone bad, she panicked."

"And the commune had you to take care of them."

"And I turned it around." He shoved his hands in his pockets and a muscle popped in his jaw. "In case you think you're going to seduce me into letting you go, think again. Just because you're spreading your legs now doesn't mean I want you any more than I did back then."

It took years of control to school her expression. She'd expected him to assume what her intent was, but she hadn't expected him to be so disinterested. The Carlos she'd known had liked the chase.

But he didn't need it anymore, did he? Everyone came to him. He didn't have to pursue one single person and he preferred it that way.

She lifted her chin. "You might've wanted it, but you didn't need it. There's a difference, Carlos, and you're holding a grudge because I didn't want or need *you*. And then I had the audacity to do a good job living a straight life."

"How did that turn out?" He pulled a hand out of his pocket. A small key dangled from his thumb and forefinger.

A gasp escaped her and she slammed a hand against the pocket she'd hidden the cuff's key in. Empty.

The corner of his mouth kicked up. "You've lost your touch."

"Tell Juliette she's not going to get away with it." She waited for his reaction. And was disappointed.

"Good try, Tosca."

He wasn't acting as she'd predicted again. The glass sphere in the ceiling corner didn't help either. She was under surveillance. "What are the chances that you're sending me back to a senator who framed me for murder because she was trafficking our females? Now you can make another deal for the commune. You need the realm to look the other way, right? So you can keep working with the demons?"

Shadows crowded his face. "I'm not listening to a murderer."

"Everyone knows I didn't kill Jean Luc, but good try. What people don't know yet is that you're allowing demon activity in the area." She tapped her chin. "I can't help but think it's all connected."

His expression crumpled with rage. "You should've stayed out of it, Tosca." He stepped close to the bars but stayed far enough away she couldn't get the key back. "You've just signed your own death warrant."

"Don't blame me for the evil you do in the world."

His nostrils flared and he straightened. "I'm using humans, just like we did before—just like you did before."

He spun on a heel and strode to the door. When he looked back, his gaze stroked over the cell that held nothing but a cot and a bucket. "I'm glad you had a chance to say goodbye to your father."

The threat wasn't aimed at her. He was going after Papa, because Carlos thought she was behind bars she couldn't pick her way out of.

But he would return to Papa's cabin and find it empty. She settled on the cot and leaned her head against the wall. At least that part of her plan was still on track.

CHAPTER 17

"I don't like it." Bronx paced the living room, veering into the kitchen. "She should've been in contact."

Urban perched on the edge of the couch, his fingers steepled. "She went there to be taken—she can't contact us. She's not in custody in Numen, so we know she's still at the commune."

No, they fucking didn't. "What if they killed her?"

"Why would they kill her? They go from stealing a few cows and swindling women on Tinder to letting demons do all the work while someone in Numen probably pays them off. Carlos hasn't had to do any heavy lifting his entire life. He's not going to get his hands dirty with her. He's probably figuring out what the hell to do."

"Why would he keep her alive?"

Urban clamped his mouth shut. Right. That was Bronx's issue. She was supposed to get in, get intel, get back out.

"She said she was good enough to get back out." So where the hell was she?

"I doubt she lied. Look, it was a risk, she knew that—but she also might be staying there for a reason."

The doorbell rang.

There was no reason for Tosca to use the doorbell. She could transcend to the privacy nook by the sliding door.

Bronx peeked out. Fucking Stephen. He didn't know if he had it in him to deal with a clueless damn human.

He took a minute to erase any anxiety from his expression. Casually stuffing a hand into his shorts pocket, he opened the door. "Stephen, my man. What's up?"

Stephen lifted his chin as a greeting, then frowned as he took in Bronx's warrior garb. "Not much. Hey, did you hear about Gena and Bennie's home invasion?"

The shock lighting Bronx's features was genuine. His team had been good. Gena and Bennie shouldn't have been able to tell their home had been broken into. Harlowe and Urban had dealt with the sylph quietly and efficiently. Ransom had taken care of the gnomes.

"Yeah, Gena said she swore she saw dark figures in her home. Said they knocked her out."

Yanking a demon out of or off of a host often knocked them out. "Oh?"

Stephen nodded, enjoying being the bearer of bad news. "And their lawn ornaments were destroyed." He leaned in and muttered out of the corner of his mouth, "Though between you and me, they were ugly AF."

"AF," Bronx said in way of agreement. "Is she sure? Did she call the police?" He'd have to explain why he didn't know the police had been in the neighborhood in the middle of the night.

"No, they can't prove it. Said their camera system blinked out at the same time." He squinted at the Barkleys' house next door. "So did theirs. You?"

Bronx shrugged. "No problems here. Just normal daily bliss."

"Yeah, well, I wanted to let you know. They're pretty spooked. Not their usual selves."

Or they were their usual selves and Stephen didn't like that Gena wasn't as receptive to his long embraces, and that he couldn't provoke Bennie as easily as before. The fear the couple was experiencing was likely left over from their demon problems, not the home invasion they suspected. But all he said was, "Sorry to hear it."

The human bobbed his head and waited for a few moments, like he was expecting Bronx to invite him inside, or at least step outside so they could chat. Bronx would rather gouge his wings out with a spoon.

"You two want to come over? Bring your swimsuits." Stephen craned his neck to look over Bronx's shoulder.

Piling on regret he didn't feel, Bronx shook his head. "Tos—uh, Julie's out of town for work. I've got plans with a buddy. Uh . . . paintball." That would explain his attire.

"Seriously?" he scoffed. When Bronx gave him a flat stare, he wiped his expression. "Okay. I'll let you go."

"See ya." Bronx shut the door before Stephen turned around.

Urban eyed him, then out the window where Stephen wandered down the sidewalk. "Played that *real* cool."

He scowled. "It was cool enough."

He hadn't made one lap around the living room when the doorbell rang again. "Fucking Steve," he growled as he went to the door and whipped it open. Stephen wasn't doing anything wrong, but Bronx didn't have it in him to humor anyone today.

But it wasn't his smooth neighbor. Familiar light-blue eyes stared back at him under dirty blond hair, but on a tall dude. "You're Tosca's father."

The male pushed his way in. "Call me Xavier."

Bronx cocked his head at the four-door gray sedan parked in his driveway. "Is that your car?"

"No, and they're a lot harder to boost these days," Xavier huffed, as if he couldn't believe the audacity of car manufacturers. He zoomed through the first floor, peeking in doorways and flipping on lights in the pantry and bathroom. "But I'm out of practice."

His appearance was particularly unnerving. Tosca had said she would tell her father everything, so it wasn't a surprise he might show up here. The problem was his frantic, paranoid behavior. "What's wrong? Where's Tosca?"

Xavier stopped. "I don't mean to snoop. Tosca trusts you and that says a lot."

Streaks of dirt stained his skin and clothing. His shoes left trails of dust behind him. Just like Tosca's had after running through the brush. Bronx's heart hammered harder. The male must have fled the commune the same way.

"Carlos took her." He started pacing and Bronx had taken the role of Urban, watching the male streak back and forth. "Everything went according to plan. I barely got away. We'd planned it, but I didn't have time to prepare, and they chased me through those damn trees. It took every skill I had to keep out of their reach and find a vehicle I could actually hot-wire. Do you know for sure where they have her?"

"She's not in Numen," Urban said. "At least not with the enforcers."

"Where can he keep her?" Bronx assessed what other weapons he had in the house. He had his angel fire vial concealed under his shirt. A dagger sheathed in each boot. He'd have to put his shoulder holster on and—

"Peacequarters. It's the only building in the commune that's been updated in the last few decades. Since Carlos has taken over, only a select few are allowed farther than the gathering room off the main entry."

Bronx ducked into the office. He never used it, but it had also been furnished, like the rest of the house. He grabbed a sheet of paper from the printer and a pen. In the great room, he slapped both on the island. "Here. Draw everything you remember about the layout."

"You're going after her?" His tone was hopeful.

Urban cleared his throat. "We'll meet with the director and update him and—"

"Abso-fucking-lutely." Bronx wasn't waiting on anyone. He'd hated this idea from the beginning, and it was only getting worse.

Xavier bowed his head and scribbled on the paper. Bronx watched as he drew a large square that must be the gathering space for the commune, probably where Carlos displayed his glory for everyone. Then a row of locker rooms and showers.

"Those are from the early days," Xavier explained. "From before the cabins were equipped with running water. I honestly don't know if they're still there."

Bronx filed all the information away.

"It's one level," Xavier said as he sketched a long hallway and an office space with living quarters. "Carlos lives and works there, like his mother did." Xavier scratched his head with the pencil. "When he came to take Tosca, he said he would call his aunt."

Urban rose from the couch and crowded around the island.

"Who's his aunt?" Bronx asked. "Juliette?"

"I don't know. His mother used to make trips to Numen, but she never gave us the reason."

Urban was already thumbing a message into his phone. "I'll ask Odessa."

If they found the aunt, the likelihood they'd also find answers was high. But they'd need more than a familial connection. "How can I get inside Peacequarters without being caught?"

Xavier tapped his chin with his pen. "Carlos has increased surveillance over the years. He didn't hide that, but of course he sold it as being for our safety. He knew exactly when Tosca arrived."

Urban leaned over the sketch. "But if he's communicating with someone from the realm, they have to be able to travel back and forth." He exchanged a look with Bronx. Cameras meant Sierra could get to them. Carlos would've gotten the best. He didn't seem like a guy who wanted to pinch pennies.

"They could just call," Xavier suggested.

"They could," Bronx agreed, "but if they're smuggling goods—or angels—then they need to be hidden so they can transcend back and forth."

Xavier's brows drew together and he leaned forward. "The roof. There's enough peaks to conceal transcending. But you two have never been up there. Neither have I. And I don't care how they come and go. I want to find my daughter."

"The more we know, the better equipped we are for a rescue mission." He settled his unwavering gaze on Urban.

"She shouldn't have done this. You shouldn't have let her." Xavier threw the pen across the kitchen. It rebounded off the wall and landed with a clatter on the counter. They'd have to fix the divot it made before they moved. "Goddamn Numen using their people like they're disposable and don't have loved ones who care."

Bronx's rising irritation plummeted. The male had lost

his mate. He was as scared for his daughter as Bronx was. But that didn't stop reality from sinking in—for himself and for Xavier. "Could you have stopped your mate from responding to the call that killed her?"

He hated himself for pointing it out, but maybe he had to point it out to himself too. Tosca was dedicated to her job, to her mission of keeping their people safe from themselves. Yet all he'd been focused on was what *he* had to give up. Why hadn't he thought about what she'd have to give up for him? What she would even be *willing* to give up for him? Why had he thought that either of them could be together in bonded bliss and ignore their callings?

He wanted to support her; he didn't want her to leave. But at the same time, this sucked. It fucking sucked not to know whether she was dead or alive.

Xavier deflated and he dropped onto a stool. "I can't lose her. It was hard enough knowing she was an enforcer, that she could be killed like her mother, but she's in danger because of the life I dragged her into."

"I'm going." Bronx went for the sliding door.

"Fuck." Urban charged after him. "Bronx. Come on, at least let me call it in."

"It'll take too long. I can transcend to the trees and figure out how to get through their security." He'd call Sierra first but he couldn't use her name around Xavier.

"Bronx." Urban's warning tone didn't make him stop.

"Call it in," Bronx said as he stepped out the door and was gone without closing it behind him.

Tosca reclined on the bed. The cuff was still on her wrist. Her ankles were crossed and she was waggling one foot, her nervous energy shaking the entire cot.

"What?" Carlos's voice drifted through the door.

She froze and cocked an ear. She wouldn't risk creeping closer. It was only a few feet and Carlos didn't need to know how well she could hear him in his office.

This cell wasn't the sturdiest construction. The door had a gap underneath and was only hollow core. The cage was little more than a large kennel. She wouldn't be surprised to walk into a farm supply store and find the same thing. Add some chicken wire around the outside and no fox was getting in.

Which told her that very few people knew about Carlos's hidey-hole. He'd used the same equipment they used for the commune's chicken flock, only he'd added an electronic lock.

Who did he keep in here? If he wasn't holding one of their own prisoner, then why an iron cage?

"I told you I need another female." His heated tone made her scoot closer to the edge of the cot.

Was he talking about her? He'd said she'd signed her death warrant, yet she was still alive. And waiting. For what?

"I can't give her to them. She's not docile. What if she gets away?" She fit that description. "I don't care. She's too skilled to trade. I need someone else." A pause. "I don't care who—that's your job. Fertile, lonely, and dumb, that shouldn't be hard to find up there."

Pieces were clicking into place. She was using assumption for glue, but based on what had been happening in the realm, it all made sense.

"No, you know why she's not dead."

Tosca's breath froze. If it wasn't her life in danger, it was some other female's. Or both.

No, she wouldn't be leaving until this was dealt with.

"Fuck me over and I let her go. She has a helluva story to tell."

She was blackmail. Her figurative death warrant didn't have a signature on the bottom. He needed her in case whoever he was talking to screwed him over.

"I can take care of myself." Another pause, then an irritated, "Fuck the commune. You'd better hurry. That warrior who was eye-fucking her when he was here last time is going to figure out she's here. Xavier got away."

She sat up. She'd told Papa to prepare for the possibility, but she'd hoped Carlos would want to be discreet. Offing a longtime member of the commune was the opposite.

But he'd tried.

Red colored her vision. That bastard. She'd kill him if she had to claw through his neck to do it.

The door to the room banged open. A splotchy blush covered Carlos's face. She recrossed her legs and started waggling the other foot. "Is everything okay?"

He narrowed his eyes on her. "Were you listening?"

"Your face says everything."

"And you care?" His tone was so harsh he could've sandpapered the walls with it.

Taken aback, she scooted to the edge of the cot. "We were friends once. I didn't quit caring when I left the commune."

"If you had stayed, maybe . . ." He shook his head. "Maybe you could've kept me out of this mess."

"I'm here now."

"You're not the same, Tosca. Neither am I."

There was a crack in his resolve and she needed to wedge herself into it. "When you first came to Forgotten Peace, you seemed so worldly. I had never left the commune, and you were so knowledgeable about Numen.

About our kind. I had to go back. I had to find myself." She let out a theatrical breath. "And maybe I swung too far in the other direction. Maybe *we're* not so different. We just found ourselves in a bad place."

Instead of storming out, he relaxed and leaned against the wall. "It seemed so fucking easy for you. Living here. Leaving. Coming back. Getting away."

"I couldn't escape this time." She crossed to the bars of her cell. "And it sounds like you're stuck too."

"My life was determined from the beginning, baby girl."

She'd hated that nickname. "You still have the power to change it. I could help."

His humorless chuckle died between the four walls. "You have no idea how untrue that is." He leaned close to the bars. The prized cock of the commune, the arrogant, confident male she'd known, was still there. So was panic. "When she couldn't use you, she tried to destroy you. And that's what she'll do to me."

Tosca wrapped her fingers around the cool bars of the cage. "Who?"

He blinked and stepped back, but not before she caught his hand. Seduction wouldn't work, but maybe the allure of a lifeline would. He was clearly alone.

He didn't jerk his hand away, and she gave his fingers a squeeze. "Carlos. I've got nothing to lose. I can't go anywhere. I *can* help." His pride had proven to be his weakness, and if she'd stayed, she'd have been as stuck as him. Conflict raged in his eyes. She pressed. "I don't want what happened to your mother to happen to you."

Sadness hung on him like a second skin. "You gave up on me once, baby girl."

"I didn't sleep with you, because I thought your mother would find out and she'd make me seduce old, rich human men, make me have sex with them until their hearts gave out."

The corner of his mouth lifted, but there was no humor, only regret. "Yeah. She would've. She didn't want to be under the control of her sister."

Tosca willed him to say the name, the bars digging into her breasts, but he didn't elaborate. He let go of her hand and slumped against the wall once more.

His gaze brushed over the swells of her boobs poking through the bars. "But now I'm the one under her control. And you left me alone to deal with it all."

"The arrangement with the demons wasn't your idea?"

"No. Mother refused to agree to it."

And then she'd never returned from Numen. Had she walked into the fire, or had she been pushed? That would've been Tosca's fate had she stayed with Carlos and gotten dragged into this mess. "How's she doing it?"

Defeat entered his gaze. "My aunt always gets what she wants, or you wouldn't have woken up naked in a pool of blood with a dead guy on your wings."

She smothered her frown, keeping her expression as introspective as possible. The way he spoke . . . It was possible he knew the details because he was corresponding with someone in Numen. But the specificity of what he'd said bothered her. Jean Luc had been on top of her wing, like someone had dumped him right next to her.

"You helped that night. Didn't you?" She had to fold her arms to keep from shaking. Keeping the anger out of her voice took even more effort.

His eyes widened and he straightened. Tugging at the cuffs of his white shirt, he avoided her gaze. "Framing you was her idea."

And again, he'd gone along with it. Hurting others was

the easier route for him. "Your aunt is cleverer and more powerful than both of us?"

He snorted softly. "More powerful, anyway."

Yet Carlos had chosen self-preservation, had agreed to hurt others. "I imagine supplying demons with young angels gives Juliette a definite advantage over the rest of the senate."

His gaze turned shrewd, then he released a humorless laugh. "You haven't lost your touch, have you? And here I thought you really were just trying to be my friend." He tipped his head, a glint of respect in his smirk. "Do you have all the information you wanted? It's not going to do you any good."

"I can still help you." She didn't care about him. She despised Carlos. If it'd been possible before, she was confident there was no way to redeem him now. It was the "fertile, lonely, and dumb" female who needed her help.

"Forgive me if I doubt your intentions, baby girl." His shadow of a smile vanished. "Did you know there're over three hundred years between my mother and Juliette?"

The circle was connected, but she couldn't celebrate her triumph. She knew all the details, yet she was still stuck in a cage. "So many years, people forgot either one had a sibling."

"It's easy enough to bribe an archivist to wipe the records."

And then kill him, most likely. Juliette was a monster. "I'm your leverage while you wait for a girl to trade to the underworld?"

"The demons are desperate to overthrow the halfling in control of the mines."

Sandeen. The underworld was trying to breed another half demon to take him on. She imagined titanium lining her bones, keeping her body from shaking and her teeth from clenching. Anything to cap her mushrooming rage. Carlos was willing to send an innocent to a demon, to make her suffer brutally until she was with child. The young would suffer as well. The underworld wouldn't make the same "mistakes" they had with Sandeen. Her words came out even. "It backfired on them before."

"The half-demon bastard is just as clever as her."

"Carlos, save yourself. I can help you." After she dealt with the hag who'd masterminded this plan.

"If you could, you wouldn't be here." He stepped closer to the bars.

"The warriors will aid us. And I can help you escape."

Mere inches away, he could dip his head and claim her mouth. Her stomach turned, but she willed her chin to stay lifted. He wasn't playing to a script, but she was.

He swayed until his lips were an inch away. She pictured an entire cauldron of molten titanium holding her feet in place. Being so close to him was revolting.

"Rest up, Tosca. Enjoy your last hours."

He left, locking the door after him.

Well, that had been informative. Using the time to process the conversation, she sat back on the cot with her back against the wall. She didn't know how much time went by before the lock on the door jostled.

She stared as the knob moved, then went still while metal clicked. Seconds later, the door pushed open.

"Bronx?" She pressed her lips shut. She'd been too loud. His dark hair hung over his forehead. He was a walking shadow.

Easing the door closed behind him, he whispered, "Are you all right?"

She didn't bother to answer. She wrapped her hands around the bars and hissed, "What the hell are you doing here? They have cameras everywhere."

"And they're all getting footage from earlier rerouted through their feed."

She straightened. "That easy?"

He lifted a shoulder. "It's hard to pay attention to the monitors when you're having an orgy in the security room."

"What?"

"A little tidbit Megan told your father once. It's a daily occurrence. You'd think they'd change their routine with you here, but Sierra got quite the eyeful when she hacked their webcam."

"Papa's okay?"

"He's fine. It's you we're frantic over. We can't risk going so long with no communication. I'm getting you out. We can transcend from the roof." He crowded around the electronic lock.

"I'm staying."

He paused. "Tosca, they're not going to let you live."

"Carlos is waiting for them to deliver a female to trade to the underworld. He's not going to touch me until they deliver her. Then I'm assuming they'll try to take me with them."

He shook his head. "The others are on their way. We can surround the place—"

"Call them off!" she whisper-yelled. "Some girl is in grave danger. I'll be right here to help her when it happens."

"You can't guarantee that."

"He won't trade an angel just anywhere. They'll bring her here first. Everyone will think she's left Numen for the commune and they'll try to forget about her. If someone comes looking, Carlos will say the life wasn't for her and she left to live among the humans. But he'll need this cage to keep her in until his underworld contacts come for the handoff. That's when he'll trade me."

"Or kill you."

She shrugged.

His expression was incredulous. "And you're willing to just wait?"

"We wouldn't know any of this if I hadn't been sitting here. He told me more than he wanted, but he thinks I'm still trying to pretend to help him. He doesn't know I can hear his conversations." She pointed at the gap under the door. "He talks more freely because he thinks he's got me. If you scare him off, we'll never catch him or Juliette."

Bronx's brow furrowed as he considered her information. "Did you confirm Juliette's behind this?"

"Cordelia was Juliette's sister, and she erased the link in the archives."

He wedged his hand between the bar to stroke her chin with his thumb. "You sure you're okay?"

She rubbed her face into his hand. She'd been in the cell for only a day, but she missed him, missed his touch. "I'm fine."

"Somehow I suspected you wouldn't leave with me, so I brought surveillance equipment to plant."

He really would be the male of her dreams if he'd get over his one-or-the-other thinking.

He withdrew his hand. "What about the cuffs? I can give you something to pick them."

She glanced at the silver circling her wrist. It was a simple handcuff lock. She reached behind her head and withdrew a hairpin from her hair. "I lifted the keys and let Carlos steal them back. This will work on the cuffs. I already tried it."

His gaze heated. "Fuck, that's hot." Then desire ebbed and concern took over.

"I'll be okay."

"I'm not going far. I'll be watching." He grabbed a device from one of his cargo pockets and placed it on the inside of the bars close to the ceiling.

"Okay. *Go.*" She had no idea how long Carlos was going to be gone.

He snaked a hand through the bars and drew her to him. The slats were wide enough for a solid kiss and nothing more. Unlike when Carlos had been close, fire swept down her spine and she got light-headed with anticipation. Could she pick the lock fast enough for a quickie?

Too soon, he pulled away. "I'll be watching." He didn't hide his regret as he left her behind.

She flung herself down on the cot. Left alone with her thoughts, she was grateful that it didn't matter if Bronx had changed his mind. She'd have to live through this first in order to find out.

CHAPTER 18

Updates buzzed through Bronx's phone.

Harlowe and Urban were waiting at the diner he and Urban had encountered the symasters. Dionna and Ransom waited in the same bushes he'd hidden in with Urban when Tosca had fled Numen.

Dionna was back. Had she mended things between her and her mate? Or was that why she was back at work?

Bronx glowered through the trees. Could he let Tosca go after this?

Leaving her behind, in a goddamn cage, festered in his gut. He hadn't been able to eat since he'd snuck out of the office.

He watched through the feed on his phone. The little cameras he'd hidden hadn't been discovered. Carlos had entered his office an hour after Bronx had left. Jack had come in shortly after. Carlos had yelled at him as Jack had discreetly adjusted his crotch.

He'd nearly chortled when Carlos had shouted, "And put your shirt on the right way. She can't think we're rookies!"

He'd then paced his office like a damn zoo tiger. Every few laps he stopped at the door and glared at the doorknob. Bronx had put a camera in the cage room. He'd know if Carlos opened the cage to get to her, but Bronx didn't know if he could make it there in time.

Anxiety twisted his stomach but he remained still, watching the commune from the bushes Xavier had told him about. The huckleberry thorns had it in for him, and he'd have to take a piss before long.

Carlos better make a move quick.

The third screen in the security app lit with a red dot. Movement.

He tapped on it. Bronx tensed, his gaze flicking from his phone to the commune.

His screen filled with Senator Colbert and—*Persephone?* He turned the volume as high as his earbud would allow.

The girl in grave danger couldn't be Persephone. Could it? She was young, and sure, Tosca had mentioned she was desperate for a mother figure to give her attention. And, okay, Persephone was the stereotypical mean girl who hadn't learned to work through the trauma of her childhood, dishing it out to others who wouldn't be sorry to see her disappear.

She was the perfect target for the senator.

But how did the senator think Persephone's parents would react when their daughter vanished?

Persephone's face screwed up like she was sniffing the air. "Ew. This is Florida?"

"It's an acquired taste. Carlos is waiting to meet you."

Persephone's robe hung to her knees. Bronx couldn't make out her expression, but her tone was excited. "Did he really say he was fascinated with me?"

"Yes, dear. Of course. He wants a refined angel after living with these . . . heathens."

"But this place is smaller than my parents' house."

"Persephone," the senator snapped. "You can't expect the height of luxury if you're unwilling to do the work. Carlos said he'd marry you—or would you rather return and leech off your parents while aimlessly wandering the market?"

He could picture the shame on Persephone's face that Senator Colbert's condescending tone was designed to elicit.

The senator cocked her head, adjusting her robe like she didn't have time for the other female's nonsense. "Carlos is the leader here and he's interested in you. You were rejected by a *warrior*. You can't exactly afford to be choosy, unless you'd rather face your parents' perpetual disappointment."

Persephone drew back, her hand flattening on her chest. "I'm sorry, Juliette. I—I wasn't thinking."

The poor, attention-starved female. She was a prime target for Juliette Colbert. And there was no way Persephone could fight off even a sylph. She'd be at the complete mercy of the demons the senator was feeding her to.

The senator wrapped her robe tighter around herself and went to a doorway that was concealed from the rest of the commune. "Come. He's waiting."

"Why are we hiding if I'm going to be living here?"

"Don't ask questions you know nothing about, dear."

The females vanished from the view of the cameras. He'd put cameras on the roof, in Carlos's office, and where Tosca was being held. But now they were going into a dead zone.

He switched to Carlos's office. The male stared out his window. With a tap of a button, the tint on the window deepened. The senator had funded him well.

A minute ticked by. Then another. Bronx sent a message to Urban and Harlowe that he'd go in at the first sign of trouble. They had their own access to the feed.

Juliette shoved through the door of the office.

"Dear Aunt, you're doing your own dirty work nowadays?" Carlos asked in a cool tone.

"Don't be snide. You want her parents to come asking about her?"

Persephone glanced between them, a delicate frown on her beautiful face. "What do you mean?"

The senator sighed. "It means that I will miss you, darling, but you've proved useless to me in every other way."

"Juli—"

The senator cut her off with a swipe of her hand. "I can't stand your whiny voice." She faced Carlos. "You make sure Vermin knows that if he doesn't keep me informed about his progress, that bastard Sandeen will get a tipoff."

"Understood."

"And kill Tosca while I'm here."

Carlos recoiled. "Now?"

"Don't use her as blackmail if you're not prepared for the consequences. Your mother learned that lesson too late." Persephone backed toward the door, but the senator barked, "Stay."

Persephone jumped and curled her arms around herself, but she stopped moving away.

Carlos pointed a finger at the senator. "Don't you dare talk about my mother—"

Juliette slapped him, a hard whap to the cheek that whipped his head to the side. He worked his jaw but remained standing in the same spot. She jutted a finger at him. "We have an agreement. You decided to be strong when your mother couldn't. But you failed to handle that female once already. I cannot allow you to fail again. She won't be used against me."

"She's not that clever. Her seduction routine is pathetic and I can string her along as long as I want." He loomed over her. "You didn't complain about how I handled her or your mate."

Persephone covered her mouth with her hands. Even in the tiny picture on his phone, her body shook from head to toe. The girl could be rude and manipulative, but she was nothing like Carlos and the senator.

Juliette drew herself up. "You earned my trust that night. But you must maintain it. My operation has taken some hits in the last several months, and I have to work double time to get around that mammoth of a half demon."

"Half demon?" Persephone screeched.

Carlos's gaze darted to the girl.

The senator brushed her off. "We don't have to worry about her. You have the trade set up?"

Persephone squeaked and grabbed the doorknob with both hands. Bronx shoved his phone in his pocket and transcended to the roof of the building. From there, he sprinted down the narrow concrete stairs hidden in a janitor's closet behind what used to be locker rooms.

He charged out of the janitor's closet and into a long hallway, ready to confront the entire underworld if necessary.

It was empty. He charged past the locker rooms and through the gathering area. Numen mingled outside as if they'd tried the outer door but found it locked. He pounded down the hallway to Carlos's office.

Two males sprinted down the hall ahead of him, probably the ones Xavier had described, Jack and Roscoe. Had they heard everything? They had to be in on it. Carlos couldn't do all this himself.

The office door was open and Carlos was trying to drag Persephone backward. Senator Colbert was out of view.

"Nothing's wrong," Carlos called to the guys charging down the hall. "This is all so new."

His gaze landed on Bronx just as Persephone's did.

"Help!" She strained out of Carlos's grip, but she couldn't break free.

"Get the warrior!" Carlos snapped.

The two males turned on Bronx, shock widening their eyes, the girl struggling in Carlos's arms forgotten. Too loyal to question their boss, too clueless about his plans. As one unit, they rushed Bronx, trying to clothesline him. He yanked a knife out of his belt and another out of his shoulder holster. Dropping to his knees just as they reached for him, he slid on the hardwood floor and slashed each of them in the thigh.

The blond cried out and staggered. Bronx spun and buried his blade to the hilt in the back of the dark-haired male. He didn't doubt he'd hit the male's heart. The guy dropped, his face rebounding off the floor. He'd stay there until someone took the knife out.

Persephone screamed, but Bronx couldn't break off for her yet. The males were unarmed, but if he didn't put them both down, they could still attack him and prevent him from getting to Persephone and Tosca.

The blond charged him, but Bronx buried his second knife in the male's gut, then stabbed him again in the chest. The second male dropped. Bronx spun, digging another blade out of his belt, and rushed toward the office.

Just as he careened through the door, Tosca tackled Carlos. He toppled to the side, taking Persephone with him. She let out another scream. Carlos tried to right himself, but Tosca locked the crook of her elbow around his neck and her legs around his arms.

"I'm all rested up, jackass," she gritted through clenched teeth.

Carlos was unarmed. Senator Colbert had been knocked down and was trying to get herself off the floor. He crouched to tug Persephone free of a thrashing Carlos.

The prickles on his neck warned him to look up. The senator staggered as she charged, her brunette hair wild around her face, and reached into her robe. She yanked at a vial on a chain around her neck, uncapping it as she moved.

Angel fire. He spun to kneecap the senator. Persephone curled into herself with her butt in the air like she was preparing for the roof to cave in.

Just as the senator tipped the vial, he plowed into her. His knife clattered to the floor. The vial flipped in the air, tiny drops of burning plasma splattering free. The senator fell backward and Bronx twisted. He had to stop the loose angel fire.

The vial landed on Persephone's back and bounced, clattering on her robe and spilling its fluid on her skin.

Carlos's face was purple, his body going limp. Tosca's eyes were wide as she watched the vial arc through the air.

Bronx leaped for Persephone as she let out a shattering scream. The vial thunked to the floor, one last drop of fluid spilling out.

The robe burned away, baring Persephone's skin underneath. Her scream rose in pitch. He dove for her, lifting her off the floor, grabbing hold of an untouched part of the robe and ripping it off her body.

Carlos passed out and Tosca dropped him, his head slamming on the hardwood. She rushed to Persephone, kneeling by the female's head.

Bronx did the same, watching the path of the angel fire. It burned what it touched out of existence, leaving wounds no angel could recover from. But the robe had taken the brunt of the substance. Still, there was little he, Tosca, or Persephone could do other than wait for the fire to burn out.

The wound spread, searing past flesh into muscle. Persephone's voice grew hoarse, her cry turning to a rough wail. Tosca gripped her hand.

An enraged snarl ripped from the senator as she pushed herself up once again. Rage twisted her face until she resembled an archmaster. She yanked a second vial from around her neck.

Bronx reached for a blade, but the one he'd entered the office with had fallen during the scuffle. Tosca lunged over Persephone, snatched it off the floor, and launched it at the senator.

Her throw wasn't the best. It was hurried and unpracticed, but the blade bumped the senator's hand. The handle hit the vial with a ting and it shattered, flinging its contents into the senator's chest, where her robe gaped open.

Tosca gasped and lunged for the senator, instinctively wanting to save the female, but he shoved Tosca back. She dropped to a knee next to him, glancing between Juliette's writhing form and Persephone's, clad only in lacy red lingerie that had been half burned by angel fire. Tosca clenched her jaw and nodded.

There was nothing they could do for the senator. Her robe hadn't taken the brunt of the hit.

As Persephone quieted, whimpering and moaning into the cool hardwood, Carlos groaned.

Bronx got up, stood over him, and decked him. They had a lot to clean up and they didn't need to juggle Carlos on top of it.

Urban rushed into the office. Harlowe's voice drifted

into the room as she reported to either Dionna or the commander what was going on. Someone dealt with the downed males in the hallway.

Compassion filled Urban's gaze when he figured out what had happened to Persephone. He shrugged out of a shoulder holster holding two daggers and yanked his shirt over his head. Ripping through the back, he helped a sobbing Persephone get her arms through it to cover her front.

Harlowe popped her head in. "The director has another team waiting to take these fuckers to the senate." She pointed to Carlos. "That bastard has some confessing to do."

"It's over?" Tosca asked, her question barely reaching his ears.

He nodded, wishing he could gather her into his arms. But this wasn't the time or the place. "Yeah. It's over."

CHAPTER 19

When Bronx had reassured her it was over, she hadn't thought he meant he was also done talking to her. But that was what had happened in the days between the battle in Carlos's office and now.

His team had brought back three prisoners. Carlos had sung like an aging rock star on his last world tour. He refused to accept the legacy of any of his aunt's crimes.

Now Tosca sat in on the senate hearing to decide what would be done with Carlos, Jack, and Roscoe. A coliseum of senators faced her. She sat in the front, next to Felicia. She hadn't had much to do with the female before this, but she was the closest to a friendly face.

Director Vale had been her staunchest supporter, and he stood next to her today. He'd refused to allow the enforcers to throw her in jail to await the hearings. She hadn't been given her old job back, and she wasn't sure she ever would be.

Wearing a long, traditional white robe was unusual. She felt both exposed and more covered than she had been most of her life. The relief of having her wings out was almost worth it.

Bronx and his teammates stood with her as well—Bronx as far away as he could get.

The senators had refused to update the males on what was happening with Forgotten Peace. Tosca didn't know either.

Senator Thomas, the oldest and longest-serving senator, scowled at the three. "Taking your wings wouldn't be the justice it should be for the three of you."

"I want to walk into the fire," Carlos said. Jack shook his head, disbelief registering on his face. Roscoe cleared his throat, like he was trying not to cry.

"Your wish will be granted." Senator Thomas's heavy voice resonated, as if centuries of service still hadn't prepared him for the hard decisions. "But you will be escorted. As for the other two, you will lose your wings. After, Winger will place you somewhere on Earth befitting your crimes. You will have no friends, no family. They will be ordered to forget you ever existed and will face their own trial should they try to contact you."

Ransom folded his hands and bowed his head. His tension radiated into her. She didn't have to ask to know the warriors around her, the ones who still supported Sierra, didn't agree with the policies of the realm. But that was a fight for a different day.

The males were ushered away. Senator Thomas beckoned her to stand in the middle of the stage in front of the senators. Her body prickled with uncomfortable awareness. The urge to tap dance or deliver an awkward monologue daunted her, but she remained stock-still.

"You expressed your desire to return to work when you were questioned."

She tipped her head. Returning to work meant

reclaiming some sense of normalcy. She was in a strange purgatory. Once before, she'd left everything and started anew. She couldn't do that again. She had nowhere to do that again.

"You realize we can't allow that," he said, his tone full of pity.

She let her gaze drop from his bushy white brows and shock-white hair. The male was one of the oldest in the realm. Giving a regretful nod, she said, "I understand."

One side of his mouth turned down. "It's unfortunate that you really do. It means you're a good enforcer and you want what's best for the realm. But for anyone else in disagreement"—his cloudy teal eyes scanned the warriors behind her—"she was fooled once. She learned, but the former Senator Colbert left a legacy of deceit. Distrust. Dare I say evil. And that will always cling to this young ex-enforcer. It will prove too challenging of a taint to shake." He lifted his thick brows. "So what do we do with an angel who's shown such dedication to our realm? An angel who had every reason to run away from the trouble and the lies she was charged with and instead raced headlong into saving humans and Numen females from a nightmare?"

He made it sound honorable, and yeah, it was. She couldn't brush it off as just doing her job. She could've behaved a thousand ways. Given how she'd been raised, she could've disappeared into the sea of seven billion humans. But she hadn't. She'd used her history to keep others from going through what she had.

But Senator Thomas didn't answer the question. "We have a community of angels who have turned away from us. They cannot be allowed to shun our rules and live in seclusion. We are angels for a reason. We may not be divine, but we're not pickpockets." He said the word with such disdain, it was as if *his* valuables had been pilfered.

"We have duties. To our people. To humanity. But we cannot yank them from the home they have made for themselves. They'll need guidance. We need guidance on how to handle them."

She agreed with everything he said. The poorly kept secret of the commune was out. There was no going back and it couldn't be allowed to function as it had been. "I'd be happy to help in any way."

"You can best do that as a senator."

She jerked, her feathers ruffling behind her. Murmurs trailed through the senate. Some of the older, more prestigious senators' voices grew louder. She knew their arguments before she heard them. They'd been born into leadership; she was nothing. They'd had years of scholarship and apprenticing under the most honorable of the realm. She'd grown up learning how to pick pockets and scam humans.

Senator Thomas raised his weathered hand and a hush fell over the coliseum. "I am able to directly appoint a senator as I see fit, and we're due for another angel who's a bit more worldly."

A female sitting halfway up spoke. "She has my support." Worry imprinted the lines of her face and her black hair fell over one shoulder. Persephone's mother. "Our children are being targeted. Our females. We need more senators who have a rapport with warriors. With enforcers—without making them their pets."

Senator Thomas shrugged and flashed a kind smile, as if he was saying he didn't need anyone's support to make the decision, then turned to Tosca. "I'll give you some time to give me your final answer."

"It's a yes." She didn't need to muddy her instinctive answer worrying about what others thought. Papa might be proud, he might be horrified. Her fellow enforcers might have lingering resentment she'd gotten the ultimate promotion. And Bronx.

Well, his feelings were no longer relevant, now were they?

Senator Thomas grinned and waved his arm to an empty seat. She was aware enough to know he was also using her as a warning. That spot was where Senator Colbert had sat. Senator Thomas was telling the rest of the senate that he had no issues replacing them.

She sat on the round marble stone carved into a seat with a low back to make room for wings. Since she was wearing a robe for once, she fit in. This was her new uniform.

From her place, she studied the warriors. Bronx's jaw was hard enough to chisel a marble chair for each of his teammates. He lifted his gaze to hers and shot her a quick, sad smile.

Loss sank low in her belly. She'd miss him, but at least she'd have a new role in the realm to keep her busy.

CHAPTER 20

$\mathcal{B}$ronx listened as the elderly senator simultaneously chastised and praised Director Vale in front of the senate. Senators sat side by side in semicircular tiers, facing the director, Bronx, and the rest of his team. Wings of varying shades of gray were the only color in the otherwise white senate coliseum. Some of the senators watched Director Vale's dressing down with undisguised glee. No doubt they'd cheer if a lion were released, like the Romans once had.

"Without your team, this realm would've ripped itself apart." Senator Thomas straightened. The gray of his feathers had faded with his age, matching the dirty white of his brows and hair. "Perhaps you now realize the prudence of open communication between the director of the warriors and the senate?"

Director Vale's gravelly voice was just as light. "I realize there are times when information shouldn't be spread, when I don't know who to trust, and that the senate has placed a lot of confidence in me to determine when secrecy is necessary."

Senator Thomas's wings twitched, but his expression was one of grudging acceptance. "Very well. I realize your warrior team is one short. What are your plans?"

Meaning—was the director still digging into shit he refused to tell the senate about? "They are familiar with the area around the commune. I'd like to task them with demon cleanup. News of Senator Colbert's demise will have reached the underworld, but they won't have vacated their hosts or given up on the humans they're meddling with."

The old senator tipped his head. "Very well. The warriors are excused." He beckoned one of the guards from the entrance to the senate. "Tell Winger we're ready for him."

Just like that, they were dismissed. The debacle of Senator Colbert was well and truly over.

Relief should make his wings sag to the floor. He should want to skip out of the coliseum. But he was leaving behind Tosca. *Senator* Tosca. She'd have training. A proper anointment. Then she'd be busy.

Good for her. She'd be good in the position. She'd be the opposite of Senator Colbert, and the enforcers wouldn't be able to get away with shit with her watching over them and other senators.

But . . . damn. Bronx walked away from the senate auditorium with a hole the size of the realm in his chest.

Once they were outside and clear of the marble building and its columns, Director Vale turned. "Go. Take the rest of the day off. Tomorrow, meet me in my office and we'll go over your next assignment and find a new safe house."

Which meant Sierra was already on it. "Brandon and Julie" no longer lived in Lakeland.

The thought made his wings twitch. Urban took flight.

He'd been absent a lot since they'd returned to the realm with their prisoners and an injured Persephone.

Harlowe vanished midstep, probably returning to her mate.

Acid climbed its way up his gullet.

Jagger and Ransom both took off, chatting with each other. Bronx could do the same. His parents had been on edge. There was only so much he could tell them about his job, but they knew a morning with the senate wasn't a good thing. Father had told him he'd be ready with a meal when Bronx was done.

He couldn't face his parents and their smothering quite yet. If coming home to a fraught mate was anything like fraught parents, he'd made the right decision.

But it ate at him like angel fire.

Dionna didn't leave. She fell into step next to him. "Everything okay?"

She'd been more talkative. He'd even heard her chuckling with Harlowe when getting updated on all that'd happened with Sandeen while she'd been gone.

Dionna had spent most of his career quiet and dedicated. She'd left without much explanation, and now she was back. And she was different. Had she lived his worst nightmare—a failed bond? Did she have regrets?

Perhaps that was why he answered honestly. "No. I'm not. Do you regret mating and continuing to be a warrior?"

Her usual composure slipped, so many emotions playing across her face. Shock that he had asked about something that was none of his business. Regret. Then contemplation. "Do I regret continuing my calling after I mated Charles?" She frowned. "Short answer, yes." Just when the dark cloud over his head threatened to form teeth and chomp his damn heart out, she continued, "The long answer is much more complicated. What I regret is how I handled it. The lack of communication between me and Charles. The years that turned into decades when each knew something was wrong but refused to acknowledge it."

He absorbed her answer, the longer version that his brain clung to. "My parents have the perfect bond. But they both gave up their jobs and raised me. You and I have both seen mated pairs drift away from each other because of our calling."

"You should talk to your parents." She leaned closer. "No couple is perfect. The sooner you realize that, the easier it is to admit there are problems, and the sooner you can work toward a solution that doesn't include moving to Earth for years of the silent treatment."

She patted his shoulder, a motherly move that pricked at his conscience. His parents were anxiously awaiting news.

"Thank you." He took flight and within minutes had landed in his parents' small front yard.

His mother was working in the garden, pruning flowering vines that thrived in the realm under her touch.

Images of Tosca in designer sweats bending over radishes bombarded his mind.

The long answer is much more complicated.

Had he made a mistake? Was there anything he could do about it if he had?

Mother's shoulders went taut as if she sensed someone. She peeked over her shoulder, muscles bunched to spin and fight, then she grinned.

"Bronx!" She dropped her trowel and flicked her gloves to the ground. He met her halfway for a hug. "I can't help but fret when it comes to the senate. They can be unpredictable, yet stereotypical at the same time." Her smile was wry. "And either one can be dangerous."

"Is Father around?" Of course he was. His parents didn't go anywhere. Their life was each other.

She studied his expression, her doe-brown eyes narrowing. As if her motherly alarm was going off, she ushered him into the house. "Bronx needs to talk to us."

He couldn't help his small smile. She'd judged correctly. He sat on the backless settee, letting his wings hang over the edge. Had Tosca noticed they'd practically dragged on the ground since he'd returned?

Probably not. He'd been avoiding her like a fucking coward.

Father rushed into the living room and dropped next to Mother on the backless love seat. "What's wrong? Did the senate—"

Bronx shook his head. "Not the senate. Why did you two quit being warriors after you met?"

A line formed between Mother's dark brows. "We told you this story before. What is it you really want to know?"

"I fell in love with Tosca, but you two are the only strong warrior pair I know and it seems like it's because you quit after you met."

Father gave his head a little shake. "We didn't quit after we met."

"Well, it was only a few years," Mother interjected.

Father bobbed his head. "Right. She got pregnant really quickly, and"—he spread his hands—"we figured it was a good time for a hiatus."

"A hiatus?" Had he missed something?

"We live a long time," Mother filled in. "We've both lost teammates. Friends. Known others who walked into the fire. And after we synced, we talked about it. Our lives are so long, we become our own worst enemies. I've seen warriors burn out, take it out on their loved ones."

Father pressed his fingertips together. "What's a century on vacation when we can work for a millennium?"

To make sure he understood, he said, "You never said you'd go back to work."

Mother shrugged. "We're having a good time. We don't even know if we will go back, and if we do, if we'll be warriors again. I served for centuries, Bronx. I saw a lot of atrocities, and this?" She held her hands up to encompass the house. "This is heaven. There are no demons in Numen. I'm actually thinking about doing something else. The point is—when you think you can only do one thing in life, that's when we've seen others quit trying. They quit trying in the field, making stupid mistakes that get them or others killed. They quit trying in their relationships."

But Dionna hadn't quit trying. She'd come back smiling, saying something similar to his parents. "I'm scared," he whispered. "I want what you two have."

"Do you want what you and Tosca have?" his father asked quietly. "Because that's what you need to ask yourself. You're not me. You're not your mother. And you're young yet. We met when we were older."

His mother scooted forward, her wings lifted. "What if you get gravely injured, and you're gifted a mate to help you heal, to save you?" She pressed to the very edge. "And what if it's Tosca because you were meant to be together, and you wasted time together out of fear?"

"It's not easy to find someone you want to spend eternity with." Father mimicked Mother's position. "I imagine it's even harder if she moves on and you have to watch her enjoy eternity with someone else."

Bronx scrubbed his hands over his face. "I messed up. I need to talk to her."

Mother popped up. "You can bring her some dinner."

Their cooking was amazing, but was it amazing enough to make up for being an epic dumbass?

~

Felicia nudged her. "Overwhelmed yet?"

"Most definitely." There was nothing like feeling underqualified, unless she counted having a hard time paying attention. This was her life now.

She wandered out of the senate coliseum, the taller female at her side. Felicia had sought her out at every break, checking on her. The sun had set. The realm was quiet.

Angels flew overhead. Senators launched themselves into the sky to go home to their mansions on the edge of the realm. She had her tidy little house by enforcer headquarters.

She might need to move. Just in case there was lingering resentment.

Felicia aimed another winning smile her way. "See you tomorrow?"

Excited to return despite everything, she grinned. "Absolutely."

Jagger landed several feet away, the poster child for gorgeous angels. But he didn't have dark, mischievous eyes or steel-gray wings better than any blanket.

She stuffed her longing away as he held his arm out for his mate. When Felicia linked her hand in the curve of his elbow, he curled her into his side and launched into the air. Watching them fly together, since the wounds in Felicia's wings made it impossible for her to take to the air on her own, was commonplace. Tosca had never paid much attention before. But now, seeing them cling to each other, crazy in love, made her chest ache with a force that could drive her to her knees.

She walked a few more blocks, avoiding taking to the air. Alone. She'd never flown with anyone before. When she'd first arrived in the realm, she'd had to hide on the fringes and practice flying like a new foal learning to walk.

She loved flying, but after seeing Jagger and Felicia together, she couldn't bring herself to take flight. Then she'd be forced to watch the other couples out for the equivalent of a night stroll.

She walked the shortest route to her house. When she approached, she spotted a male sitting on her front step, his knees bent and his arms draped over the top.

She stopped on the path to her front door but went no farther. "Is something wrong?"

"Yeah." He rose, a fluid motion of grace and power, but different than it had been at the safe house. His wings were out, the tips dragging the ground. "I'm in love with you and I'm not sure I can ask for take backs."

"Take backs?" she echoed because she couldn't comprehend anything else he'd said.

"I talked to my parents. And Dionna. Look, I've had it so fucking easy in life. Yes, I'm a warrior and it's dangerous and I've been hurt before. But it's still easy, know what I mean?"

The guy who flitted from woman to female with no entanglements was scared of just that. "I know what you mean. You're good at it and the world needs you."

"I need you," he said hoarsely.

She forced herself to stay rooted. "What are you saying?"

"That I'll do my damnedest to work on us. Because you're fucking mine and eternity is a hell of a long time without you."

She was his. She crossed to him but didn't touch him. "Hmm . . . that sounds like a deal. Because I love you too."

His sexy smile was all for her. "I thought maybe you'd make me beg. You're a senator and all now."

Feathering her fingers over his chest, she asked, "How do you feel about that? Really?" His team had essentially been fighting corrupt senators since Odessa was targeted.

He pulled her close. "I'm relieved that they're getting worthy angels to run the realm. I'm relieved that you and Felicia will have my team and the rest of the warriors at your backs. And I'm relieved the enforcers will be so fucking irritated you got promoted over any of them."

"So many of them were so salty I wouldn't break the rules."

"Not me." He touched the tip of her nose with his. "You're my little enforcer and I wouldn't have it any other way."

A pinching pain on her wrist made her hiss. Bronx did the same, tilting to catch the moonlight.

A pink spot, like a birthmark, appeared on her wrist, the outline like a wing. "Is that . . ."

"A sync brand." He grinned, hugging her to him again. "It's official. You're mine."

"Say it again."

He placed a soft kiss on her lips. "You're mine, and I'm going to keep telling you that until I'm buried to the hilt inside you and you're calling my name."

Her body lit like the stars in the sky were inside her. "Promise?"

He lifted her, and thankfully her robe parted so she could wind her legs around him. She'd have to consider a different work wardrobe if it hindered her. He seemed to like picking her up—and she loved it just as much.

"I promise you eternity, Tosca. Even when I'm not here

physically, you'll always be in my thoughts and in my heart."

"I promise the same. Because you're mine too." He carried her into her house. Work might force them to be apart more often than they'd like, but they'd work through it together. And they'd start with tonight.

URBAN LANDED at the edge of a mansion, hiding behind bushes like he'd done so long ago outside of Juliette Colbert's place. Only then, he'd been investigating.

Tonight, he was breaking and entering.

At some point, he'd get caught, but she'd asked him to hide. She'd asked him to keep it between them, and fuck, whatever she asked, he was in danger of torching everything he'd worked for to give it to her.

The moon was half full, but still obnoxiously bright when a guy wanted to sneak across a yard without being seen.

Why did she still have to live with her parents?

But it would be harder on her if she didn't.

With that thought, he crouched and darted from manicured shrub to manicured shrub. The one he hid behind was shit for concealment. Corkscrew-shaped greenery wasn't meant for ducking behind.

Lights shone out the windows of the lower level. Blinds were drawn. He couldn't see anyone, but they were there. Two second-floor balconies hung over the back of the house. Large glass French doors opened to each balcony.

He aimed for the one on the left. The door would be locked. Her parents checked it every night, and every night he picked the lock.

His wings gave his jump enough lift to bring him level

with the carved railing. Gripping it, he flipped himself over and landed silently. Digging in his pocket, he crept to the door and pulled out his lockpick set.

Moments later, he cracked the door open and listened. If someone else was in the room, he'd have time to get away, preferably without being seen.

Or she could tell them why he was there, but he wouldn't add more stress to her life. He'd done enough.

Hearing nothing, he crept in and eased the door shut once his wings had cleared the opening.

He turned to the bed. A form was curled on her side in the middle. Black hair made a halo of darkness around her head and her hands were tucked under her face.

Persephone.

Her sheer night shirt was cut open in the back, and all the material that usually surrounded the wings had been removed.

The raw, ravaged flesh was still visible in the dark, thanks to the lifeless heap her wings made. She couldn't morph without severe pain, nor could she roll over without help—and a lot more pain.

Director Vale had sympathized with her, commenting that the thought of what she was going through during the healing process had made the memories of his own agony fresh again. The side of his face showed the trauma he'd experienced, but Urban knew the damage spread down his neck and shoulders. But the director was strong.

No one equated strength with the richest, most spoiled daughter of the realm.

"It hurts," she whisper-moaned.

"Do you need more salve?" He crossed her spacious bedroom, his boots sinking into the plush carpet surrounding a bed that could fit five angels.

"Yes."

A chaperone who escorted souls into the afterlife had made her own salve for warriors with angel fire burns. She'd acquired topical pain relief from Earth and added it to her product. She also charged handsomely for it, but Persephone's parents could afford it.

He scooped some cool gel out of the little round container and carefully sat on the edge of the bed. This had become their nightly routine. She'd caught him watching her outside of her window. He'd gotten sloppy, thought she was out of it, but she'd caught a glimpse of him and would've screamed had he not flailed around like a jackass until she'd nearly laughed. Then cried from the pain.

He would've done anything he could've to help her, so now he did this. Applying salve. Sitting with her.

Gingerly dabbing salve in the middle and deepest of her wounds, he worked his way out. As the numbing agent took effect, she relaxed, but only slightly.

"Can you lie with me?"

He almost jerked, but that sudden movement next to her raw wounds would've cost her. "What?"

"Just tell me something that isn't everyone else getting on with their lives while I waste away in my castle." The bitterness in her tone was unlike anything he'd heard from her before. She was catty. Snide. Definitely superior. But he'd seen none of that since he'd found her burning on the floor of the office.

"Uh . . . okay. Let me think." A joke. He fucked around with Bronx but his jokes were never intentional. Digging his phone out, he punched in a search with his greasy fingers.

"You don't know a joke?"

"Hard to believe?"

"I actually know a joke."

"Seriously?" He hadn't meant for the disbelief to ring so loud.

"Did you know nine out of eight people are bad at fractions?"

A chuckle burst out of him and he immediately smothered it before her parents could catch him. He didn't know what would happen. Persephone was an adult. Younger than him, but still well into her twenties. He normally didn't care about getting on the wrong side of senators, but Persephone's mother was a family friend of Odessa's and Felicia's. She helped the warriors. Would she think he was trying to take advantage of their sheltered daughter?

Because that was what Persephone was. He saw that now. Sheltered and ignorant of life outside the little circle of groupies she'd made for herself.

"Okay, let me try." He found a silly one. "What are the laziest shoes?"

The first smile he'd seen in days graced her face, chasing away the strain suffering had left behind. "Loafers."

"Are you going to ruin all the jokes I try to tell you?"

"Are you going to find a good one?"

Was this the real Persephone coming out? "Is that a challenge?"

"What do you call a fish with no eyes?"

"The fuck if I know."

She giggled and winced, but her smile didn't vanish. "A fshhhh."

He almost barked out a laugh, but he held the sound in. "Fine, little jokester. I'll up my game next time."

Slowly, her smile faded and her eyes clouded over. The salve was working, but it wouldn't last long. "I used to love telling jokes. Then Mother said they were silly and I should behave more appropriately for the privileged station I'd been given in life."

Damn, he didn't know what to say. Tosca's words rang through his mind. Persephone and her folks were complicated. His were long gone. "It's important to laugh."

"Yeah." The words came out on a breath and her eyelids fluttered shut. "Can you stay until I fall asleep?" she murmured.

How long would she ask him to do that? At first, he'd come out of a sense of obligation, of remorse for the way he'd talked to her, but now he wanted to stay and learn more about the female underneath the facade she'd crafted —and whether she'd keep it in place after she healed. But for now, that didn't matter. He'd been just another dick who'd driven her closer to Juliette. He wasn't leaving her side. "I'll stay right here the whole time, little jokester."

————————————————

WILL Urban help Persephone heal her mind and her body, or will she carve her own path and leave him behind in Eternal Fire?

FOR NEW RELEASE UPDATES, chapter sneak peeks, and exclusive bonus content, sign up for Marie's newsletter.

THANK you so much for reading. I'd love to know what you thought. Please consider leaving a review of Corrupt Fire.

ABOUT THE AUTHOR

Marie Johnston lives in the upper-Midwest with her husband, four kids, and an old cat. Deciding to trade in her lab coat for a laptop, she's writing down all the tales she's been making up in her head for years. An avid reader of paranormal romance, these are the stories hanging out and waiting to be told between the demands of work, home, and the endless chauffeuring that comes with children.

www.ingramcontent.com/pod-product-compliance
Lightning Source LLC
Chambersburg PA
CBHW050833190726
48286CB00007B/2067